Berkley Prime Crime titles by Diana Killian

Death in a
Difficult
Position

Diana Killian

BERKLEY PRIME CRIME, NEW YORK

THE BERKLEY PUBLISHING GROUP
Published by the Penguin Group
Penguin Group (USA) Inc.
375 Hudson Street, New York, New York 10014, USA
Penguin Group (Canada), 90 Eglinton Avenue East, Suite 700, Toronto, Ontario M4P 2Y3, Canada
(a division of Pearson Penguin Canada Inc.)
Penguin Books Ltd., 80 Strand, London WC2R 0RL, England
Penguin Group Ireland, 25 St. Stephen's Green, Dublin 2, Ireland (a division of Penguin Books Ltd.)
Penguin Group (Australia), 250 Camberwell Road, Camberwell, Victoria 3124, Australia
(a division of Pearson Australia Group Pty. Ltd.)
Penguin Books India Pvt. Ltd., 11 Community Centre, Panchsheel Park, New Delhi—110 017, India
Penguin Group (NZ), 67 Apollo Drive, Rosedale, Auckland 0632, New Zealand
(a division of Pearson New Zealand Ltd.)
Penguin Books (South Africa) (Pty.) Ltd., 24 Sturdee Avenue, Rosebank, Johannesburg 2196,
South Africa

Penguin Books Ltd., Registered Offices: 80 Strand, London WC2R 0RL, England

This is a work of fiction. Names, characters, places, and incidents either are the product of the author's imagination or are used fictitiously, and any resemblance to actual persons, living or dead, business establishments, events, or locales is entirely coincidental. The publisher does not have any control over and does not assume any responsibility for author or third-party websites or their content.

PUBLISHER'S NOTE: The recipes contained in this book are to be followed exactly as written. The publisher is not responsible for your specific health or allergy needs that may require medical supervision. The publisher is not responsible for any adverse reactions to the recipes contained in this book.

DEATH IN A DIFFICULT POSITION

A Berkley Prime Crime Book / published by arrangement with the author

PRINTING HISTORY
Berkley Prime Crime mass-market edition / September 2011

Copyright © 2011 by Diane Browne.
Cover illustration by Swan Park.
Cover design by Lesley Worrell.
Interior text design by Laura K. Corless.

ISBN: 978-0-425-24381-7

BERKLEY® PRIME CRIME
Berkley Prime Crime Books are published by The Berkley Publishing Group,
a division of Penguin Group (USA) Inc.,
375 Hudson Street, New York, New York 10014.
BERKLEY® PRIME CRIME and the PRIME CRIME logo are trademarks of Penguin Group (USA) Inc.

PRINTED IN THE UNITED STATES OF AMERICA

10 9 8 7 6 5 4 3 2 1

To Lisa and Megan—
and the friendships that last a lifetime.

Acknowledgments

Sincere thanks to my editor, Faith Black, for her on-going and much-tried patience—and of course a big thank-you to everyone at Berkley Prime Crime.

One

✄

"The Reverend David Goode says you're going to hell."

"Me?" A.J. Alexander stared at Sacred Balance receptionist Emma Rice's severe features. "What? Why?"

"Not for the reasons you might think," Emma said obliquely, laying a stack of neatly sorted mail in A.J.'s in-box. "Reverend Goode says yoga is rooted in demonic practices. That even one little yoga class is playing right into the hands of evil."

"You've got to be kidding me. How could anyone—" A.J. stopped and eyed Emma doubtfully. *"You* don't believe that, do you?" At sixty-something, Emma probably didn't fit anyone's image of a yoga studio receptionist. She was a short, slender black woman who favored Worishofer orthopedic sandals and Chantilly talcum, but she had a memory like a steel trap and organizational skills that many a five-star general would envy. A.J. didn't even want to think about replacing her.

Emma snorted. Not a ladylike snort, a snort like a workhorse facing a pitchfork of moldy hay. "Honey, if I thought there was something profane about all this stretching and bending, I wouldn't be here. I'm old enough to know right from wrong."

And yet from the minute the Reverend David Goode had turned up in Stillbrook with his dog and pony show, Emma had been in attendance at every Sunday service. Well, perhaps *dog and pony show* wasn't quite fair. A.J. liked to think of herself as both hip and tolerant, but evangelism made her uncomfortable. Especially the made-for-TV brand that Goode touted.

"Did he mention me by name?"

Emma nodded. "You and Lily Martin."

"Me and Lily?" There was some kind of cosmic irony to that. Lily Martin was A.J.'s business rival. Formerly A.J.'s co-manager at Sacred Balance, Lily had received what she considered a better offer and was now managing Yoga Meridian, a chic, upscale studio and spa in neighboring Blairstown.

"The reverend sees you as the biggest threat, though," Emma added as though that was somehow reassuring news.

"*Threat?* What am I threatening?" Except maybe stiff backs and bulging waistlines? If only she could laugh this off the way it deserved to be. Unfortunately, though New Jersey was not a particularly conservative state, Stillbrook was a small town with many small-town attitudes.

Emma shook her head in part commiseration, part bemusement. "I don't know, but I see a lot of familiar faces every Sunday."

Meaning a lot of Sacred Balance clients were also buying what the Reverend Goode was selling?

"Great." A.J. chewed her lip, thinking. "Maybe I should try and talk to him. Maybe he honestly doesn't understand what we do here."

Emma shrugged her bony shoulders. The phone was ringing in the front lobby, and she went to answer it. A.J. studied the photo on her desk of Diantha Mason, founder of Sacred Balance studio. The woman in the photograph smiled back with serene confidence. No question what Aunt Di would do. Aunt Di would head straight into town and have it out with the good reverend.

A.J. wasn't afraid of confrontation, but she didn't relish it either. After a moment's thought, she reached for the phone on her desk.

"Oh my God! Did you *hear*?"

A.J. dropped the handset and sat back in her chair. Suze McDougal, the most junior of her instructors, stood in the office doorway, blonde hair standing on end. That wasn't alarm. That was the way Suze's hair always looked.

"Did I hear what?"

"About John Baumann's cows."

It sounded like the start of a folk song. "Oh, did ye hear about John Baumann's cows . . . ?"

"I haven't even got through my e-mail this morning, let alone—"

"Something attacked them last night."

"When you say attacked—"

Once again Suze interrupted. "A bunch of John Baumann's cows had their throats ripped out last night!"

"What?" A.J. knew she was gaping. She couldn't help it. Not that Mondays didn't have their own strange dynamic, but this was just . . . weirder and weirder.

"Everybody's talking about it."

A.J. spoke cautiously. "You mean ripped out as in . . ."

Suze made an uncannily vivid gesture—sort of like a monster yanking his bowtie off with both claws.

"Oh my gosh."

Suze nodded. "Really sick."

A.J. assumed Suze was going by what she'd heard others saying, which meant there could easily be some exaggeration. In fact, there was almost certainly some tall tale telling in this sort of situation, right?

"What are people saying? I mean, what's the theory? Bears?" Warren County was home to the Delaware Water Gap National Recreation Area, and as such, the area had its share of wildlife, including the occasional black bear. Bear attacks were fairly rare, although the more people pushed into previously uninhabited areas, the more likely they were to encounter critters.

"I don't know if there is an official theory," Suze said. "It's weird, no?"

"It's weird, yes." A.J. lived on a fairly remote farm outside of Stillbrook. She wasn't exactly thrilled at the idea of marauding bears.

"Are they going to hunt the bears?" She was nearly as unenthused at the idea of hunters as she was bears.

"I don't know. It might not be bears."

"What else could it be? Wild dogs?"

"Wolves?"

"Werewolves?"

Suze said, "No, seriously."

"There are no wolves in New Jersey," A.J. said firmly.

"Yes, there are," Suze said, to A.J.'s surprise. "There's the Lakota Wolf Preserve at Camp Taylor Campground. That's not that far from here. Maybe a wolf got out."

First bears, now wolves. It made A.J.'s issues with the Reverend Goode seem quite tame by comparison.

"Oh!" Suze beamed, abruptly changing mood. "I saw your mom on TV last night. That was the *best* episode yet. An old boyfriend from your mother's past turned out to be a hit man."

A.J. smiled feebly. Her mother, Elysia, once the darling of British B films, had a new career these days on the hit television series *Golden Gumshoes*, a show about three "mature" lady detectives. One critic had described the series as "*Charlie's Angels* on Geritol and crack." In A.J.'s opinion, he'd nailed it. Not that she was a regular viewer.

The show did seem to be popular with the fickle public, and at least it kept Elysia out of trouble. Unless she was getting into trouble in California. A.J. listened with half an ear as Suze burbled on about the details of what sounded like another insane plot.

"So finally your mom had to shoot him in order to save Gina's life. . . ."

"Oh dear."

Should she try to confront Reverend Goode? Maybe the best thing was to ignore his ranting and raving. If she went up against him, she was liable to bring more attention to his charges, even lend them credibility.

"He died in your mom's arms."

"Sounds . . . great."

"Oh, it *was*. Your mom's *such* a good actress. I can't believe you don't watch the show. *Oh my God*. Look at the time!" Suze departed in a flash of sage green unitard.

A.J. gave her head a little shake like she had water in her ear. She picked up the phone again but replaced the handset slowly. It was probably wiser not to give Goode advance warning. If she really *was* going to beard the lion in his den, there were advantages to not ringing the supper bell first.

* * *

"**Have** a seat, please," the grave young man told A.J. "I'll see if the reverend can spare you a few minutes."

The nameplate on the tidy desk of the Reverend Goode's administrative assistant read *Lance Dally*. Dally was thin and bespectacled but, nonetheless, attractive. His eyes were green and long-lashed behind wire-framed glasses. His mouth seemed naturally inclined to a wry smile despite his gravity, which A.J. read as an encouraging sign.

She seated herself on the tan sofa in the lobby of the New Dawn Church headquarters in the Stillbrook Shopping Center and gazed doubtfully out the windows at the busy parking lot. People in raincoats splashed back and forth from their cars to the shops, heads ducked against the pelting rain.

"He'll be right with you," Lance said, closing the door between the lobby and the mysterious inner hallway. He took his seat at the desk once more and began busily sorting the just-delivered mail.

A.J. sighed inwardly and gazed out the window. They'd been having rain and thunderstorms all day—not unusual for November in New Jersey—and the parking lot was starting to flood. That meant the country roads would also be less and less traversable, which could making getting home that evening problematic. If A.J. did get stranded, she could always stay over at Jake's. Thinking of the possibilities of an impromptu sleepover made it hard to suppress a smile. She bit her lip hard, not wanting the Reverend Goode to find her grinning like a loony in the church lobby.

Assuming the reverend deigned to speak to her demonic self. There had been no sign of him so far, and A.J. wasn't sure how much longer she could take the sappy, soulful Muzak drifting through the office speakers.

"Have you worked for the New Dawn Church long?" she asked Lance, mostly out of boredom.

He smiled. "I've been with the reverend a little over six months."

"Do you enjoy your work?"

"I do. Yes."

A.J.'s cell phone vibrated, and she picked up her bag and fished it out.

A photo of her mother looking uncharacteristically relaxed and maternal flashed up.

Speak of the Devil. Elysia would be phoning with her travel plans. *Golden Gumshoes* had finished shooting for the season and Elysia planned to return to her home in Warren County for the break.

A.J. was a little surprised at how much she was looking forward to seeing her mother. Their relationship had not always been as close as it was these days, but A.J. found that she'd missed Elysia during the long months she was filming her new series. Though A.J. had been frequently invited to visit Los Angeles, she just couldn't bring herself to leave Sacred Balance for more than a day or two. In fact, every time Jake suggested they go away for a real vacation she reminded him that without Lily to co-manage, there was no one to handle any possible emergencies at the studio. The truth was, even when Lily had been her co-manager, A.J. hadn't trusted her enough to leave Sacred Balance in Lily's unsupervised hands. Ironically, Lily had felt the same way about A.J.

No doubt that inability to trust had contributed to the strain between them.

Conversations with Elysia often led in unexpected directions, so A.J. let the call go to voice mail and then listened to the message. It was brief and to the point. Elysia gave her flight info and requested that A.J. pick her up in Elysia's Land Rover rather than A.J.'s own car. A.J. raised her brows at the imperial directive, saved the message, and put her phone away.

Still no sign of the Reverend Goode. A.J. sighed.

"He's really very busy," Lance said apologetically with a glance at the phone on his desk. "His line is still in use."

A.J. nodded, gazing restlessly around the small room.

The lobby was generic to the extreme. Neutral walls, neutral carpet, tan furniture, and a couple of potted silk plants. A rental space in a mall was not A.J.'s idea of church, and she assumed that worship services were held elsewhere. For one thing, no way could this space be large enough to contain the crowds that the Reverend Goode supposedly drew each Sunday.

A tidy bulletin board notified the faithful of an upcoming bake sale, a cross-country bike ride, and a youth group secret slide show. A picture of a giant glass and steel cathedral with a small brass plate inscribed New Dawn Church hung on one wall. On the opposite wall was a large formal photograph of a plain woman in a plain navy dress and an extremely handsome man wearing a smile that would put most toothpaste models to shame. A.J. had seen enough photos in the local paper to recognize the Reverend David Goode, but she had no idea who the woman was. Mrs. Reverend?

Beneath the portrait was a tower of clear plastic shelves offering brochures with titles like *Praying Your Way to Sobriety*, *Praying Your Way to Heterosexuality*, *Praying Your Way to Weight Control*, *Praying Your Way to . . .*

Something buzzed on Lance's desk. He smiled wryly at her as though they shared a private joke. *Your table is ready?* "He'll see you now." He sounded like God himself had agreed to a quick five minutes.

He rose and walked over to the door leading to the back offices. He held the door for her, and A.J. rose. She followed Lance down a short bare hallway to a small office with bookshelves, a desk, and a pair of comfortable chairs. Frankly, the office could have contained a bed of nails and an iron maiden—the only thing A.J. really noticed was the man seated behind the desk.

The Reverend David Goode stood. "Miss Alexander. What can I do for you?"

He had a wonderful speaking voice, deep and mellifluous. It matched his looks. He was, quite simply, the most handsome man A.J. had ever seen—and as a former freelance marketing consultant she'd seen one or two prime specimens in her time. Her boyfriend, Detective Jake Oberlin, was ruggedly good-looking, and her ex-husband, Andy, was almost beautiful, but the Reverend David Goode was in a class all his own.

He was probably about forty, but every feature—from his smooth, unlined forehead to the dimple in his chin—was flawless. His hair was dark and glossy, his eyes sparkled a heavenly blue, and his mouth was sensitive but firm—with just a hint of sensuality.

A.J. stuck her hand out automatically. "Thank you for seeing me on such short notice."

"Not at all. I'm very glad you've taken this first step." Goode gestured to one of the chairs in front of his desk. "Please sit down."

"Well, I felt I had to take this step. I'm hearing some really disturbing things."

"I imagine so." Goode smiled briefly and sympathetically. He waited for A.J. to sit before taking his own chair
once more.

"Friends are telling me that you've denounced my
business, denounced yoga in general and me in particular.
In fact, I've heard myself and my work described as
demonic."

She felt silly saying the word. It sounded so ridicu-
lously overdramatic, but Goode didn't refute it. Instead,
he said with that same maddening sympathy, "And you're
naturally upset and beginning to question things you've
previously taken for granted."

"Sort of. To start with, I'm questioning why you didn't
have the courtesy to talk to me before saying such defamatory things to your congregation."

"As you would say, if the mountain won't come to Muhammad, Muhammad must go to the mountain." Goode
smiled the breathtaking smile of the photograph in his
front office.

"Actually, I wouldn't say that," A.J. replied. "What I
would say is that before you started spouting a lot of ig-
norant and possibly libelous nonsense, you should have
had the courtesy to speak to me."

Goode's benign expression never wavered. "And what
is it you would have told me?" he inquired politely.

"First of all, I would have asked you where you got
such bizarre ideas about yoga. And me."

Goode sighed. "I'm afraid you put me in a difficult
position."

"How am I putting you in a difficult position?"

"A.J.—I'm sorry. May I call you A.J.?"

A.J. nodded curtly.

"You're an intelligent young woman—certainly a very

attractive woman." He winked. A.J.'s mouth parted indignantly, but Goode overrode any objection she might have
made by continuing. "Intelligence, however, is a two-
edged sword. I'm sure you believe sincerely in the work
that you do. I'm sure you believe sincerely that your efforts to convert—"

It was an effort to keep her voice level. "I'm not trying
to *convert* anyone."

Goode held his hand up. "Please. You're angry because you feel the truth of what I'm saying, but if you'll
be quiet and listen with your heart rather than allowing
your thoughts to confuse you, I'm sure you'll begin to
understand."

"Understand what? That exercise is bad? That medita-
tion is unhealthy?"

Goode looked pained. "You're far too smart to believe
that yoga is simply about physical activity. It's not possible to separate the philosophical and spiritual aspects of
the practice."

"There's nothing harmful or even anti-Christian in the
philosophical or spiritual aspects of yoga."

The pitying look he gave her sparked a very unspiritual
response within A.J. She smothered it. Or tried to. It kept
rising up like a cobra beneath a carpet.

"You can't see it yet. Your yoga is descended from
Eastern religion. It's a heathen practice, pure and simple.
And the funny thing is, even other Eastern religions say
the same thing."

"I think this was a waste of time." A.J. stood up.

Goode rose, too. "Not at all! Not at all. The fact that
you sought me out is a very positive sign." He came around
the desk and placed both hands on A.J.'s shoulders.

A.J. stiffened. Maybe it was a Man of the Cloth thing.

Or maybe he didn't get the concept of personal space. Maybe he was just very, very friendly. Laying hands on someone with whom you were having an argument seemed inappropriate to A.J., but maybe it was different for ministers.

She stepped back, and his hands fell away. "I can't stop you preaching against yoga, but if you continue to make defamatory statements about me, I'm going to seek legal counsel."

Goode's blue gaze held her own. "We're not enemies, you know. Your coming here today proves that."

"My coming here today proves that I'm a reasonable person who would prefer to work things out civilly."

Goode nodded. "I know. My actions may seem harsh. In time you'll come to see that what I'm doing is for your good as well as the good of our community."

"So in other words, you're not going to stop?"

He cast a sorrowful look at her, and A.J. couldn't help thinking Goode was playing to the nonexistent studio cameras. She knew what he would say before he opened his mouth.

"No, A.J.," he said solemnly. "I'm afraid I can't stop now."

Two

❧

Back at the studio, A.J. was still fuming over her waste-of-time meeting with Reverend Goode when Emma ushered in Michaela and Mocha Ritchie for their four o'clock appointment.

Given the weather, which was getting steadily worse as the afternoon poured by, and the disheartening phone conversation she'd had with Bradley Meagher, her lawyer, A.J. had been hoping the Ritchies would cancel. What kind of people named their daughter Mocha, anyway?

But Michaela Ritchie was there at four o'clock on the dot, Mocha in tow.

"Please have a seat," A.J. invited as the women were led into the upstairs conference room. "Can I offer you coffee? Tea? Cucumber water?"

"No, thank you." Michaela Ritchie was very short and very trim. She looked a well-cared-for forty. Her makeup could have been applied by a professional artist; her hair was a lovely, if premature, silver cropped close to her head.

Mocha was probably about fifteen, although the dyed black hair, heavy kohl eye makeup, and sparkly lip gloss made it difficult to be sure. She was—there was no polite word for it—fat. Technically obese. Clothes couldn't camouflage the problem, but the black thigh-high boots were a mistake, and the oversized purple Benetton-style sweater she was wearing as a dress certainly accentuated the problem.

A number of problems—because what kind of parent let their child out of the house looking like an overfed hooker? It was especially disconcerting given how severely chic Michaela Ritchie was.

A.J. smiled at Mocha. Mocha stared stonily back.

"You're certainly out in the middle of nowhere." Michaela threw a disparaging look at the conference room's long windows, which framed glistening pine trees rising out of the rainy mist. She sat down at the oval table and pulled out her cell phone, checking messages in a businesslike fashion.

"Less and less so," A.J. said. "There used to be nothing around us for miles, but now we've got the Carriage House Inn right down the road. Bikers still love this stretch."

"Sit down, Mocha." The snap in Michaela's voice startled A.J., but Mocha didn't bat a black-rimmed eye. Enigmatic as an Egyptian princess, she seated herself next to her mother and folded her woolly purple arms.

A.J. finished pouring herself a cup of tea. "Are you sure I can't get either of you anything?" She carried her mug to the table and sat down opposite the Ritchies.

Michaela dropped her phone in her Gucci bag and said

without preamble, "Mocha's pediatrician recommended we try yoga. Mocha's father is in favor of it, so we'll give this a shot. I think six months is a reasonable amount of time, don't you?"

A.J. spared a glance at Mocha's impassive face. Nothing. Michaela looked equally removed from the proceedings.

"I'm sorry? I feel like I'm missing something. Six months is a reasonable amount of time for what?"

Michaela made an exasperated sound. "I think one look at my daughter should make it clear what the problem is."

Well, that was brutally frank. A.J. smiled warmly at Mocha, who looked right through her.

"What do you hope to achieve by enrolling at Sacred Balance, Mocha?"

"I want to get my stepmother off my back."

Michaela made an amused sound and met A.J.'s gaze in cool challenge. A light dawned. This, apparently, was the part where A.J. was supposed to concede defeat, say there was nothing she could do with such an attitude, and send Mocha and Frosty Freeze on their chilly way.

And that, at one time, was exactly what she would have done. But at one time she wouldn't have been running a yoga studio. Not for love or money or anything in between.

She removed a form from her folder, slid the membership enrollment sheet across the table to Mocha. "Please fill this out to the best of your ability, Mocha. Take your time and feel free to ask any questions you like in the section on the back page. Candidly, the more honest you are and the more questions you ask, the better. We want to make sure we tailor a program to suit *you*."

Mocha snorted, sounding uncannily like her stepmother.

A.J. smiled at Michaela with all the professional sincerity she could muster. "Would you like to see the facilities? Perhaps talk to some of our instructors or other students?"

"Oh, by all means." Michaela sounded bored as she rose.

"Please excuse us," A.J. said to Mocha, who was hunched over the table, filling in the form in tiny script.

"You're excused."

Michaela met A.J.'s gaze with something unpleasantly like satisfaction. A.J. led the way from the room.

"I thought it might be helpful if you shared your expectations for the next six months," she said as the door to the conference room swung shut.

"Honestly? My expectation is zero. You'll get zero cooperation from my stepdaughter, and you'll get zero results. But this is what the doctor suggested, and it's what my husband wants, so this is what we're doing."

A.J. didn't love all her clients, but she could rarely remember disliking one as immediately and intensely as she did Michaela Ritchie. Perhaps her expression gave her away, because Michaela added, "Sorry, but we're not all living a version of *Leave It to Beaver*. Mocha and I don't get along. It's that simple."

A.J., knowing firsthand that family relationships were anything but simple, restrained herself and led the way to the showers, steamy and pleasantly scented by shampoo and soap at that hour. She extolled the efficiency and beauty of their up-to-the-minute plumbing to Mrs. Ritchie, and then asked, "Does Mocha have any health issues we need to be aware of?"

"Not according to her doctor. If you want my opinion, Mocha's weight is merely another form of acting out. If you decide to take her on, I'll have her doctor forward her medical records."

"I can't see any reason we wouldn't take Mocha on."

"No?" Michaela smiled. But her smile faded. In fact, her face fell, as a tall woman wrapped in a white terry robe and holding a blow-dryer approached the built-in table and mirror of the blow-dryer station.

A.J., too, did a double take. The woman's face was oddly familiar, but thanks to the white toweling around her hair, it took a few seconds to place her as the Reverend Goode's companion in the portrait that hung in his Stillbrook office.

The woman smiled at her politely, smiled at Michaela— then her expression also froze.

She nodded curtly to Michaela. Michaela nodded curtly back. Turning abruptly away, Michaela left the shower area. A.J. followed, still trying to put a name to the client in the white terry robe.

She was sure she had seen the woman at the studio before, but no particulars came to mind. That was odd. A.J. prided herself on, at the very least, knowing all her clients by name.

The moment in the shower room had been too obvious to ignore—at least in A.J.'s opinion. "Do you know—" she began.

"No, I don't," Michaela said. "I know *of* her, of course. That's Mrs. Goode. The Reverend Goode's wife. Look, can I be honest? I don't need the grand tour. I'm quite sure your facilities are state of the art. In fact, I know they are. My husband and I did our homework. I'd just as soon wait for Mocha in the car. I'm sure she'd prefer that, too."

"If that's what you'd—"

Michaela Ritchie was already walking away toward the main staircase.

"I don't think I'm imagining things either." A.J. set down her wineglass. She and Jake were having dinner at his house, A.J. having opted for Jake and Jake's homemade lasagna over a rainy drive home, cold leftovers, and an aging Labrador retriever who, though he would be delighted to see her, would spend most of the evening snoring atop her feet.

So it was a doggie door and dry kibbles for Monster tonight, and no doubt A.J. would hear about it tomorrow.

Jake served himself another helping of lasagna—lasagna with meat sauce. Though red meat was something A.J. now limited in her diet, she refused to feel guilty over her thorough enjoyment of the meal. Jake was a surprisingly good cook. The beef was very lean and there was just a hint of fennel in the sauce. "What do you think is going on?"

A.J. shook her head. "According to Emma, Oriel Goode uses one of our free guest passes every couple of weeks or so. That's really not the idea behind the promotion. The whole idea is that the guest will realize what a terrific place Sacred Balance is and enroll, but it's not something we're going to make an issue of."

"She'd have trouble enrolling given her husband's view of yoga, right?"

"Right. True."

"As for the Ritchie woman's reaction, I'm sure you've heard some of the rumors about the good Reverend Goode."

"Well . . ." A.J. flashed Jake a quick, rueful smile,

reaching for her wineglass once more. "I don't believe everything I hear, but he does seem to take a . . . hands-on approach."

Jake's dark brows drew together in a formidable line. "Did he come on to you?"

"I doubt it. I think he's probably a little weak on the concept of personal space. It probably goes with the job."

"Yeah, well, reverend or not, the guy's already got a reputation as a womanizer. I'm guessing that was what was behind that little moment in the ladies' locker room."

A.J. snorted at the idea of calling her tile floors, granite counters, and stylish, ergonomic fixtures anything so plebian as a "locker room."

"That visit to see Goode was probably a mistake any way you look at it. I feel like I played right into his hand. Not that he could have known I'd come calling."

"Sure he did." Jake chewed, swallowed. "He was lying in wait for you."

"How do you figure that?"

"He'd have to be stupid not to know you were going to pay him a visit. And one thing I don't hear is that David Goode is stupid." Jake put his fork down and pushed his plate away. "He threw down the gauntlet at Sunday's service. He had to know you'd pick it up. Either you or Lily. Or both of you."

"Do you think I should have ignored him?"

"Hard to say. You not noticing him would certainly annoy him. But ignoring him wouldn't make him go away."

"I don't know that there *is* any way of making him go away. Mr. Meagher thinks suing for slander is liable to give the Reverend Goode the very thing he wants."

"Free publicity," agreed Jake. "Yep. There's nothing like a messy lawsuit."

"And the more I think about it, the more convinced I am that that's what this whole thing is about."

Jake's eyes were very green in the muted light of the candles. The candles were there less for romantic effect and more because the power had been knocked out an hour earlier, though there was no denying the softened illumination added a certain cozy intimacy. "You don't think the good reverend is sincere?"

"I don't know that for a fact, but it's hard for me to believe an educated person could seriously believe that there's anything in the study of yoga that would be contradictory to Christianity, let alone dangerous."

"You're not religious," Jake pointed out.

"I'm not *anti*religious. I've just never been a big churchgoer."

Jake's nod was noncommittal.

"Are you?" Sometimes it caught A.J. off guard how many things they still didn't know about each other.

"Not something I think a lot about either way," Jake said. "So Meagher advised you not to sue?"

"He said we should keep an eye on the situation."

"Seems like good advice. You don't think the reverend is really harming your business, do you?"

"I think it's too early to tell. Given the financial climate, I can't say I'm thrilled with someone coming up with more reasons for clients to cut us out of their monthly budgets."

"If the reverend's own wife isn't taking his preaching to heart, it doesn't seem like you have a lot to worry about."

"Maybe she's spying for him."

Jake's lashes rose, his gaze alert. "Do you think she is?"

A.J. shook her head. "I honestly have no idea."

"Why suggest it if it's not on your mind?"

"Because it seems like such an unusual situation. *He's* condemning us and *she's* using our free passes. Have you heard something that makes you think I'm right?"

He shook his head. "More rumors. Speculation." He reached across to refill A.J.'s glass.

"Speaking of speculation and wild rumors. What's this story about something attacking John Baumann's cows last night?"

Jake sighed. "What's the theory now? Aliens mutilating livestock? I've heard everything else today."

"So it *is* true?"

Jake lifted a broad shoulder in dismissal. "It's not the first time livestock has been killed in this area. The Baumann farm is right on the edge of the Delaware Water Gap National Recreation Area."

"So you think wild animals attacked the cattle?"

Jake hesitated just a fraction too long.

A.J. had started to lift her glass. She lowered it. *"No?"*

"I didn't say that," Jake said quickly.

"Didn't say what?"

"Whatever you're thinking."

A.J. started to laugh. "You know, you sound just *a little* paranoid."

Jake grimaced. "So would you if you'd had the day I did."

"Come on. Tell me. I share all my problems."

His expression was unexpectedly serious. "Do you?"

"I'm happy to say I don't have a lot of problems these days, but . . . yes. I do. It's one of the best things about, well, having someone. In my life."

Jake's eyes tilted. "As opposed to—"

"You know what I mean."

He chuckled. "Yeah. I know what you mean. And yes,

I agree. It's nice having someone to talk to. Even if I don't always take advantage of it."

"So? What are people saying about your dead livestock case?"

Jake sighed. "They're saying it's the Jersey Devil."

When A.J. stopped choking on the wine she'd inhaled, she gulped out, "You're kidding."

"I wish."

"People are seriously suggesting that the Jersey Devil is roaming the countryside killing cows?"

"I know. Believe me, I know."

"It's got to be a joke."

"If so, it's an expensive and brutal one." Jake pushed his chair back from the table.

A.J. glanced at the clock over the stove. It was nearly ten o'clock. The steady rhythm of the rain on the roof made a sleepy, soothing sound.

"Dishes?" she asked.

"Nah. I thought we'd have dessert now."

"Oh? What's for dessert?"

Jake grinned, his expression wicked in the wavering light. "You."

A.J. started to laugh.

Three

∞

Some things never changed. Lily Martin was one of them.

Well, perhaps that wasn't quite fair. Though Lily looked very much as she always did, she was wearing a new shade of lipstick—an unlikely peony—and her hair was longer. She wore it tied back in a severe ponytail. Spring-toned lipstick aside, she looked as tired and edgy as usual, so perhaps finally managing a big, successful yoga studio all on her own was not the twenty-four-hour picnic she'd expected.

"Hi," A.J. said, taking the lattice-back chair across from Lily. "Sorry I'm late. I had a call from Vi McGrath at Zen Zone as I was about to leave. She says hello and she's in on whatever we decide to do."

The waitress, a petite brunette in cargo pants and camo tee, arrived with the menus, cutting off Lily's response—

assuming she'd had one. The choice to meet at Juice Junction had been hers. A.J. would have preferred somewhere a little more comfortable and a lot more private, but Lily had initiated this meeting with a surprise phone call that morning.

A.J. ordered the pad thai with tofu and Lily spent several minutes interrogating the waitress about the ingredients and preparation of the lentil burger.

"All right, what are we going to do about him?" Lily asked briskly as the cowed waitress escaped, menus clutched to her chest.

So much for social niceties.

"I don't see that there's a lot we *can* do," A.J. said. "If we take Goode on publicly, we just provide him with the free publicity he's seeking."

"You may be willing to sit back and let that lunatic ruin your business, but I've worked too hard to get where I am."

And A.J. hadn't? *Choose your battles.* She sighed inwardly. "If you've got an idea, I'm willing to hear it."

"We start by hiring a private detective."

"Seriously?" Whatever A.J. had expected, it wasn't that. Granted, with Lily, anything from staging a sit-in to firebombing the church headquarters could not be ruled out.

"Dead serious." Lily's expression was grim. Grimmer than normal.

A.J. sipped from her glass of ice water. It tasted like it had come from a hose. All part of the Juice Junction dining experience? "What is it you think a private detective might uncover?"

"If I knew, I wouldn't suggest we hire a private detective, would I?"

"I mean," A.J. replied, grabbing onto her patience, "what makes you think there's anything to find out?"

"Instinct. There's something *off* about that guy. I know a huckster when I see one."

"Really?" A.J. wasn't challenging Lily; she was genuinely curious. Maybe Lily did have life experiences that enabled her to pick out a phony baloney at ten paces.

They were silent as the waitress returned with their lunches. The speedy service might be the mark of spectacular efficiency, but A.J. couldn't help wonder if the fact that the small eating area was mostly deserted at lunchtime was a sign of things to come. The only other customer was Sarah Ray, a lanky thirty-something blonde who hosted a local TV cooking show. She was dividing her attention between her lunch, *Food and Wine* magazine, and the window facing the street.

Maybe Sarah was there to do an exposé of Juice Junction. Or maybe the food was much better than the presentation would suggest. The scent of cayenne and fish sauce wafted up from A.J.'s plate. She picked up her fork and gave the noodles a cautious poke. "There *is* one odd thing, although I don't know that it's significant. Goode's wife is a client."

"Of *yours*?" Leave it to Lily to find something in that to be miffed about.

"Of Sacred Balance."

Lily seemed to weigh this. "If she *is* his wife."

A.J. chewed and swallowed hastily. "Is there really a question of that?"

"For someone with a reputation for sleuthing, you really haven't done much background checking. Goode is boinking half the female population of Stillbrook." Lily selected a sweet potato chip and crunched it briskly.

"*Half* the population?" A.J. didn't care about the slur on her supposed sleuthing skills, but surely the rest of it had to be gross exaggeration?

Lily nodded indifferently and took a big bite out of her burger.

"Even if that's true, it doesn't mean they're not married. Marital infidelity—"

Lily shook her head. "Have you had a good look at her? If they are married, it's strictly a business arrangement."

"And that's it? That's why you want to hire a PI? You think they might not be married? That's not much of a sin these days."

"It is for a minister."

"True." A.J. had to give her that much. "But that being the case, why take a chance? Why not just marry?" Lily's hypothesis that the Goodes might not be married because they didn't seem like a great match seemed almost touchingly naïve.

"Maybe they can't marry."

"Because?"

"Because he's already married." Lily added pointedly, "Or maybe he's gay."

A.J. cleared her throat. "Do you have anything else to go on besides some rumors and a hunch the Goodes aren't married?" She lowered her voice as Sarah looked up from her magazine and glanced at their table.

"How would I? That's why I want to hire a PI. So we can catch Goode in the act."

"What act?"

"Any act. If we can discredit him, then no one is going to be interested in anything he has to say about the rest of us."

There was certainly an ugly logic to Lily's reasoning,

but A.J. found the idea of a smear campaign—even if the smears were legitimate—more than a little revolting.

"I'm not happy about what Goode's saying about us and about yoga, but this all sounds a little extreme to me."

"Why am I not surprised to hear that you're happy to take a passive approach to the problem?"

"I'm not being passive, Lily. I'm trying to be practical. Imagine if word got out that we felt so threatened by the idiot comments of this man that we felt we had to hire a PI to dig up dirt on him? I think that could do us more harm than good."

"How would word get out unless you blabbed?" Lily fixed A.J. with a hard eye.

"It's a small town. News spreads. Look at the rumors circulating about Goode right now."

"There's no smoke without fire."

"First of all, that's not true. Sometimes dust looks like smoke from a distance, and people still yell fire. Secondly, you're missing my point. If Goode really is the hypocrite you think he is, then it's going to come out."

"Eventually. Maybe after we're ruined."

A.J. made an exasperated sound. She was honest enough to recognize that part of her resistance to Lily's idea was due to the long-standing antagonism between them, but she also really didn't think hiring a private investigator was the way to go. It seemed overly dramatic for the circumstances, but maybe she was underestimating the threat posed by rumor and innuendo.

"I'll think about it. How's that?"

"Don't bother." Lily's chair scraped noisily as she pushed it back. "I'll deal with it myself. As usual."

"Come on, Lily. Don't turn this into—" But A.J. was talking to Lily's back as the other woman strode briskly to the front entrance. A.J. rose, then realized they hadn't paid for lunch. She checked her pocketbook but she only had a couple of dollars in cash. She retrieved a credit card and took it to the front where there was no sign of a waitress or cashier.

Through the plate glass window she could see Lily marching down the street.

By the time the harassed-looking waitress appeared to run A.J.'s credit card and A.J. got outside, there was no sign of Lily.

She shook her head and started toward the small parking lot behind the café. The sound of raised voices caught her attention. She looked around and spotted Lily a few yards down on the other side of the street, arguing with a tall, dark-haired man.

A.J. let out a little groan as she recognized the Reverend Goode. A woman in a raincoat stood next to him while Lily read the good reverend the riot act. Fortunately, the rain had cleared the streets of Stillbrook of most pedestrians, but there were still a few people going in and out of the various shops, throwing curious looks at Lily and Goode.

A.J. spared a quick look for traffic and sprinted across the street. She didn't particularly have a plan—in fact, she wasn't sure getting involved in a public showdown was a good move—but it didn't seem right to calmly get in her car and drive away. Tempting though the idea was.

As she approached the other three she heard Lily's harsh tones. "Oh, you'll be sorry. Believe me. I'll personally see to that."

"Are you threatening me, young woman?" Goode asked, although he was probably no older than Lily. He smiled in a way that sent unease slithering down A.J.'s spine. Despite the wide, white smile, his eyes were dark and dangerous.

"Lily, let's not do this here." A.J. reached Lily's side.

"You're damn right I'm threatening you." Lily's voice carried clearly in the cold autumn air.

A.J. met the eyes of the woman with Goode. She recognized Oriel Goode from the Sacred Balance showers. Oriel's brown hair was piled in a careless upsweep. She wore pink makeup that did nothing for her sallow skin tone. Her brown gaze met A.J.'s without any sign of recognition before returning to her husband's profile.

"I'd be careful if I were you. I could have you arrested for making threats," Goode told Lily.

"That wouldn't help any of us," A.J. interjected before Lily could snarl a response. She reached for Lily's arm, but Lily shook her off.

"You might fool some people. You don't fool me." Lily continued to glare at Goode, who abruptly looked bored. He looked down at his watch—a Rolex, unless A.J. was mistaken.

"You'll have to excuse us. My wife and I are already late for our lunch appointment." Goode took his wife's arm and hustled her in the direction of the Happy Cow Steak House.

Lily took a step to follow, and A.J. moved in front of her. "You're kidding, right? You're not really going to go harass him in front of fifty witnesses at the most popular restaurant in town?"

"Why? Would it be awkward for you?"

"It would be *stupid*. Even more stupid than accosting him on the street in broad daylight was."

Lily's face was tight with anger. She was still trembling.

"I'm sorry I can't be dispassionate like you, but everything I have is tied up in the success of Yoga Meridian."

"I understand. Everything I have is tied up in Sacred Balance. But this isn't the way."

"The difference is you have eighteen *million* dollars to cushion you if you lose the studio. If I lose Yoga Meridian, I'll have nothing left."

A.J. opened her mouth, but what was the point? She could try and explain to Lily that most of her money was invested in the various subsidiaries of Aunt Di's empire, and that, like everyone else in the country, she'd suffered hits during the current recession. This wasn't really about money for either of them. Lily couldn't see it—would never see it—but they were equally vulnerable. Each of them needed their respective studios to succeed—and for more than financial reasons.

"Then you can't afford to make mistakes in how you handle this. You need to step away for now. When I get back to the studio, I'll call Vi and a couple of the other studio owners in the county and tell them what we discussed and get their input on how we should proceed. I think we need to keep a unified front on this—and we need to keep it impersonal and professional."

Lily's face screwed up in utter disgust. She flung herself away from A.J. and marched up the street.

Wearily, A.J. watched her go. She was feeling the lack of sleep from the night before. The thought of Jake was unexpectedly comforting. She smiled at the memory and then sighed as Lily climbed into her battered Renault and the engine screeched as though in pain.

A.J. turned and walked back toward the parking lot and her own car.

* * *

One of the first changes implemented by A.J. when she took over Sacred Balance was weekly staff meetings. Though initially the Tuesday afternoon meetings had not been greeted with universal joy—even on A.J.'s part—gradually they had evolved into a relaxed forum for everything from airing grievances to brainstorming. Now A.J. actually looked forward to the opportunity to touch base with her busy colleagues. The excuse to eat the occasional pastry certainly didn't hurt either.

She was proud of the team she was building. She both respected and genuinely liked her staff members. It gave her a good feeling to know they cared as much about the success of Sacred Balance as she did. But if they honestly thought the way to bolster studio memberships was camping trips, she needed to check their green tea for hallucinogens.

A.J. was not, by any stretch of the imagination, an outdoors girl.

She *liked* the outdoors, in moderation. She liked being able to look up and see the stars at night. She liked being able to take walks in the woods or swim in unpolluted waters. She recycled faithfully, voted responsibly, and typically did her bit to preserve Mother Earth for future generations.

But *camping*?

Camping was . . . well, really too much of a good thing in A.J.'s opinion. She kept starting to object and then restraining herself as her staff got more and more enthusiastic about the idea of a weekend camping retreat for their students.

"This is brilliant. It's something none of our competitors have thought of," Denise Farber, the Pilates instructor, enthused.

And there was a very good reason no one else had thought of it, in A.J.'s opinion. But once again—with difficulty—she held her tongue.

"I've always wanted to do one of those yoga camping holidays in Spain," Jaci said. "You know, horseback riding and wine tours and river fishing at one of those organic olive farms." Jaci was their newest instructor, hired to replace Lily after she had left to manage Yoga Meridian. She was a curvy strawberry blonde in her early twenties. Despite her youth and easygoing attitude, she was a highly experienced instructor, and A.J. rejoiced on a regular basis that they'd snapped her up before Lily and Yoga Meridian had gotten her in their clutches.

"I like the idea of wine tours in Spain, too. This is camping in the Pine Barrens. In November," A.J. couldn't help pointing out.

"It doesn't have to be the Pine Barrens," Simon said quickly. "I just threw that out as an idea. We could find someplace closer to home."

"Especially with the Jersey Devil on the loose," Suze put in, through a mouthful of soft pretzel. This month A.J. had made an effort to provide more healthy snacks for their weekly staff meetings rather than the pastries she personally loved.

"The Jersey Devil . . . ?" Jaci was staring at Suze.

"Didn't you hear about John Baumann's cows?"

"Okay, that's great." A.J. spoke over Suze, who was clearly readying to launch into a ghoulish retelling of the recent attacks on livestock. "Back to camping in November. Never mind the fact that we're not giving ourselves a lot of time to prepare, it's . . . camping in November. Maybe we should postpone to the spring. The weather will be warmer and there'll be more flowers."

"And snakes," Simon said. "And ticks, yellow jackets, and other insects, not to mention a host of varmints just waking up from their long winter's nap."

A.J. closed her eyes. "Great."

"A little rain won't hurt anyone," Denise said. "Better early in the season than later when we might have to deal with snow."

"Snow?" A.J. opened her eyes and gazed reproachfully at Denise, who—before the meeting—had been as unenthusiastic about the idea of camping as A.J. Simon had been very persuasive on the topic, however, and it was beginning to look like a camping trip was in A.J.'s near future.

Denise smiled sheepishly.

"No, no," Simon reassured. "We'd have to cancel if snow was in the forecast. Of course. The idea is to have fun and learn something."

Suze said, "And offer something the competition doesn't."

A.J. knew when she was defeated. "Right. Then I guess the next question is what's the focus of the retreat? Adults only? Women only? Teens?" She gazed around the table.

"I'd love to take my teens and young adults on a camping retreat," Jaci said. "I think they'd really get into that."

"But looking at this from a commercial standpoint, I think maybe we should start out with adults only. Maybe a working women's retreat weekend," Denise suggested.

A tap on the doorframe had them all turning around. Emma stood in the doorway with an uncharacteristically grim expression. "The Reverend Goode is here to see you," she told A.J. "And he doesn't look happy."

Four

Goode was gazing down at the silvery water pouring over the glinting stones of the mini-fountain in the corner of A.J.'s office. He turned as she entered the room, and his expression fell into stern lines.

He quoted, "'The wife must willingly obey her husband in everything, just as the church obeys Christ.'"

"I'm sorry?"

"Knowing my feelings regarding the heathen practice of yoga, you still encouraged my wife to come here and take part in your ungodly activities."

"I didn't encourage her." It occurred to A.J. that she might have let indignation trip her into an indiscretion. She added, "If your wife is a student here, I'm not aware of it."

"The mouth of them that speak lies shall be stopped."

"I can't wait." A.J. met Goode's gaze steadily. He didn't look away. Neither did she. The seconds ticked by, and the ridiculousness of trying to stare each other down struck her. A.J. resisted the hysterical impulse to burst out laughing, but it wasn't easy.

"Is there something I can do for you?" she asked briskly, finally.

Goode, seemingly feeling he'd won the encounter, relaxed ever so slightly. "Yes. Yes, you can, A.J. You can pray with me."

A.J. expelled a long, exasperated breath. "Thank you, but no. Is there something else I can do for you?"

"You can bring me my wife. *Or* I can search these premises."

For real? Did people honestly live like this? A.J.'s marriage had had its problems, no doubt about it, but compared to this, it seemed to her a model of civil interaction.

"I'm sorry, but I can't allow you to disrupt classes. Your wife is not enrolled at Sacred Balance. I'd know if she was one of our students."

"Unfortunately, I can't take your word for such a thing. I'll have to check for myself."

This could go a couple of ways and none of them were very pretty. A.J. said with a calmness she didn't feel, "Fine. Will you take the word of our front desk administrator? Emma can confirm or deny whether your wife is enrolled as a student at Sacred Balance. Emma's a member of your . . . congregation."

Goode got a little glint in his eyes at the mention of Emma being a member of his flock. He nodded graciously, and A.J. leaned out the door and called, "Emma? Can you come here a sec?"

Emma hustled down the short hallway. Her brows rose inquiringly as she reached A.J. A.J. shrugged and nodded at Goode, who waited with impressive sangfroid for a guy who had to realize how very unpopular he was—although perhaps he didn't realize it. Or perhaps he simply didn't care.

"Is Mrs. Goode enrolled as a student at Sacred Balance?" A.J. trusted Emma to read between the lines.

Emma didn't miss a beat. She shook her head. "No."

"Is my wife attending this facility under another name?" Goode asked shrewdly.

Emma leveled a dark glance his way. "She is not. We've only got one class in session right now, and it's our Sunset Seniors."

Goode frowned. He looked from Emma to A.J.

A.J. said, "Tuesday afternoons are our staff meetings. We resume classes in the evenings."

"I see. Very well. Thank you."

A.J. nodded to Emma, who left the office.

Goode, however, didn't appear to be in any hurry to depart. He turned to A.J.'s bookshelf, scanning the titles. "*Fourteen Lessons in Yogi Philosophy and Occultism.* Do you still insist that yoga is nothing but physical exercise?"

"I never said that yoga was simply a form of exercise, although I suppose that's true for many of our clients. Yoga is, of course, much more than that. But nothing that should contradict or conflict with Christianity. That particular book you're looking at is a 1909 edition of a series of lessons that made up a correspondence course for a Masonic temple in Chicago. My aunt kept it mostly as a curiosity."

"Do you believe the men who wrote this book were sincere in their beliefs or do you believe they were con men and charlatans?"

"Maybe a little of both."

"A little of both? That's a certainly a . . . tolerant viewpoint." Goode smiled faintly. "A little of both," he repeated to himself and returned the book to the shelf.

"Is that it?" A.J. asked.

"Hmm?"

"Is there anything else I can help you with?"

Nothing. She might have been talking to the bookcase itself.

"You'll have to excuse me, Reverend. I have a staff meeting to get back to."

Goode at last turned unhurriedly, making it very clear that he was on his own timetable and not being rushed by her. "What? Oh. Of course."

He turned and left the office.

A.J. followed Goode out to the main lobby. Emma, on the phone, met her gaze in silent inquiry. A.J. resisted the desire to roll her eyes.

Standing at the glass door, she watched Goode stride down the walk and cross the parking lot to a Mercedes.

"What on earth was that about?" she murmured.

Emma put the phone down. "What's that, honey?"

"What kind of a relationship must the Goodes have if she feels she's got to hide the fact that she's taking yoga lessons—or that he feels entitled to track her down. What would he have done if she'd been here?"

"Dragged her out of class?"

"That could have been messy. What if it had gotten physical? What if she'd punched him in the nose? What if I had?"

Emma laughed. "Brings out your violent streak, does he?"

Watching the black Mercedes pulling out of the parking lot, A.J. said moodily, "I bet that man brings out a lot of people's violent streaks."

Elysia's flight from LAX was late, and A.J. spent half an hour strolling around Liberty International Airport drinking very bad coffee and window-shopping for items she would ordinarily never consider buying. Just how many styles of *Everyone Loves a Jersey Girl* T-shirt *were* there?

When she finally spotted Elysia by the baggage carousel, surrounded by a small but noisy throng, A.J. inevitably wondered what her mother had done now. Hopefully nothing liable to incite an international incident.

As she approached the madding crowd she realized two things: a number of people seemed to be asking for autographs, and Elysia was not only at the center of the maelstrom, she seemed to be directing it.

She swept her stylish long pageboy out of her face as she spotted A.J. "Oi! Anna Jolie. Darling!"

"Mother!" A.J. was slightly thrown by the fact that her mother seemed to have had a complete makeover in the months since they'd last met. In addition to the new haircut, Elysia now had a striking streak of silver framing the left side of her face. It wasn't the silver that shocked A.J.; it was the fact that Elysia would admit to, let alone flaunt, even one single strand of gray. Her jeans and black cashmere coat were decidedly less flamboyant than her typical wardrobe. In fact, she looked disconcertingly . . . well, like a stranger.

They pressed cheeks and A.J. was reassured by the familiar maternal scents of cigarettes and Opium. The fragrance, not the drug, although Elysia had had her substance abuse problems. Happily those seemed to be safely in the past now.

A couple of cell phones turned in A.J.'s direction, photos were clicked, and then the crowd seemed to trickle away. Elysia and two other vaguely familiar-looking middle-aged women bade them a fond, smiling adieu.

"What was that about?" A.J. asked.

"What was what about?" Elysia's feline gaze turned her way.

"All that . . . fuss. Is it like that everywhere you go now?"

"That was nothing, pumpkin. No one recognizes us here. You should see the reception we get in Beverly Hills."

The other two women nodded enthusiastic agreement, apparently tickled at the idea of autograph hounds and photographers.

"We?" A.J. asked cautiously.

Elysia made the introductions briskly. "This is Marcie, pet." Marcie was red haired and freckled and had probably been adorable at twenty. She was still very attractive in her leather jacket and jeans. Elysia waved vaguely at the other woman. "And this is Petra." Petra was a very thin, weathered blonde in braids and wire-rimmed glasses. She looked vaguely like Diane Keaton, but A.J. was sure that wasn't the only reason she seemed so familiar.

She said hello and shook hands, sparing an uneasy glance at a fair-haired man trying to load a ridiculous amount of luggage onto a small trolley. He was clearly not a porter, and he didn't appear to be a fan either.

Which must mean . . .

"Are we dropping you somewhere?" she asked, trying not to sound too hopeful.

Marcie laughed. She had a cute little laugh, a sort of pixie giggle.

"Don't be daft. They're coming home with me, darling." Elysia pawed through her bag, searching for what turned out to be cigarettes.

"You can't smoke here, Lucy," Petra objected.

"Oh, bother all these bloody rules and regs!"

Lucy? Wasn't that the name of the character Elysia played on TV? That explained why Petra and Marcie looked so familiar. A.J. hadn't recognized them without their sequins and guns.

Which meant that the rather handsome man struggling with the luggage was probably not a random Good Samaritan—surely no one would be unwise enough to voluntarily tackle that Everest of suitcases and tote bags—but yet another member of the *Golden Gumshoes* cast?

He dived to save a Gucci makeup case and threw a slightly harassed look over his shoulder as A.J. said, "I'm sorry. Have we met?"

"This is Dean," Elysia purred, resting a possessive hand on Dean's broad shoulder. "Dean Sullivan. He plays Danny O on the show."

"Oh!" A.J. said brightly. She was trying to remember who the heck Danny O was in the *Golden Gumshoes* universe. A cop? A PI? Someone's son?

Dean smiled, straightened a precariously balanced makeup case, and offered a hand. "I've heard a lot about you, Anna."

"A.J.," A.J. corrected with a forbidding look at her mother.

"Nicknames are for children under thirteen." Elysia's expression was pained. "If your father and I had wanted you to be named Scooter or Skipper, we'd have formalized it on a silver mug. Or possibly a pet dish."

"Gee, I've missed you," A.J. said. "How soon till you start filming again?"

Elysia sniffed.

"We've got the green light for February," Petra responded, taking A.J.'s comment at face value.

Elysia asked, "Where are you parked?"

The official introductions and greetings over with, A.J. led the way, and the others filled her in on what Elysia had been up to in the months she had been in California.

During the short trip by mini train to the parking structure, Elysia asked about Sacred Balance, and A.J. described the situation with Lily and the Reverend Goode.

The night air smelled of rain and plane exhaust as they disembarked and walked to where A.J. had parked. Elysia stopped short at the site of A.J.'s ancient Volvo.

"You're joking. You're not still driving *that*?"

"Why not? It runs beautifully. And it belonged to Aunt Di."

"Yes, very touching, I'm sure. But how on earth are we going to load all these people and all this luggage into that little car?"

Clearly they weren't.

Dean offered to rent another car. This was greeted by relief from all concerned. He went off to find the rental desk and the others did their best to load the luggage into the back of A.J.'s car.

"Sort of like a team-building exercise, isn't it?" Marcie inquired, giving a final shove to a makeup bag that could have doubled as a knapsack. Petra nodded, leaning against the side of the car and wiping her face. Even her braids seemed to be drooping.

"Now what did I do with me . . ." Elysia's voice trailed as she poked through her purse.

"Whatever it is, you better hope it's not in a suitcase," Marcie said.

Dean returned, slightly out of breath, and Petra and Marcie volunteered to drive with him.

"Just don't lose me," he requested of A.J. His smile was warm and rueful. A.J. had to admit he was a very attractive man.

"I'll keep an eye on you," she promised.

He departed with Petra and Marcie, their voices echoing cheerfully as they vanished down the rows of gleaming cars and cement pillars.

A.J. and Elysia got in the car. Elysia heaved a sigh and smiled the first relaxed smile A.J. had seen from her. "It is nice to be home, I must say."

"It's nice to have you back." A.J. started the Volvo.

"How is everyone? How *is* darling Andy?" Elysia rooted around in her purse again. "I brought you a lovely prezzie. Now where is the bloody thing?"

Andy was A.J.'s ex, and a year or so ago that would have been a sensitive question. They had been college sweethearts, and after college they had married and set up a freelance marketing consulting firm together. A successful business, an indulgent and affectionate husband; at the time A.J. had believed that was about as good as life got. And then Andy had dropped the bomb on her. He was in love with someone else. And the someone else in question was a man.

But that was ancient history now. Or at least so much had happened since her divorce that it felt like ancient history to A.J. One of the blessings of her new life was that she had been able to let go of her old bitterness.

"Andy is doing great. The business is thriving, even in this economy, and his health seems to be stable for now, which I personally think is largely due to Nick."

"How so?" Elysia's voice was muffled as she continued to dig through her purse.

"Just . . . the fact that he has someone to love him, someone to stay well and healthy for. Plus I think Nick watches him like a hawk and makes sure he's not overdoing things."

Elysia sat up abruptly. "'And in these degrees have they made a pair of stairs to marriage.' As the Bard says."

"Does he? Well, he was right about Andy and Nick."

Elysia pored over something that looked unsettlingly like an iPhone. "What about you and that big brute of a copper?"

A.J. said warily, "What about us?"

"Has he popped the question or whatever the ghastly term for it is over here?"

"He's popped a number of questions. None of them have to do with marriage." A.J. spared a glance from the road. "Mother, what are you doing?"

"Checking my Facebook, pumpkin."

"Ch . . ." A.J.'s voice failed. When she had recovered from the shock, she managed, "You have a Facebook account?"

"Of course. Well, actually it's the show's Facebook but we all post in character." Elysia added with an innocent pride that brought an unexpected lump to A.J.'s throat, "I—Lucy Bannon, that is—am the most popular."

"That doesn't surprise me." A.J. felt the look her mother threw her. "The fact that you actually bother to *post* does."

"Oh, I have to post. The fans expect it. We have to be accessible."

"Oh. My. God. Who *are* you and what have you done with my mother? Next you'll tell me you're on Twitter."

"Of course I'm on Twitter. Aren't you?"

"No. Absolutely not."

Elysia sighed. "You sound so like your aunt sometimes. That's not necessarily a good thing," she added quickly.

"All right. I admit the studio has a Facebook account. Suze maintains it."

Mention of Suze distracted Elysia momentarily, and A.J. spent the next few minutes catching her mother up on everyone in Stillbrook from Suze to A.J.'s neighbor and friend, Stella Borin.

"So, Stella's standing by her jailbird beau?" Elysia's pointed nails tapped and clicked on the iPhone keys like an old-fashioned telegraph operator signaling trouble.

What on earth was she communicating so urgently to her Facebook friends? The traffic stats outside of Liberty International?

"Yes. She firmly believes Stewie was more sinned against than sinning."

Click. Click. Click. Elysia said vaguely, "I suppose everyone needs a hobby."

"I see it as a good thing. Stella needs someone in her life. Everyone needs someone."

Elysia stopped clicking and sat up straight. She stared out the rain-starred windshield.

"I know you and Stella have had your differences, but you have to admit she deserves more in the way of company than a houseful of cats and a spirit guide from the Great Beyond."

"I always thought she was happy with Slap Happy, or whatever her ghostly crony's name was, and the cats."

Her voice altered. "How's Bradley Meagher? You haven't mentioned him."

"Mr. Meagher? He's fine. Busy. Aren't you—" She stopped, suddenly aware that she had seemingly and inadvertently stepped out onto slippery ice.

Elysia began to type once more. "You should come out to Los Angeles in the spring, pumpkin. You haven't seen the house yet. It's really lovely. And it has a wonderful swimming pool with nearly year-round sunshine. We could shop and spend time together. I think you'd enjoy it."

"I probably would, but it's difficult for me to leave the studio for any length of time."

Elysia sighed. "Of course. The devotion to duty that verges on mania."

"*Mania?* That's not exactly fair."

"Just the other night Dean and I were watching a film on that poor man Howard Hughes. All that money, and he could never relax enough to *enjoy* it. It's like this, your insistence on driving this heap."

Well, here was an abrupt change of subject. A.J. forced her hands to relax on the steering wheel. "Mother, I didn't realize why you needed me to bring the Land Rover, that's all. I'm not driving this car because I've forgotten how to enjoy myself or I've developed an obsession for forcing as many people as possible into a backseat. Yes, the car has sentimental value for me, and yes, it is taking me a while to adjust to the idea that I can do things like buy a new car when I need one—or even when, strictly speaking, I don't *really* need one. But I've been considering getting a new car. I just didn't realize it was an emergency."

Elysia dropped her phone in her bag. "It would be so nice if just for once you would obey me without question."

A.J. nearly swerved off the road. "I'm sorry, your majesty. I didn't realize it was a royal command. I thought it was a suggestion."

Elysia muttered something and then said briskly, "Don't mind me, pet. I'm nervous, and I'm making a muddle of it."

A.J. looked away from the road for an instant. "Making a muddle of what?"

"Of what I have to tell you."

A.J. swallowed. "What do you have to tell me?"

"It's good news."

"*What* is good news?"

"Dean and I are engaged to be married."

Five

"You're right. You win," Jake said. "Your night was def-initely worse than mine."

"Thank you." A.J. took a bite of her cinnamon dough-nut and dusted at the crumbs that fell to her lap. She and Jake had met for a very early, very quick breakfast at Tea Tea! Hee! They were seated on the newly built enclosed patio. Even with the space heaters it was a little chilly, but they had the room to themselves with the exception of a group of groggy-looking college students hunched over laptops and notepads. Through the glass doors she could see the sleepy baristas. "Marcie's in the middle of her third divorce, Petra's farmhouse in the Berkshires is being repainted, and Dean is . . . whatever he is, so they're all staying at Mother's for the time being."

"Cozy."

"It's not that I don't want my mother to remarry. I think she *should* remarry. I know she's lonely. I know she still misses my dad. I'd just prefer she didn't marry someone who's going to be mistaken for my brother."

"Is this one younger than you, too?"

"No. Dean Sullivan's about forty, I think. Still a minimum twenty years younger than my mother."

"Your mother's ageless. Like a diamond. Or a national disaster."

A.J. snorted. "So what happened to you last night?"

Jake gave a little grunt. "I got called out on an attempted break-in at the Goodes' place."

A.J. perked up. "At the Goodes'? A burglary? Really?"

Another one of those noncommittal grunts from Jake. A.J. eyed him curiously. "What?"

"Supposedly . . ." He stopped again.

A.J. nudged him in the ribs. "Will you just spit it out?"

"Goode is claiming that he got a good look at the prowler."

"What's wrong with that?"

"He's claiming it—the prowler—was over seven feet tall, hairy, with hooves instead of feet, a horse's head, and small wings."

A.J. stared at him. "Let me get this straight. Goode is claiming the Jersey Devil tried to break into his house last night?"

Jake nodded grimly.

"Seriously? He actually put that in a police report?"

"Yep." Jake dunked his glazed doughnut in his coffee.

"And did you find cloven hoof tracks beneath Goode's bedroom window?" A.J. teased.

She nearly spilled her coffee when Jake said calmly, "Sure did."

"You did?"

He nodded.

"Somebody is obviously messing with Goode."

"That's my thought."

"How close did the Jersey Devil come to actually breaking in?"

"It—he—tore the kitchen screen door off its hinges and did some damage kicking in the doorframe."

"Wow. Someone was pretty angry."

"It looks that way. Angry enough not to care that anyone inside the house was bound to hear him kicking in the back door."

A.J. stared at Jake, trying to imagine the scene that must have taken place. "And so Goode looked out his window and saw a guy in a costume or what? What did he see?"

"Pretty much what I told you. Goode came downstairs to find out what all the ruckus was about. He says he thought one of his parishioners might have come to him with an emergency. He switched on the back porch light and saw what he describes as 'an unholy creature' running for the woods behind the house."

"He didn't think it was someone in a costume?"

"He insists he would have been able to tell if it was someone in a costume. He said the wings unfurled and flapped."

"It *flew*?"

"No. Haven't you ever seen pictures of the Jersey Devil? The wings are too small to support flight."

A.J. opened her mouth, then closed it. She restrained herself to a mild, "Uh, right. It's an aerodynamic thing, not a that-creature-was-a-total-fake thing."

"According to Goode that was the giveaway. He says you couldn't fake wings like that. So now he's going around claiming that the appearance is a sign."

"A sign of what?"

"I'm not sure I got all the details. It seemed to boil down to the sinners of Stillbrook are about to reap what they've sown."

A.J. shook her head. She looked at her watch. "I don't think I can listen to any more of this. Just hearing about this man is making me nuts. I don't understand why he's so popular. Honestly. The Jersey Devil?"

"He's popular because he's entertaining." Jake dunked the last bit of doughnut in his coffee. "He's like reality TV or a traffic accident. It's hard to look away even though you know watching isn't doing you any good. Have you heard him preach?"

"No. Have you?" A.J. gazed at Jake in disbelief.

"I went online. His sermons get uploaded onto YouTube right after he delivers them. They're interesting. He's a showman. He understands the value of entertainment."

"I admit I'm not an expert, but one thing I don't think I'm looking for in a religious leader is showmanship."

"People like to be entertained. I don't think anyone in Stillbrook is really changing their religious affiliation. I noticed the parking lots at both the Catholic and Presbyterian churches were packed as usual on Sunday. Folks are still making the trek to the synagogue in Deerfield Township. Personally? I think Goode is a kind of novelty. Once the novelty wears off . . ." Jake shrugged and swallowed the last dripping bit of doughnut.

A.J. checked her watch again. "Now I *am* late." Jake rose, too, and she gave him a quick kiss.

"I'm supposed to have dinner at my mother's tonight. You're invited, too. Do you think you can make it or are you going to grab the excuse of chasing the devil?"

Jake's impassive face softened into a brief smile. "I'll try to make it."

"Great. You can meet my future stepdaddy."

"He's probably a very nice guy."

"I know. He seems like a very nice guy. Ignore me." She turned away, but Jake caught her arm to a deliver another, more deliberate kiss—despite the interest of the college kids in the corner.

"That's easier said than done," he said. "See you tonight."

A.J. was still smiling as she climbed into her Volvo.

The sunrise studio was the easternmost space on the top level of Sacred Balance. The long picture windows faced the mountains and offered a glorious view of the sun rising over the woods. The first rays of light stretched pale fingers across the shining wood floor, and the windows seemed to blaze as soothing music played—in this case Jeff Beal's moody but lovely melodies.

Seated cross-legged on the floor, facing her eight faithful Sunrise Yoga students, A.J. rested her right hand on her left knee, inhaled slowly and deeply as she stretched her spine. She exhaled and twisted to the left. She drew in another controlled breath and returned to center. She switched sides, left hand on her right knee, inhaling in smooth, deep breaths. She returned to center.

By making these simple exercises part of her morning routine, A.J. found that she was no longer troubled by the stiffness and minor aches and pains that had gradually begun to creep up on her. The slow stretches were a great way to gently transition from the inactivity of the night without adding any stress to a typically busy morning.

The students in this class had been attending before A.J. took over the studio, and there was no need for speech as they moved together through their routine. In fact, A.J. was aware of a sense of peaceful community, enhanced by the haunting music and the misty sunlight.

Even that lump of doughnut in her stomach didn't unduly bother her, though she generally didn't eat on the mornings she led the sunrise sessions. Generally speaking, the ideal way to start the morning was never going to be with coffee and doughnuts. Usually A.J. opted for a glass of lukewarm water with a slice of lemon followed by her morning asanas and then a light, healthy breakfast before heading to the studio.

This was not to say she had sworn off Pop-Tarts and Cocoa Puffs for all time, but she did try to limit her consumption of them. The truth was she not only had more energy, she felt better overall when she ate right.

By now the class had moved on to lunges. The lunges were inevitably easier to demonstrate than explain. Balanced on all fours, A.J. slid her left foot forward so that her toes lined up with her flexed fingers. She slid her right leg behind until her knee touched the floor while keeping her spine straight and stretched, her shoulder blades down. She tilted her face ceilingward.

The class held the pose for a silent eight count, continuing to breathe slowly, evenly. They switched sides and repeated.

The sun rose higher and gilded the floor and students in golden light.

On her way back down to her office, A.J. spotted Mocha in a gray sweat suit on her way to her first class.

"Good morning!"

Mocha's heavily made-up eyes stared at her blankly.

"I hope you have a good session this morning. Let me know if you have any questions or if there's anything you need."

Mocha didn't exactly roll her eyes but the impression was roughly the same. She continued on without comment at all. A.J. sighed and continued downstairs to her office.

She poured a cup of green tea and sat down at her desk to go through her e-mail. There were the usual offers of credit cards, diet supplements, and holiday getaways as well as a note from Andy asking if she and Jake wanted to come to Manhattan for Thanksgiving.

A.J. read the invitation ruefully. It said something that she could even consider the idea of spending the holiday with her ex and his partner. But the truth was, Andy had been her best friend for most of her adult life. She missed him.

She typed out a quick response saying she would have to check with Jake and see what Elysia's plans were, but if everyone else was up for it, she'd love to.

There were a few other e-mails to deal with. The usual kind of thing. Nothing too urgent. She clicked on the link in the notice from My Yoga Journal and quickly scanned an article on attracting more men to yoga.

Yes, recruiting men might compensate for losing a few students to the economic crunch. In fact, recruiting men might even wind up bringing in more women students, but figuring out a way to do that was more daunting than tackling all the Vedic mysteries in one go. A.J. had tried to get Jake to commit but though he occasionally attended a class, it quite obviously had more to do with pleasing her than any concern with gaining flexibility or experiencing alternative forms of training.

Even though yoga was historically taught and prac-
ticed by men, in Western culture it was perceived as a pri-
marily feminine endeavor. And the male instructors and
students A.J. encountered were, typically, a bit more sensitive and enlightened than the guys shooting pool down
at Terry Mac's Pool Room. That was probably part of the
difficulty in attracting male students. A lot of guys felt
that yoga just didn't seem very . . . masculine.

Suze poked her head in the doorway.

"Did you hear the latest?"

"About?"

"The Reverend Goode. He was on the news this morning. Well, Channel 3."

A.J.'s heart sank. "Oh no. What now?" She was prepared to hear something dire like the reverend was urging
a boycott of all yoga studios.

"He claims that he had to do spiritual battle with the
Jersey Devil last night." Suze grinned cheerfully, apparently untroubled by the idea of good and evil duking it out
in her backyard.

"How does an attempted break-in turn into spiritual
battle?"

"I don't know, but that's not all. He was talking about
how all these sightings of the Jersey Devil are a sign
that our unthinking and godless behavior is leading up to
disaster."

"Disaster? What kind of disaster? You mean like the
Apocalypse?"

"Well, he didn't go *that* far."

"What *does* he mean?" A.J. was bemused. It was almost funny, and yet . . . not really. "Higher gas prices?
More dead cows? Are people really buying into this?"

Suze shrugged. "I don't know. I was at home watching with my cat."

"What did your cat think?"

"She likes fishy things. Anyway, it's not like he's getting national coverage."

"No. That's true. Not yet anyway."

They chatted for a few minutes more and then Suze ducked out only to be replaced by Denise.

"Traitor," A.J. told her without heat.

Denise looked guilty, but then she laughed. "I hate camping, too, but it *is* a good idea. Simon and Jaci sound like they've had a lot of experience. It'll probably be fun."

"If by *fun* you mean we probably won't all die of exposure, you're probably right."

"Have you ever been camping?"

"No. My parents were not the camping types. Neither was my husband."

"You might like it."

"Stranger things have happened."

They discussed issues with a couple of clients and then Denise departed to conduct her first class.

A.J. turned back to her laptop and Googled the New Dawn Church. More than six hundred thousand hits popped up in .20 seconds.

Holy moly. And no pun intended.

"Great." She studied the page and quickly determined that New Dawn Church was a very popular name for a lot of religious entities that had absolutely nothing to do with one another.

She refined her search to include David Goode and New Dawn Church. This brought up more focused results. *Women's Bible Study Group led by Oriel Goode*. That was more like it. *Christian Couples Counseling led by the Reverend David Goode.* A.J. snorted. *Tour de Christ Cycling Club.* She kept reading and finally found what she was looking for.

The New Dawn Church had been founded in the 1960s by a man named Kirkland Bath. Bath, from what A.J. could discern, had been the well-educated only son of a wealthy but strict Presbyterian New England family. For reasons unclear in anything A.J. read, Bath broke with his family while in his early thirties and moved out west to establish a small, fundamentalist sect. There was a lot of information on the church's doctrine, which was something to do with Dispensationalism. Dispensationalism, according to a quick side trip to Wikipedia, was "the rediscovery of early Christian millennialism." At that point, A.J. conceded defeat and went back to searching out what information she could find on David Goode.

The timeline on when he had joined up with Bath was vague, but at some point in the last decade he had married Bath's niece, Oriel Hatton. A.J. studied the tiny web photos closely. Oriel Hatton did appear to be the current Mrs. Goode. The church had continued to grow. Bath had dropped out of the picture, which wasn't surprising considering that he'd be in his eighties by now. Goode had decided to take his ministry east.

Why he had settled on Stillbrook was anyone's guess. A.J. would have expected him to aim a little higher than Warren County. Not that Warren County wasn't a wonderful place to live, but it was largely rural and not densely populated. Of course, maybe that was what Goode liked about it.

Remembering what Jake had said about listening to Goode's sermons, A.J. surfed over to YouTube and searched for the Reverend David Goode. She blinked at the number of video clips that came up. Someone had been a very busy boy.

She pressed play on the most recent video. There was a clip of a dove flying through the spring blue sky and a snippet of music from a popular Christian group, and then there was a surprisingly skillful cut to David Goode delivering an impassioned sermon to a packed community center.

"Some of you have asked about a seven-year pretribulation rapture. I'm here to tell you that the start date of that rapture was 2005."

There was nervous laughter from the audience. Goode laughed, too, his eyes seeming to light with wicked amusement, and for the first time A.J. began to see what some of the appeal might be.

"Yes, 2005. Do the math."

More laughter.

"Have you heard about the mass evacuation? Have you heard about alien rapture tricks? Have you heard of reptiles devouring the ascending?" Goode chuckled, and it was so infectious a sound that A.J. found herself smiling as she watched the clip.

Goode's smile faded. His voice lowered. "But brothers and sisters, I'm here to tell you that monsters *do* exist. Monsters walk among us. . . ."

Six

❧

A.J. was reading over Mocha Ritchie's medical history when Emma's voice crackled through the intercom. "Lily Martin's on line one." Emma had never been a fan of Lily's. Probably because Lily had treated all of A.J.'s hires with a condescending patience that was worse than downright rudeness.

A.J. set the file aside and picked up the phone. "Lily. Hi."

"Are we going ahead or not, A.J.?" Lily's manners were just as bad on the phone as they were in person. "I've been waiting to hear from you. Did you talk to Vi and the others?"

A.J. felt a little flare of guilt. She had sort of assumed that Lily, being Lily, would charge ahead with hiring a PI regardless of what A.J. and the other studio owners decided. Plus she'd been a little distracted with her own personal concerns.

"Not yet. Things have been hectic. I'll call as soon as I get off the phone with you."

"I've found the perfect investigator. He's based right here in Blairstown, but he's expensive."

"How expensive?"

"More expensive than I want to shell out on my own. I'm not the only one whose livelihood is in jeopardy here."

As a matter of fact, out of all the local studios, A.J. would have thought Lily's position was the least endangered. Yoga Meridian was owned by a pair of business entrepreneurs with a strategy of buying up a number of the nation's largest and best-known yoga studios in a bid to create their own national chain. If anyone could weather this kind of tempest in a chai tea pot, it would be the employees of Tussle and Rossiter, surely.

But when A.J. suggested this, Lily replied, "It's not that simple."

"Why isn't it?"

Lily hesitated and then said shortly, "It's like anywhere. When someone comes in from the outside, the existing employees are resentful. Nobody wants change, and because I came in at the time of the buyout and Mara Allen's departure, I'm seen by some as the enemy."

Now there was irony. It was almost an exact replay of Lily's reaction to A.J. when A.J. had inherited Sacred Balance after Aunt Di's death.

But Lily only managed Yoga Meridian. She didn't own it, and reading between the lines, A.J. suspected there had been enough complaints that Lily wasn't sure she could survive much more bad press. And by openly confronting the Reverend Goode, she was liable to have put herself right in the line of fire. No wonder she was looking for backup in the form of a united front of local studios.

"Let me talk to the others." A.J. was unwilling to commit to hiring a PI, but she did, unwillingly, sympathize with Lily's plight. Or maybe it was just the fear that if Lily couldn't make a go of it at Yoga Meridian, she'd be back knocking on the doors of Sacred Balance. A.J. wasn't sure what the legal ramifications of that were. Lily had left Sacred Balance of her own volition, but the terms of Aunt Di's will were vague, and A.J. could imagine a case being argued based on what Aunt Di's ultimate intent might have been.

"Will you please make it a priority?"

In all the time A.J. had known Lily it was the first time she could remember Lily actually saying "please" for anything.

"I'll call now. In the meantime, stay away from Goode. The last thing you need is another public confrontation with him."

"I know." Lily sounded uncharacteristically subdued.

A.J. hung up and immediately dialed Vi McGrath of Zen Zone. Vi, a contemporary of Aunt Di's, had always seemed as down-to-earth as they came, so it was a surprise to hear her voting in favor of Lily's plan to hire a detective.

"You don't think maybe that's a slight overreaction?" A.J. inquired cautiously.

"Goode's not the first soldier of the religious right to demonize yoga as a vehicle for his ambition, but he's by far the most photogenic. The camera loves that man. Have you noticed?"

"But being really, really good-looking isn't enough."

"Of course not. But he's also articulate and personable. There's a cumulative effect to this stuff. In this case, killing the messenger can only help."

That seemed to be the consensus of opinion. Greg Kern of Golden Kernel gave Lily's plan two thumbs up. "Have you heard the rumors about that guy? You *know* there's a story there."

Lori Faith of Faith in You concurred. "I think discrediting Goode will go a long way to discrediting his message. I'm not suggesting we frame him, but it's obvious from the stories circulating about him that there's something not right there."

And Zenobia Graham of Graham Studio said, "Have you seen YouTube lately? Stupidity is viral. We need to fight fire with fire."

Suze brought in a rough draft of a flyer as A.J. was hanging up from her conversation with Zenobia.

"What's this?" A.J. studied the flyer, which turned out to be an invitation for the women's camping retreat. "Wait. You want to try to schedule the retreat for *this* weekend? I thought we were agreed on next weekend."

"We were, but Jaci and I were thinking with next weekend being Thanksgiving, we're probably not going to get many people participating, and after that we're into December. It's now or never."

A.J. raised her hand. "I vote never."

Suze made a face. "Come on, A.J. You're always saying we're a team and we should take initiative about the direction Sacred Balance goes."

It Could Happen. That was the Sacred Balance motto, right? So she could hardly complain when it *did* happen.

"But this gives hardly any time to get people interested."

"We've been talking it up with everyone, and we've already had a couple of students sign up."

"It just seems like we're rushing this."

"If we're going to do it this year, we have to do it

now. It's only going to get colder and wetter from here on out."

"But if we can't generate any interest, we might as well wait until the spring, right?"

"But we *are* generating interest. Like I said, we've got three people signed up already. Besides, we're mostly looking at this as a trial run for next year when we really make a big deal of it. The main thing is, regardless of how many students sign up, we still get the benefit of the promotion for it."

A.J. studied her junior instructor with surprise. That was unexpectedly shrewd of Suze.

"You're right." She quickly read over the flyer, tweaked a couple of things, and handed it back. "Okay. Let's run with it—though I'm personally praying for snow and a cancellation. 'Cause we'll still get the promo value that way, too."

Suze spluttered, shook her head, and departed. A.J. phoned Lily to give her the good news. Not that A.J. really thought of the decision to go ahead with hiring a PI to dig up dirt on their adversary as good news, but Lily would probably see it that way.

However, Lily was not in her office, and A.J. ended up leaving a message.

She spent the afternoon going over the reports on the various subsidiaries of Sacred Balance.

Though A.J. made a conscious effort to get away from the studio at lunchtime, at least a couple of days a week she found herself eating at her desk while she went over paperwork. It was a bad habit, she knew, but it was hard to break it. That day she bought a chicken cranberry walnut salad from the catering van that visited daily. While she ate her salad, she dialed Bradley Meagher and spoke to him about the possibility of Lily returning to Sacred Balance if she lost her job at Yoga Meridian.

Mr. Meagher greeted her as always. "Sure, and if it isn't me own favorite client. How are you, me wee darlin' girl?"

A.J. could hear Mr. Meagher's pet cockatoo shrieking rude commentary in the background and what sounded like a nearby vacuum cleaner. She raised her voice to reassure her legal advisor and friend that all was well in her world with the possible exception of the return of Lily. Mr. Meagher was unnervingly noncommittal on that point, saying vaguely, "Grand, grand. No need to shout, me darlin'. Nothing wrong with my hearing. Speaking of which, have ye heard from your mither?"

Awk.Ward. A.J. was never exactly sure what the relationship was at any given moment between her mother and Mr. Meagher. She knew that Mr. Meagher had great affection—and possibly even deeper feelings—for Elysia, and she knew Elysia was very fond of her old friend and advisor, but beyond that? Angels feared to tread. Let alone A.J. "As a matter of fact, I picked her up at the airport last night."

She needn't have worried about having to break bad news. Mr. Meagher launched into commentary, concluding, "And did she tell you she was planning on marrying the man?"

"Er, she did say something along those lines."

"And himself a great big handsome booby with no more than cotton wool for brains!"

That seemed a little harsh. Dean was certainly handsome, but he hadn't seemed particularly boobish. It was hard to say *what* he'd seemed, given that he'd barely had a chance to string a sentence together between Elysia's running commentary and that of her fellow Golden Gumshoes.

She volunteered, "For what it's worth, I don't think Dean's anything like . . . the last time."

The last time having been particularly painful for all involved, there was a minute pause before Mr. Meagher launched into another tirade, ending with, "It's time the wee woman learned to act her age!"

"I hope you didn't say that to the wee woman."

Mr. Meagher made a sound like an aggrieved billy goat, which A.J. took to mean no, but if the circumstances were right, he just might.

"Maybe when we get to know him a little better," A.J. began.

"Oh, aye. She's invited us to supper this evening, so I expect we'll cop an eyeful."

The evening sounded less and less congenial, and A.J. fervently hoped no urgent police business came up to prevent Jake from attending. Then Mr. Meagher's words actually registered.

"*We?* Are you bringing someone to dinner?"

Mr. Meagher coughed as though he'd swallowed cockatoo feathers. "Indeed I am! I'm bringing Sarah."

"Sara?" Sara Munsen was Mr. Meagher's elderly—and married—housekeeper.

Mr. Meagher read her mind. He clarified, "Sarah *Ray.*"

"Sarah Ray? You mean *Cooking with Sarah* Sarah Ray?"

"Aye. That'll be the lass."

"Are you and Sarah—?"

"And why ever shouldn't we?" Mr. Meagher was sounding more and more like an irate leprechaun.

"Go for the gold, boyo!" screamed the cockatoo in the background.

A.J. said hastily, "No reason at all. I just wasn't . . . I didn't know." Wasn't there about the same difference in age between Mr. Meagher and Sarah Ray as there was between her mother and Dean? Dinner was liable to be an experience. "Well, then, I'll see you both there."

Mr. Meagher concurred and rang off.

A.J.'s days were typically a mix of teaching and administrative work. She enjoyed teaching the most—particularly the children's classes she conducted (to the grateful relief of her associates)—but more and more she was finding herself stuck in her office going over reports. Of course, she could have hired someone to do the boring stuff, but she believed it was her aunt's expectation that A.J. would try to be as hands-on as she herself had been. From the first, A.J. had done her best to meet that unspoken expectation. Sometimes, though, it was a relief to get into the studio and simply work out as another student, to stretch just that little bit further, to push herself just a little harder.

That afternoon A.J. took Simon's intermediate class during her own office time, and found the break from routine physically invigorating and mentally relaxing.

Afterward, she was blow-drying her hair—and trying to decide if she ought to cut it short again—when Suze, Jaci, and Denise burst into the shower room.

"You've got to come downstairs," Suze yelled.

A.J. switched off the dryer. She was thinking *fire*, *flood*, *famine*. Thank goodness, whatever the disaster was, Simon hadn't also felt it necessary to join them in the ladies' showers.

"What on earth is the matter?" She was conscious of a handful of students who attended the afternoon courses watching them in surprise.

"The Reverend Goode is dead," Suze told her. "And Lily's been arrested for his murder."

Seven

"No Jake?" Elysia asked when A.J. arrived for dinner at Starlight Farm that evening.

A.J. shook her head. "He's stuck working on the Goode murder case."

Elysia took her coat. "Oh yes. Of course. Poor Jake." She didn't sound particularly sympathetic. "He might as well be a doctor with those hours. Minus the pay, of course, and plus the added danger to his life posed by all the nutters that are out there."

"Thanks for pointing that out, Mother."

"Best to be realistic, pumpkin. Do you think Lily did it?"

News certainly traveled fast. As a matter of fact, A.J. had been thinking of little else all afternoon. Lily had her flaws, no question there, but murder? That was pretty hard to believe.

"I doubt it. I know Lily has a temper, but if there's one thing yoga teaches, it's restraint."

Elysia led the way to the living room. She'd had the farmhouse redecorated once again while she was in Hollywood. The new décor was streamlined and modern. White custom sofas from Schaefer Studio, glass-topped cubic tables, blackened steel lamps, and modern primitive paintings in muted yellows and tangerine.

Dean sat at the piano near the front windows, tinkling abstractedly at the keys. He looked up and smiled at A.J.'s entrance. "There she is," he said cheerfully.

Marcie was clicking on a laptop. Facebooking? Petra was signing a stack of 8 by 10 glamour-shot glossies depicting the Golden Gumshoes in a pose that seemed to parody the old *Charlie's Angels* promo pics.

"A.J. doesn't believe Lily Martin did it," Elysia announced. "Exonerated on grounds of her yoga training."

"I didn't exactly say *that*."

"Then you *do* think she did it?"

"No. I think it's unlikely. I don't know. I haven't heard enough to make my mind up either way. The news has been pretty sketchy."

"It'll make the national news tonight." Petra paused to sip her coffee. She went back to tapping away at her computer.

"We never really know anyone, do we?" Marcie asked brightly, continuing to scribble her signature across photographs with a broad, flamboyant hand.

"Gina, er Petra, thinks Lily is the perp." Elysia turned away. "Come help me in the kitchen, pumpkin."

"She did it, all right. One look at those eyebrows and I *knew*. She's got Joan Crawford eyebrows."

A.J. met her mother's eyes. Elysia shrugged and nodded for A.J. to join her at the sidebar. A.J. followed Elysia to the newly refurbished kitchen, which smelled tantaliz-ingly of roasting meat and fresh herbs.

"Dean seems nice," A.J. volunteered, taking a stool at the counter. She selected a slice of orange from a plate.

"He's lovely, isn't he? The girls and I have been think-ing what a marvelous promotional opportunity this mur-der case is."

A.J. avoided her mother's eyes. "What happened to Morag, by the way?"

Morag was the dearly beloved pet ferret of Elysia's friend Maddie Sutherland. Elysia had "inherited" the fer-ret (in a manner of speaking).

"Morag is with my trainer in Beverly Hills."

"What's Morag training for?"

"Ha. Very amusing. Beth had a ferret of her own, which was apparently suffering from a broken heart, so I gave her Morag, and they all lived happily ever after. I'm quite serious about the girls and me solving this crime."

A.J. groaned and dropped her head in her hands.

"Now don't be silly, pumpkin. We have an excellent track record. One hundred percent solve rate of our cases so far."

"That's a TV show, Mother! It's in the script that you solve all your cases."

"I'm not talking about the show," Elysia snapped back, equally exasperated. "*You and I* have a one hundred per-cent solve rate on *our* cases."

"Cases? You make it sound like we had a plan. We just stumble into other people's personal disasters."

"Oh tosh. You're selling us both short. We have a knack for this kind of thing. We're born detectives."

A.J. could hear Jake now. "Detectives aren't born.

They're trained. We're not trained. We're lucky. And one day our luck is going to run out."

"Now that's where you're wrong. The girls and I have a police advisor on the show and we've received quite a bit of instruction over the last few months."

A.J. shook her head and reached for another slice of orange. Lunchtime's chicken walnut salad was only a fond memory by now. "What's in the casserole dish?"

"Baked beetroots for the salad. Orange salad with beetroot and fennel."

"Sounds dreadful. Whatever happened to iceberg lettuce and Wish-Bone dressing?"

"I sobered up." Elysia gave her a chiding look. "Quit trying to change the subject. We're going to solve this case with or without your help."

"It's going to be without my help, then."

"Very well. But don't—" The doorbell, which consisted of the opening bars of the old British crime show *221-B Baker Street*, rang through the house, cutting Elysia short. Her cheeks pinked. "That will be Bradley. Have you met that *creature* he's seeing?"

"Sarah Ray? I've seen her around. I've never been formally introduced to her. What makes you think she's a creature?"

But Elysia was already on her way to answer the front door. A.J. stole a final slice of orange and followed.

By the time she reached the living room the introductions were being made.

"The creature" was very tall and very thin. She had long blonde hair pulled back from her face by a trademark tortoiseshell clip, and eyes of nearly the same shade as the tortoiseshell. Sarah Ray wasn't pretty exactly, but hers was the kind of bone structure that might have been designed with a television franchise in mind. "Oh my gosh! I've been a fan ever since I was a little girl," she cooed to Elysia.

Mr. Meagher blanched and met A.J.'s eye.

"Mmm. Sweet child," Elysia murmured in a voice that would have freeze-dried acid. She delivered a look to Dean that had him at her side in an instant. "Help me with the hors d'oeuvres, darling."

She vanished down the hallway, Dean in her wake. Mr. Meagher watched them go. Feeling A.J.'s gaze, he met her eyes and offered a crooked little smile.

He was quite a bit shorter than Sarah, and definitely a bit older, but he was very fit. He still had a full head of perfectly groomed silver hair and a year-round tan. In the year or so since she had moved to Stillbrook, A.J. had grown fond of Mr. Meagher. In fact, she wouldn't have minded if her mother had discovered her feelings ran deeper for her old mate.

But some things were simply not meant to be.

Elysia's partners in crime were making nice with Sarah in a manner that reminded A.J. of the way her cat Lula Mae used to bat a mouse around before having it for a snack.

"She's lovely," A.J. said under her breath to Mr. Meagher. "Where did you meet?"

Mr. Meagher beamed. "I was being interviewed at the local TV station. They were doing a segment on reverse mortgages for seniors. Sarah was cooking Irish stew in the studio next door."

Elysia and Dean returned, Elysia carrying a tray of fig and blue cheese nibbles and Dean bearing drinks. It occurred to A.J. that she was finally to the point where the sight of her mother near cocktails no longer made her stomach churn with nerves.

Elysia disappeared down the hall once more. Dean joined the tableau of Petra, Marcie, and Sarah. Sarah smiled in greeting and then did a tiny double take.

Dean smiled back. His smile grew faintly puzzled.

"A terrible business, this murder," Mr. Meagher said in a quiet aside to A.J.

"Were you a member of Goode's church?"

"Saints preserve us!" Mr. Meagher replied, and that seemed to settle that.

They chatted for a few minutes. A.J. couldn't help noticing that Dean and Sarah were now talking animatedly together, though their voices were too low to overhear. That ended abruptly when Dean was peremptorily summoned back to the kitchen.

Mr. Meagher asked Marcie and Petra a number of questions about *Golden Gumshoes*. To A.J.'s relief neither woman brought up anything about the potential good publicity of solving a real-life murder.

At last Elysia reappeared in the doorway leading into the dining room. "Dinner is served. Bring your drinks if you like."

They filed into the elegant room where the table was laid in Waterford crystal and gold-rimmed Lenox china. The candles were lit, the flames throwing graceful shadows against the olive green walls and the paneled Japanese mural of a full moon behind a snowy flowering tree. Next to the mural, the real moon, bone white and luminous, seemed to fill the window.

"This is *gorgeous*!" Petra exclaimed, taking the seat

across from A.J. at the long table. "You're spoiling us, Lucy."

"Just a little something I whipped up," Elysia said airily, and A.J. smiled fondly at her. Elysia had first developed an interest in cooking when she was battling her addiction to alcohol. She had turned into a fine cook and was not unreasonably proud of that fact.

A.J.'s own culinary efforts were pretty much summed up by soup and salad. It was hard to change the bad eating habits of a lifetime. Her lack of interest in cooking was underlined by the fact that she *liked* fast food and junk food and processed food.

But she was trying. And she was making progress.

Once everyone was seated, the plates and wine began to circulate. The main course was roasted filet with Stilton and crispy shallots served over mashed potatoes.

"What's the herb in the potatoes?" Sarah inquired, her pale brows drawing together as she sampled the first bite.

"Celery root."

"Mmm. That explains it."

Elysia's eyes kindled. "I think it gives the potatoes a lovely, earthy bottom." Never had spuds sounded so risqué.

"Elysia is a marvelous cook," Mr. Meagher put in. As Sarah turned her gaze his way, he added, "As is Sarah."

It was a fine line between diplomacy and disloyalty.

"It must be true that the way to a man's heart is through his stomach. You've put on weight, Bradley," Elysia commented.

Mr. Meagher reddened and fell silent.

Dean launched into a funny story of a recent calamity on the *Golden Gumshoes* set. Marcie and Petra chimed in,

and soon everyone was safely past the moment of indiges-
tion. The meal was perfectly cooked, in A.J.'s opinion—
although she didn't care for the orange and beetroot
salad—and everyone seemed to be enjoying themselves
until the topic turned to Lily's incarceration.

Afterward A.J. couldn't recall who had mentioned the
murder itself, but Sarah dropped her glass. The crystal
didn't break, but the red wine spilled across the gleaming
surface of the table like blood.

No one moved.

"Oh, I'm so sorry!" Stricken, Sarah stared at Mr. Meagher and then at the surprised faces gazing her way. "Did
you—I thought I heard you say David . . . David Goode
was dead."

"We did, my dear," Elysia said coolly, making no effort
to mop up the spreading red tide. "He was murdered this
afternoon. Someone stabbed him through the throat with
a ballpoint pen."

"I'll just get something to mop that up." Dean rose. No
one paid him any attention.

Sarah's mouth opened and closed. She blinked like
someone waking from a trance.

"It was all over the local news," A.J. said. She didn't
mean it unkindly; it was just surprising to her that Sarah
could have missed hearing about Goode's death.

"I've been taping all day. It's our big Thanksgiving
show. I only had time to run home and change before
Bradley arrived to pick me up."

"So you knew the Reverend Goode," Elysia probed.
The other two Golden Gumshoes were watching poor
Sarah with equal intensity. Did they imagine this was the
last act of one of those manor house mysteries and Sarah
was about to confess to murder? It seemed clear to A.J.

that Sarah hadn't had a clue Goode was dead until this very moment—either that or she was a better actress than anyone at the table.

Sarah's throat moved. "I knew *of* him," she faltered. "Of course. Everyone knew David. I used to attend his church."

"Used to?" Elysia leapt on this.

Dean, who was back with a fistful of paper towels and was busily mopping at the pool of wine, threw Sarah a look of sympathy that wasn't going to win him points with his fiancée. "She's obviously not going to be attending anything but his funeral service now."

Sarah visibly winced.

Elysia, sounding like the Sunday School Police, ignored him. "When did you stop attending church?"

"I-I don't know." Sarah looked helplessly at Mr. Meagher, who seemed to finally shake off his frowning preoccupation.

"Is it the third degree you're giving the girl now, Elysia?"

"Third degree?" Elysia laughed merrily, the sound tinkling ominously off the crystal up and down the table. "What an odd comment, Bradley. I'm merely . . . making dinner conversation with my guests."

Mr. Meagher snorted. Elysia colored in annoyance.

Sarah recovered some of her composure. "To be honest, I found some of David's views to be a little extreme for my taste. I'm attending Emmanuel Episcopalian now."

"Delightful, I'm sure. So your relationship was strictly spiritual?"

"Of course!" Sarah was a shade of holiday cranberry.

"I believe that's enough of that," Mr. Meagher said, briskly. "You're not on the telly now, my girl."

Both Sarah and Elysia blinked at him in surprise. A.J. bit back an inappropriate laugh.

Elysia opened her mouth, but Sarah spoke first. "I'm sorry, but I'm not feeling very well," she apologized. "I hate to drag you away from your friends, but . . ."

"Don't give it a thought, me darlin'," Mr. Meagher said gallantly, rising to the occasion, both figuratively and literally.

The Golden Gumshoes exchanged knowing looks as Sarah also rose. She rested a hand briefly on her stomach. "I think the potatoes may have been a little heavy for me."

Elysia's eyes narrowed dangerously.

"Don't give it a thought," Dean assured Sarah while Mr. Meagher made soothing sounds.

Elysia murmured regretfully, "Oh dear. You'll miss out on the chocolate clementine cake with hot chocolate sauce, Bradley."

Mr. Meagher hesitated a fraction of a second. Sarah shuddered, and he snapped to.

"I'll have you home before you know it," he promised, fetching coats and organizing their departure in record time. Despite his orders that no one disturb themselves, everyone rose from the table and escorted them to the door.

Sarah was charmingly apologetic, managing to convey simultaneously graciousness and a conviction she'd been poisoned.

Elysia switched on the front porch light, and they went out into the crisp November night.

The door closed behind them. Elysia said acidly, "There's no fool like an old fool."

* * *

A.J. awoke to the comfortable, familiar sounds of Jake moving around her kitchen.

She rose, threw on her soft blue Nandina bathrobe, and padded down the hallway. The butter yellow stove light dappled the dark polished floor and cherrywood cabinetry. Jake stood at the counter buttering thick slices of honey oat bread. Country ham was frying in the iron skillet.

For a few seconds A.J. watched him against the backdrop of her affectionate memories of Deer Hollow. She had replaced the old-fashioned appliances with new stainless steel ones, but the navy and white tile backsplash, the copper canisters, and the pig cookie jar on the gleaming fridge top were all straight out of her childhood.

It was a lovely moment, this merging of past and present. Jake was now as familiar with her kitchen as she was.

"She'll have both our hides if I feed you this late at night," he was telling Monster, who sat licking his chops and watching hopefully.

The floorboards squeaked beneath A.J.'s feet, and Jake glanced around.

"Sorry. I was trying not to wake you." He put down the butter-smeared knife and reached for A.J. as she walked into his arms.

"I didn't think I'd see you tonight." She kissed him. Jake's face was cold against hers, his hair damp beneath her fingertips. He smelled of faded aftershave and rain and something uniquely Jake.

"Nice PJs."

A.J. looked down at her Nick & Nora baseball patterned pajama set. "I left my negligee at the castle. How's Lily doing?"

"She's well on her way to getting herself convicted."

A.J. picked up a fork and checked the sizzling ham. "She hasn't confessed, has she?"

Jake shook his head. "No. She hasn't stopped explaining why Goode got exactly what he deserved long enough to actually confess."

A.J. winced. "Even so, she couldn't have done it, Jake."

"You say that about everyone I arrest."

A.J. chuckled. "Well, not *everyone*. Eggs?"

"I was going to make do with a sandwich, but eggs would be great. I'm starving. I didn't have lunch or dinner."

A.J. took out three eggs. "Sometimes I'm right. You have to admit that."

"I admit that you've been. . . ."

"Sorry?" she asked innocently, cracking the eggs on the side of the skillet. "I didn't catch that."

"Occasionally you've been helpful with an investigation or two."

"Don't worry. I won't let it go to my head."

He got a plate from the cupboard. "Are you having breakfast, too?"

"I'm still full from dinner. I brought you a piece of chocolate cake, by the way."

"Thanks. How was dinner?" He sat down at the table, watching as A.J. moved around the kitchen.

"Interesting. Mr. Meagher was there with Sarah Ray, who's apparently his . . . I don't know. Girl toy?"

"Sarah Ray? *Cooking with Sarah*, Sarah?"

A.J. nodded. "I think she might have been one of David Goode's paramours."

"*Paramour*. There's a word you don't hear every day." He was absently, gently, tugging Monster's ears. The dog panted up at him with adoration. "You're probably going to be called as a witness. You realize that, right? You were there for the altercation between Lily and Goode outside the Happy Cow Steak House?"

"It wasn't much of an altercation. If that's all you've got, you might as well arrest me, too. I probably had more face-to-face run-ins with Goode than Lily did."

"Maybe. But so far no one has come forward with reports that you threatened him. And we didn't find your fingerprints all over the murder weapon."

"You found Lily's fingerprints on the murder weapon?"

Jake admitted, "In fairness, we don't have the forensics report yet. There were several sets of fingerprints, mostly smudged. Lily's were definitely among them."

"The murder weapon was a ballpoint pen?"

"Yep. With the Yoga Meridian logo on it, plain as day."

"Somebody's *got* to be setting Lily up."

Jake groaned, and Monster's ears perked in surprise. "Please don't tell me that you think Lily couldn't have done it because she wouldn't incriminate herself by using her own pen. We both know Lily well enough to know that in the heat of the moment she'd be perfectly capable of grabbing the nearest thing to hand up to and including her personalized license plate."

"She doesn't have a personalized license plate. Anyway, I agree with you about the lack of impulse control, but she's not violent. As far as I know Lily's never done a violent thing in her entire life. The fact that someone's not very good at interpersonal relationships doesn't mean they're potentially homicidal."

"And it doesn't mean that they're not. Most people who resort to murder do so because they're not very good at interpersonal relationships."

"But you know what I mean."

"Sure. And I hope you know what I mean. When people resort to violence, especially homicide, it generally comes as a shock to the people who know them. But the fact is, we're all capable of violence given the right set of conditions."

A.J. used the spatula to bathe the frying eggs in butter and the juices from the ham. "Let's say I agree with you. If Lily didn't try to kill *me* during the last year, I find it hard to believe she'd resort to killing the Reverend Goode. She already had a plan for dealing with him—and I and the other local yoga studio owners were with her. So I just don't see her suddenly losing it and deciding to kill Goode."

"It wasn't premeditated. It looks like someone came into the office when Goode was there on his own, argued with him, and ultimately lashed out in anger."

A.J. shivered. "People are so fragile."

"Especially with a sharp object stuck in their jugular." Jake looked apologetic at the glare A.J. threw him.

A.J. slid the ham and eggs onto the heavy china plate. She carried it to the table and set the plate before Jake. Taking the chair across from him, she folded her arms and watched him begin to eat.

Jake sighed in appreciation. "Now *this* is heaven."

"Yeah, maybe literally. That stuff will kill you."

He shook his head. "What'll kill you are preservatives and worrying about what'll kill you. Anyway, it's not like I make a habit of eggs and ham at two o'clock in the morning." He reached for his coffee mug.

"If the rumors about Goode are true, there are any number of people who might lose their tempers with him. Including Mrs. Goode. Aren't you the one always telling me spouses are always the first to fall under suspicion?"

"True. But Mrs. Goode has an alibi. Lily doesn't. Or at least not one that holds water."

"What's her alibi?"

"Whose? Mrs. Goode's alibi is she was doing one of those live radio interviews for a Christian station. Lily's alibi is that she took time out to go walking in the autumn woods."

"*Lily?* Oh." That did sound sort of fishy. A.J. never thought of Lily as the nature-loving type. But then people probably didn't think of *her* as the nature-loving type, and she enjoyed walking in the woods. Although today it had been pouring rain all afternoon. Maybe Lily also liked walking in the rain. A.J. persisted, "Are you sure this radio interview was live?"

Jake slapped his forehead. "I never thought of that! Maybe you should join the police force and solve *all* my cases for me."

A.J. scowled.

Jake shook his head and calmly went back to eating his late night supper.

Eight

The next day A.J. got a call from Lily's court-appointed lawyer. According to Ms. Martinez, Lily was requesting that A.J. visit her in jail.

A.J. drove into Stillbrook. The town was old and charming. Effort had gone into preserving the historical integrity of the houses and shops while still catering to the needs of a new generation. Victorian architecture housed bakeries, boutiques, and art galleries. A number of families had lived in Warren County since Colonial times.

Not far from the center of town with its picturesque village green was the brick courthouse and police station.

A.J. had been dating Jake long enough to be greeted by name at the front desk, though the cordiality cooled a little when she explained why she was there. There was a brief delay, and then she was informed that Lily had been released on bail.

A.J. knew where Lily lived, having mailed enough

paychecks to her. She drove to Lily's house, a beige and white ranch style with an attached garage and a generic front yard. Two news vans—one a national affiliate—were parked at the curb.

A.J. ignored the reporters and camera men who jumped out of their vehicles, calling questions and snapping pictures, as she walked up the driveway.

The screen door was locked. A.J. rang the doorbell.

After a few seconds there was the sound of a sliding bolt and then the front door opened. Lily peered warily out.

"I heard you wanted to talk to me," A.J. said.

Without answering, Lily unlatched the screen and stepped back so that A.J. could enter.

A.J. stepped inside, looking around curiously. She had never been in Lily's home before. They weren't on close enough terms to have ever paid each other visits. Family pictures lined the hall Lily led A.J. down. The carpet was white shag. The walls were a restful earth tone. Music—Kitaro—was playing softly from another room.

Lily led the way to a family room with large comfortable chairs and an assortment of colorful throws and pillows. Two Bella Dos Santos prints decorated the wall.

There was a cup of tea and a jigsaw puzzle on the coffee table.

"I went to the court complex first. I didn't realize you'd been released." A.J. wasn't accusing, she was simply searching for something to say.

Lily hugged her arms across her chest. Her face looked drawn and tired. "You probably don't think I should be."

"Lily, if I thought you were a murderess, I wouldn't have driven over here." A.J. sat down on the sofa.

Lily moved restlessly around the room. "Tussle and

Rossiter paid my bail—right before they suspended me. Indefinitely."

"Oh. I'm sorry they suspended you, but once you're cleared that will be resolved."

Lily laughed bitterly. "You think so?"

"Yes. I mean, you have to admit it's a weird situation for them, too."

Lily's black eyes met A.J.'s. She said dryly, "You have no idea."

Having once been suspected of murder, A.J. actually did. "What is it you, er, wanted to talk about?"

Lily drew a deep breath and exhaled slowly. "You're supposed to be some kind of an amateur sleuth. I want you to help prove my innocence."

"Me?"

"Don't sound so surprised. You've done it for other people. People you didn't know nearly as well as you know me."

"I know, but it's not like I—" Like you? Care about you? A.J. stopped cold. That wasn't even true. Well, it was true that she didn't like Lily, but she wouldn't want anyone to go through the pain of a police investigation. No, what she really meant was that in those other cases she hadn't had a clue what she was doing. That she had managed to work some good was surely due more to luck and providence than her own abilities.

Watching her, Lily said, "Di would expect you to help me."

There was no denying the truth of that, and A.J. knew Lily could see her words had hit home. "There are different ways of helping, Lily. You're not exactly asking for the usual fund-raiser potluck."

"I'm not expecting you to put your life in danger, A.J. I wouldn't ask that of anyone. You don't need to do anything but poke around enough to raise reasonable doubt in the mind of that pigheaded cop you're dating."

A.J. let the insult go. "It's not up to Jake. He's just one of a number of people involved in any given investigation. The DA makes the final determination as to whether they proceed with the case or not."

"I know all that. I also know that if you can uncover something—anything—that throws sufficient suspicion on someone besides me, the DA is going to think twice about prosecuting this case. The police will conduct a real investigation instead of the half-assed excuse for police work that got me thrown in jail to start with."

"What happened to this PI you were going to hire? He's got to be a lot more qualified at this kind of thing than me."

Lily sat down in the chair across from A.J. She pulled an afghan around her shoulders and huddled into it. "My lawyer is already using some kind of a professional investigator. I want someone that people won't be afraid to open up to." She gave a derisive sniff. "That's you. People talk to you. I've seen it happen often enough. People like you and they spill their guts to you."

Apparently that was a good thing, although one would never guess from Lily's expression and tone.

A.J. thought it over. "Obviously I want to help you, Lily, but I don't have any idea where to start."

"I know *exactly* where you need to start. Start with Mrs. Goode."

A.J. shook her head. "Mrs. Goode is the first person the police thought of. Their suspicions turned out to be a dead end." There was an unfortunate turn of phrase. "She's got an alibi for the time of her husband's murder."

"I don't care what she has. She's involved."

"What makes you so sure?"

"The day we went to lunch and ran into Goode? I thought the woman with him looked familiar. Later I remembered where I'd seen her. At the studio. At Yoga Meridian. She comes in every few days on a guest pass. That's where she got hold of the pen she used to kill her husband."

"I'm not saying it's not interesting, I'm saying it's not conclusive."

A.J. was on her cell phone talking to Jake as she walked from the parking lot to Sacred Balance's entrance following her meeting with Lily. "But it's definitely worth checking up on, right?"

Yellow and russet leaves skittered across her path. Most of the trees were bare now. The evergreens stood like black feathers against the slate blue sky.

"Of course. Just don't pin your hopes on it."

"No, I know. Lily's another matter. She's grasping at straws. I really believe she's innocent, Jake."

"I appreciate that, but—" The rest of his words were lost as A.J. pushed through the glass doors in time to hear hysterical screams floating down the staircase.

"I don't have to do anything I don't want to! You can't make me!"

There was no one in the front lobby. The entire ground floor seemed deserted. The screams overhead were getting louder. "Leave me alone! Take your hands off me!"

"Jake, I have to go." A.J. clicked off without waiting for an answer and sprinted up the wide staircase.

As she reached the top of the stairs she narrowly missed colliding with a large, gray mass hurtling in her direction. The mass resolved itself into a furious girl in a sweat-streaked sweat suit. Runny mascara and bared teeth made Mocha Ritchie look a little like a distraught badger.

"Mocha, was that you screaming like that? What in the world is the matter?" A.J. looked past Mocha to Jaci, who was in hot pursuit of her runaway student. Jaci looked nearly as distraught as Mocha. "What's going on here?"

Jaci shook her head.

"I don't have to stay here," Mocha cried. "You can't make me stay here."

Other students and instructors had gathered in the hall-way to watch. Emma was right behind Jaci, looking about as grim as A.J. had ever seen her look. "I don't know where you think you're going, young lady. It's miles back to town and you're not much of one for walking."

"I hate you all!" Mocha shrieked.

"Okay, enough." A.J. held up a hand. "You." She nodded to Mocha. "Go downstairs and wait for me in my office."

"The hell I will!"

There were shocked gasps—and a few snickers—from the other teens crowding the hall. Even some of the adult students looked taken aback. A.J. said, "Kid, get your butt down to my office or you *will* be walking back to town."

Mocha glared at her for a long, trembling instant and then lumbered past A.J. down the staircase.

"Could everyone please go back to class?" A.J. called to the other students. "Everything's under control." To the teens and young adults she said, "Jaci will be right with you guys."

Simon and Denise shepherded everyone back to their respective rooms.

"Before you say anything," Jaci burst out as A.J. turned back to her, "I have no idea what set her off. I honestly thought we were building some kind of rapport but she's been a pill since she walked in today."

"Who dropped her off?" A.J. asked Emma.

"Mrs. Ritchie, same as always. That girl stomped in here today looking for trouble, if you ask me."

"Great." Jaci was still flushed and angry. A.J. asked, "Are you okay to go back to your class?"

Jaci nodded. "I'm fine. She kind of took me by surprise. She seemed fine and then . . . BOOM. I mean, the poses are difficult for her, but she's already shown progress."

"Okay. I'll talk to her. Would you be willing to have her back in class—assuming she's agreeable to that?"

"Yes. Of course. She owes Emma an apology, though."

Emma said, "She does, but let's not make it into too big a deal. I taught school for a lot of years."

"What did Mocha do?" A.J. asked with a sinking feeling.

"She used the N-word," Jaci replied.

"No," A.J. said. "No way is she going to use that language and stay enrolled at Sacred Balance. That's unacceptable."

"She knows that. That's why she used it." Emma seemed remarkably sangfroid about the whole incident. "You go downstairs and talk to her, honey. She's not a bad kid. I've known bad kids. Mocha is just about as unhappy as a little girl can be. It'll do her good to talk."

"What'll it do to the rest of us?" A.J. inquired, but she let herself be swept downstairs ahead of Emma.

There was no sign of Mocha on the ground floor so she had either gone to A.J.'s office or she'd left the building. "You know, my background is in marketing," A.J. muttered to Emma. "Any tips?"

Emma said quite seriously, "Listen to her."

"I'll try." A.J. waved to Suze, who was returning from lunch, and went down the hall to her office.

Mocha was standing at the windows looking out at the windblown meadow behind the studio. She didn't turn when A.J. entered, and A.J. guessed from the defensively hunched shoulders that she had been crying.

A.J. closed the door. "Would you like some tea?"

That seemed to surprise Mocha into facing her. She had indeed been crying. "No," she said thickly.

"Well, I'm having a cup. Let me know if you change your mind." A.J. switched on the hot plate and sat down at her desk, swiveling her chair to face the girl. "Why don't you sit down."

"No."

"Suit yourself. So tell me what that was all about."

"It's none of your business."

"Actually, everything that happens here is my business." A.J. studied the stubborn set of Mocha's plump shoulders. Her gaze moved to the photo of Aunt Di. According to just about everyone, Aunt Di had been wonderful with kids, though she'd never had any of her own. She'd been a wonderful aunt to A.J. So what was the trick to dealing with teens? Could it be something as simple as Emma's suggestion that she listen?

She waited, hoping that Mocha might volunteer something.

Nothing. Mocha sniffed and rubbed at her nose.

"According to Jaci you've made excellent progress since you started. How do you feel you're doing?"

Mocha shrugged.

"Are you enjoying your classes?"

"No." It was said sullenly, without any real heat.

A.J. tried waiting again, but once again she met with no success.

"Why? Is there something that would make the classes more enjoyable?" The teakettle began to hiss. A.J. rose and poured tea into her mug. "My aunt is the one who founded Sacred Balance. She was English, and she used to always say there was nothing like a nice hot cuppa when you were upset. Except she always drank green tea and I prefer Earl Grey. Are you sure you wouldn't like a cup?"

Another one of those shrugs.

"Would you like a little honey or a little milk in your tea?"

"It's too fattening."

A.J. restrained her immediate exasperation. She had seen the girl drinking thousands of calories' worth of fruit juice, but someone had convinced her that a teaspoon of honey would make her fat. She made a mental note to make sure Mocha received nutritional counseling.

"Okay. Come sit down and drink your tea."

Mocha reluctantly left the window and took the chair near the fountain. She accepted the cup A.J. handed her, wrapping both hands around it. A.J. noted the black fingernail polish that couldn't disguise how badly bitten Mocha's fingernails were. A.J. had also bitten her nails when she had been a nerve-racked adolescent.

For a few minutes they sipped their tea in silence.

"Are you going on the camping trip this weekend?"

Mocha looked up in surprise. "It's adults only."

"We make exceptions sometimes. Did you want to come?"

Mocha's expression grew suspicious. "Why?"

"I thought you might enjoy it."

Mocha went back to sipping her tea.

"Did you want to tell me what happened in class?"

Mocha shook her head.

"You don't like Jaci's style of teaching?"

"I like Jaci," she said quickly before hurriedly resuming her sulky expression.

"What do you think of the other kids in the class?"

Mocha's tea sloshed. "I *hate* them."

Funny though it might seem, they were finally making progress. "Why?"

"They make fun of me. They say things to me when Jaci's back is turned."

"Like what?"

Mocha's face quivered. "Hippobuttamus. Elephat. When I bend over they make noises like my clothes are ripping or like I'm farting."

So much for the spirit of yoga. A.J. was mildly startled at her near visceral reaction to the news of Mocha's harassment. During the short time that A.J. had attended school in Stillbrook, she, too, had been unpopular, an outsider. The fact that she had grown into her looks and become a successful businesswoman even before inheriting her aunt's empire couldn't entirely erase those hurtful memories.

She kept her face and voice neutral. "Go on."

And go on, Mocha did. Near the end of her recital, A.J. saw the truth of what Emma had said earlier. Here was a

young girl about as unhappy as a teenager could be—
which was saying something.

By that point, Mocha had branched out to her anger
and resentment over what she saw as her father's neglect
since his remarriage. "And she doesn't even love him!"

A.J. tuned back in. "Not everyone shows their feelings
the same way. Your st—"

"She's *cheating* on him."

"How do you know that?" The words were out before
A.J. recollected that it was not only not her business, it
was probably not appropriate to ask a kid about such
things.

"I know. She lies about where she's been. She lies about
his phone calls. I saw a text message from him once. She
caught me looking and deleted it, but I saw enough."

"You might have misunderstood what you saw."

Mocha shook her head stubbornly. "He called her 'darling' and he was talking about having to sneak around
because people were watching him."

A.J. absorbed this. Conscience warred with suspicion.
"Do you have any idea who 'he' was?"

Mocha shook her head. "He didn't use a name or
even an initial. But I know it's the same one she meets
when she pretends she's going to her book club."

"Will you take some advice from someone who's been
in a sort of similar position?"

Mocha stared unblinking, her expression mutinous.

"You have to let your mom and dad work this out on
their own."

"She's not my mom!"

A.J. knew from Mocha's file that her birth mother had
moved out of state. There was a story there, no doubt, and

probably a painful one. "You know what I mean. Even if what you believe is true, that's between your father and his wife. If you get involved, it'll just make your own relationship with both of them harder—and it's probably not going to turn out the way you hope."

Mocha's mouth trembled.

"I'm sorry. I really am, but life isn't a Disney movie and you can't hurt and embarrass the grown-ups in your life and expect everything to bounce back to normal. You have to respect their privacy the same way you expect them to respect yours."

Mocha blinked.

A.J. glanced at the clock on her desk. "Jaci should be coming downstairs any minute. Did you want to wait for her in her office?"

"Wait . . . for what?"

"Well, among other things, I thought you might want to tell her you planned on signing up for this weekend's retreat." Mocha sat up abruptly. A.J. added gently, "And then I think you probably have something you want to say to Emma."

Mocha's face washed a painful red. She didn't argue, though. She rose and went out. A.J. heard the office door next to hers open and close.

She jumped as the phone on her desk rang suddenly.

The only calls that Emma put through without screening were from Jake or her mother. Remembering that she had essentially hung up on Jake, A.J. picked up even as she acknowledged that he was more likely to call her cell phone.

"There you are, pumpkin." Elysia sounded like she'd been searching through a pile of boots in her mud porch. "Do you have plans tonight?"

"I do. I'm looking forward to a nice quiet evening

spending quality time with my dog and watching *Eat Pray Love*."

Elysia made a dismissing sound. "You can do that anytime. Why don't you come by for dinner?"

A.J.'s brows drew together. "I was there for dinner last night."

"There's no reason we can't have dinner two nights in a row. We used to have dinner every night."

"How about another night? I'm bushed."

Elysia's tone changed, grew coaxing. "The truth is, I thought we might discuss my wedding plans."

A.J.'s stomach knotted. "What's the rush? You've only known the man a few months."

"I knew your father less than twelve hours before I'd decided to marry him."

"I knew my father. Dean Sullivan is not my father." A.J. was trying to joke, but somehow it hadn't come out all that lightheartedly.

"Of course not, darling," Elysia assured her, "but Dean is a lovely man in his own right. You'll see, once you know him a little better. You want me to be happy, don't you?"

"Not necessarily."

Elysia laughed her husky laugh. "You're more my daughter than you'd like to believe, you know."

That was undoubtedly intended as a compliment. It served to make A.J. cagey. "You didn't invite me over to discuss wedding plans. What's going on?"

"True. True. Dean and I are already agreed on a small, private wedding. No worries there. I thought you might like to drop by this evening and discuss whatever it was you were doing at Lily's this afternoon."

After an astonished moment A.J. put two and two together. "The news van."

Elysia chuckled. "I'm afraid so."

A.J. let out a long, exasperated breath. "Mother, it's true that I went to Lily's. Lily asked for my help, and I'm going to try and do what I can for her, but I don't really feel that discussing it in front of the entire cast of *Golden Gumshoes* would be appropriate."

"That *is* a shame," Elysia murmured, "because it just so happens that Trini—I mean, Marcie—has some information that might prove very useful to you."

"I can't keep them straight. Which one is Marcie and what information does she have?"

"Marcie plays Trini. She's our weapons expert."

"*That* much, I grasped. Well, not about her being a weapons expert. I don't understand why mature lady sleuths would need a weapons expert."

"You really should watch the show, pumpkin. It's very entertaining. The episode where Marcie found us a tank—"

"A *tank*? I don't even want to think about that. Which one is Trini, er, *Marcie* in real life?"

"Tall, slender, red hair. Looks like a jaded pixie."

"Er, right. What information does she have?"

"You'll have to pay us a visit to find out, won't you?"

"Mother!"

"We'll see you half-past six?"

"*Mother.*"

"Cheerie-bye, pet."

Elysia disconnected.

Nine

∞

"I know how much you were looking forward to seeing *Eat Pray Love* tonight, but we're going to have to postpone."

Monster took the news with his usual composure, panting cheerfully as he followed A.J. from the front door to the kitchen. A.J. sorted through the day's mail—mostly catalogs with a few bills just to break the monotony—then tossed the catalogs in the recycle bin and the bills on the kitchen table.

Monster sat down in front of his bowl and eyed her expectantly.

"Nope, we're going out," A.J. told him. "And if dinner is half as good tonight as it was last night, it *might* even be worth it. Mother got rid of the ferret, though, so don't get your hopes up."

In her bedroom she changed into a pair of faded Vince flare leg jeans and a short gray marled-knit "Greenwich" sweater by Ella Moss over a white silk tank. She looked through her aunt's jewelry box and selected a pair of elegant *S*-curved sterling and cultured pearl earrings. Diantha had been photographed wearing the earrings many times, including an iconic *LIFE* magazine layout. A.J. fastened one earring in her right earlobe.

"I just can't believe she's going to marry him."

She blinked at her reflection in the mirror, surprised that she had given voice to that thought. "Not that there's anything wrong with that. Dean's probably a very nice guy. It's just I feel like I only got her back and now . . ."

Well, maybe it was better not to examine whatever it was too closely. A.J. turned to Monster and placed her hands on her hips. "You're just going to wear what you've been wearing all day? You're not going to shave at least?"

Monster tilted his head. He thumped his tail on the wooden floor. A.J. laughed and knelt, ruffling his ears. "You're my best beau. Yes, you are." She kissed the top of his nose and stood up.

"Okay, let's go. But remember. Don't say anything about her mashed potatoes. She's very sensitive about them."

She switched off the bedroom light.

A pajama party seemed to be in progress at Starlight Farm.

Elysia, wearing a purple velvet dressing gown with a mandarin collar, greeted A.J. and Monster at the door. She led the way to the family room with its plump leather sofas, ottomans, and big-screen TV. Petra, wearing men's-style white silk pajamas, was sitting cross-legged tapping away at her laptop. Marcie, ensconced in a chair by the fireplace, was wearing one of those vintage-looking plaid Beacon bathrobes. She appeared to be going through a stack of *People* magazines and making notes. They greeted A.J. cheerfully.

A large silver tray, littered with china cups, dishes, a pot of cocoa, and a plate of brownies, took up the center of the coffee table. A couple of white pizza boxes took up the rest.

Conspicuously missing, in A.J.'s opinion, were bridal magazines and the happy groom.

"Where's Dean?" Monster cautiously sniffed the corner of a pizza box. *"Monster!"* Monster flattened his ears and threw her a guilty look.

"He went into the village to have a pint. Have a slice of pizza, pumpkin. We need to get to work before he comes home."

Chastened, Monster took the chair across from Marcie, curling up in a tight ball and burying his nose in his tail. A.J. investigated the white boxes and selected a slice of still-warm veggie pizza.

"Doesn't Dean approve of sleuthing?"

Petra gave a short laugh. A.J. gave her mother an inquiring look. Elysia ignored them both.

"Marcie believes she knows your Reverend Goode."

"Really?"

Marcie set aside the stack of magazines. "Except his name wasn't Goode." She moved over to the sofa beside Petra. "Show her."

"Petra is our computer genius," Elysia informed A.J.

"In real life or the show?"

"Both."

Petra turned the laptop so that A.J. could see the screen. *Miracle Skin Transformation* read the headline.

"Are you sure . . . ?"

Petra peered at the screen from over the top of her spectacles. She frowned. "Oops." She clicked on another window and the *Los Angeles Times* came up with the heading *Socialite Found Dead in Bathtub*. A.J. scanned the brief article that followed.

Socialite and heiress to the Smithy yacht-building fortune, Jill Smithy-Powell, 46, was found dead in her Laurel Canyon home last Monday. The LAPD has so far revealed little about the case, including how the publicist and fashion importer was killed, but Smithy-Powell's husband of two months, Maxwell Powell, is being sought for questioning. Police found the body after receiving a domestic disturbance call about 3 a.m. Monday. Smithy-Powell was well-known within social and philanthropic circles, and handled the publicity for the nonprofit Girls Can Dream annual Black and White Gala to benefit underprivileged girls. The website of Fiore Brune, the jewelry import company she founded in 1997, has been converted to a memorial page.

The date of the article was January 2001. "Interesting. I'm not sure I'm following. Are you suggesting . . . Well, what, exactly?"

Petra clicked and brought up the tribute page on the former Fiore Brune site. "Not that page," Elysia said. "Find the photos of Powell."

More clicking and Petra brought up a page showing photos of blonde and pretty Jill Smithy-Powell and a tall, handsome, dark-haired, bearded man.

"Good lord," A.J. said, peering more closely at the screen.

"You see?" Elysia said triumphantly.

A.J. continued to study the images. "It does look a lot like David Goode. A younger David Goode."

"It's a decade later. He's bound to show a little wear and tear."

"The beard makes it hard to be sure."

Elysia said, "No, it doesn't."

"The police never found Maxwell Powell?"

"See for yourself."

Elysia nodded at Petra, but A.J. said, "I'll take your word for it. Was Jill Smithy-Powell's murder ever solved?"

"No." That was Marcie. She ruffled her hair absently. It stuck up in tufts, reminding A.J. of Suze. "It never was. If you read the tribute page, her family still offers a reward for any information leading to the arrest and conviction of her murderer—*and* for the discovery of Maxwell Powell's whereabouts."

"So they're not openly accusing him of her murder? Was he ever charged?"

"Well, no. They couldn't find him."

Elysia put in, "He wasn't cleared either. He simply vanished. As though he'd never existed. You can read the details for yourself."

A.J. said slowly, "Maybe he was killed, too."

"That's one theory. Not many people subscribe to it, but it is a possibility. However, if that's the case, why was his body never discovered?"

A.J. shook her head. "I don't see how the police could have failed to find him, though."

"People do disappear even in this age of technology."

A.J. was thinking about Kirkland Bath's small religious sect living and working in the remote wilds of Baja, California. Not a bad place to hide out if you were on the lam from the law. Of course you'd have to already know about the New Dawn Church, but it wasn't impossible that it could have happened like that.

"Marcie knew Jill. She's positive that David Goode and Maxwell Powell are one and the same."

"Well, not *positive*," Marcie qualified. "I never got a chance to see the reverend close up, but his voice sounded the same. Max Powell had a distinctive voice."

"We can fix that," A.J. said. "May I?" Petra pushed aside the pizza cartons, swiveled the laptop A.J.'s way, and A.J. typed in the address for YouTube. She brought up Goode's recent interview on Channel 3.

Goode was speaking earnestly to the interviewer. "Our materialist, reality-based culture doesn't want to admit that evil exists as a physical manifestation. We want to talk in abstracts and try and rationalize away the evidence of our eyes. But evil does exist. It walks among us and it can sometimes take a terrible, monstrous form."

The perky news announcer said, "When you say 'monstrous form' do you mean—"

"I mean 'monstrous' literally. What I witnessed last night was not someone in costume and it was certainly no hallucination."

Marcie looked up wide-eyed. "It really *is* him!"

"Was," Petra said grimly. "It looks like the Smithy family eventually got justice for Jill."

The thought gave A.J. pause. She said to Marcie, "Did you actually know Max Powell?"

Marcie said, "We all knew Max. Not well, granted. But we knew him."

"What was he like?"

"Charming. I guarantee you not one of us expected what happened to Jill. Even after the murder, even after Max disappeared, we all kept thinking there had to be some mistake, some other explanation. He just wasn't the type."

If there was one thing A.J. had learned over the past months it was that there was no particular "type" of person destined to be either victim or perpetrator.

"Interesting, no?" Elysia said. "Although, frankly, I'm not in such a hurry to dismiss that little chit Sarah," Elysia said.

A.J. did a double take. "That little what?"

"Chit."

"Oh. What on earth do you have against Sarah?"

Elysia's eye kindled. "That girl is using Bradley."

Petra and Marcie exchanged tolerant looks.

A.J. said, "It seemed to me to be an even exchange of goods and services."

"That's a rather cynical attitude."

A.J. shrugged. "Mr. Meagher seems happy." It also seemed to her a case of the pot calling the kettle black.

"Did it somehow escape your notice that that girl was having an affair with the dead man?"

"He wasn't dead when they were having their affair."

Elysia pinned her with a glinting eye. *"Most* unamusing, Anna Jolie."

"Mother, you have absolutely no proof that Sarah was lying about her relationship with Goode. Even if she *was* lying, it's obvious from her shocked reaction at hearing he was dead that *she* didn't kill him."

Elysia shook her head. Marcie and Petra gave her pitying looks. Elysia said, "You can't go by her reaction at dinner. The girl's an actress."

"The girl's the host of a cooking show."

"If *she's* pretending to know anything about cooking, she's the biggest actress to ever step foot in this house."

Petra and Marcie seemed to find that hilarious. A.J. managed to preserve her expression. Just. "I see. What is it you think she was acting about? Knowing Goode or killing him? Or both?"

"Time will tell," Elysia said darkly.

The next morning brought the pleasant surprise of book galleys in the mail.

Before her untimely death, Diantha had completed work on a manuscript that was part memoir, part philosophical treatise, and part instruction manual. A.J. had found the manuscript when she'd been sorting through her aunt's belongings after she'd inherited Deer Hollow farm. She had completed the copyedits and, at the publisher's request, written an introduction to the work.

She spent several peaceful hours poring over the galleys. In a strange way it was like spending time with Aunt Di. She could hear her aunt's voice so clearly in the written words.

Jake called late morning, and they arranged to meet for a late lunch at the new pub and grill that had taken the place of their favorite Italian restaurant—another victim fallen to the recession.

Jake was waiting at a table by the time A.J. arrived at the restaurant. A.J. sat down and looked around. "This is cute."

"Mmm." Jake studied the menu.

The pub was decorated in dark wood and shining brass fixtures. The lighting was supplied by old-fashioned-looking amber lanterns, and the leather booths were large and comfortable.

A.J. spied a familiar couple near the back. Mr. Meagher and Sarah Ray were also having lunch together. She started to wave hello, but they looked rather . . . intimate. Sarah was giggling at something Mr. Meagher had said sotto voce.

A.J. sank back in the leather sofa. "What do you know about Sarah Ray?"

Jake looked up from the menu. "Not a lot. Why?"

"How long has she lived here?"

"A few years, I guess."

"Where did she come from?"

"One of the Dakotas, I think."

"Dakota? So that little Southern belle act she does is just a shtick?"

"I never noticed a Southern belle thing. I'm pretty sure she's from North Dakota. Why?" Jake glanced around and spotted Sarah and Mr. Meagher. "Oh. I see. What have you got against Sarah?"

"Nothing. Mother's sure she's going to break Mr. Meagher's heart."

"And your mother thinks that's *her* job?"

A.J. made a face. "I think Mother does really care for Mr. Meagher. I don't know why they never quite managed to . . ."

"Connect?"

A.J. nodded.

"They probably know each other too well by now. They've been friends too long."

"But you'd think that would be a great basis for marriage."

"You want my take on it?"

"Do you *have* a take on it?"

Jake laid his menu down. "I think your mom's afraid."

"*My* mother? *Afraid* of a man? Have you met the woman?"

"I think you're right. I think she's fond of Meagher and she doesn't want to risk a friendship that's so important to her."

"I never quite thought of it that way."

"I doubt if she thinks of it that way either. Anyway, I think Meagher is perfectly safe in young Sarah's hands."

A.J. watched Sarah giggling again as Mr. Meagher whispered something to her. She sniffed. "She's not that young either."

Jake laughed.

The waiter appeared at last. A.J. ordered a French dip with shaved, lean, perfectly roasted beef on a warm, crusty French roll. Jake opted for a spicy sloppy joe.

As the waiter withdrew with their orders, A.J. said, "Before I forget, Andy asked us to Thanksgiving dinner."

Jake's brows rose. "Is that something you want to do? Spend the holiday with your ex?"

"I'm as surprised as you probably are to hear it, but yes. I do miss Andy—and he makes chestnut stuffing like no one in the world."

Jake sighed. "Your mother is going, I guess?"

"As far as I know. Unless they're going to Dean's family. I assume he has family. I've really heard almost nothing about his background."

Jake's mouth quirked. "Have you asked anything about his background?"

"No. And don't give me that look. I plan to get to know Dean. We've got plenty of time if he's going to be my step-daddy."

"Okay. Well, about Thanksgiving. I'm not sure I have the day off. It's a premium holiday for the married guys, but if I do, we can spend Thanksgiving in Manhattan. So long as I get turkey and all the trimmings and not some weird tofu substitute."

"Don't worry about that."

They talked until their lunches came and the next few minutes were occupied with the simple pleasure of good food properly prepared and served.

Considering the trouble her sleuthing had occasionally raised between them, A.J. was prepared for Jake to state his disapproval of her helping Lily in no uncertain terms, but he only referred to it obliquely and in passing as he questioned her again about the encounter she had witnessed between Lily and Goode in front of the Happy Cow restaurant.

"On a scale of one to ten, ten being homicidal, she was really only about an eight."

Jake snorted and took a huge bite out of his sandwich.

"Seriously, though, I think there might be people out there with much stronger motives for having wanted Goode out of the way."

"So you said on the phone. Go on. Tell me what the Snoop Sisters uncovered."

A.J. laughed unwillingly. "Hey, you! That's my mother you're talking about."

"Believe me, it's only the thought of having Endora for a mother-in-law—" Jake cut himself off abruptly and took refuge behind another giant bite of sloppy joe.

A.J. pretended not to have heard, but her heart jumped. She launched into a slightly disorganized retelling of Jill Smithy-Powell's still unsolved murder.

Jake heard her out without comment until she finished

her story. "Okay, so let me make sure I've got this straight. Goode bore an uncanny resemblance to the missing husband of a murdered Los Angeles socialite. That's it?"

Put like that, it didn't seem like a lot.

"I know it doesn't sound like much to go on, but just consider the implications if it's true."

"Sure. But you consider this. What would be the point of Maxwell Powell killing his wife and then disappearing? He obviously didn't kill her for her money, so what would the motive be in such a case?"

"That's a whole different situation. How is his motive even relevant?"

"It's relevant because you're drawing a correlation between the two. It's your theory that someone killed Goode in revenge for Smithy-Powell, right?"

A.J. nodded. "Although *theory* is too strong a word."

"Whatever you want to call it, it only holds together if Goode can believably be suspected of killing this Smithy-Powell woman."

"You're the one always telling me motive is the least important element in building a case."

"Fair enough. If someone did believe Powell killed his wife, for whatever reason, and that Goode was Powell, then it could be argued there was motive there. But given those two things, why not turn him over to the police? You said the Smithy-Powell case was still open and that a reward had been offered for information on Powell?"

"Right."

"So why not turn him over and collect the reward?"

A.J. shrugged. "I have no idea, but there's nothing to be lost by checking Goode's fingerprints or whatever it is you do, right?"

"No. And we'll do that. I just don't want you to pin too much hope on this lead turning into anything substantial."

"Lily's convinced Goode's wife killed him. She says Oriel Goode has been a guest at Yoga Meridian several times, just as she's been a guest at Sacred Balance. She says Oriel could easily have picked up the pen that killed the reverend at any time."

Jake conceded, "Okay. It's possible Oriel inadvertently introduced the murder weapon into the crime scene, but that doesn't change the fact that she has an alibi."

"Maybe she also has a partner."

"You mean a lover?"

"Why not?"

Jake considered it. "There's no indication of that."

"But?"

"I didn't say there was a but. There's no indication that Oriel Goode was anything but a devoted wife and help-mate. Certainly no indication that she has a lover. It's not impossible, but that kind of thing usually turns up pretty quickly in a case like this. We've heard plenty about David Goode's extracurricular activities."

"I'll bet. My mother and her cronies are convinced Sarah Ray was having an affair with him, though Sarah denied it. But then, she would."

"Our Sarah? Is that why you were asking about her background?"

"That's the one. And, for the record, she's not *my* Sarah."

"Oh boy." Jake's mouth quirked but he managed to control his amusement. "Sarah hasn't turned up in our investigation so far. We've identified most of Goode's ro-mantic liaisons. None of them seem too serious."

"I'm curious how you came to that conclusion."

"Cached e-mails and old voice messages as well as interviews with the women involved. In most cases the novelty seemed to wear off fast for the ladies."

"That's interesting."

Jake agreed. He finished his sandwich with a final bite and pushed back his plate.

"But all those affairs, however trivial for the women involved, do reaffirm Lily's belief that no one had better reason to want Goode dead than Mrs. Goode."

Jake nodded. "Except, and I hate to be a broken record, Oriel Goode has an alibi."

A.J. made a face. "True."

"If it cheers you up any, we do know that Goode had been seeing an as-yet-unidentified woman. Whoever she was, she took pains to stay out of the limelight."

A.J. said eagerly, "It would make sense if that woman was Sarah Ray. Seducing ministers doesn't mesh with her wholesome image."

Jake grinned faintly. "I admit it's always the good girls who surprise you."

"Good. I like to keep a man on his toes."

"Is that a yoga thing?"

Meeting his eyes, A.J. laughed.

Ten

❀

There was a message from Andy when A.J. returned to her office. Unfortunately she didn't have time to return his call just then as she had only enough time to get changed for Beginners Yoga.

"Mocha signed up for the weekend retreat," Jaci told her as they passed in the hall. "That makes a total of seven students."

"How's Mocha doing today? Did she show up for class?"

"Today she does Pilates, but Denise said she was good as gold. It's a whole different dynamic in that class, though. Most of the students are older."

"True. Well, we'll just have to monitor her. The fact that she showed up today is a great sign, and that she signed up for the retreat is even better."

"I agree."

They chatted another minute and then A.J. went into the studio where her students waited.

As there were two new students in the day's session, A.J. took the opportunity to cover the basics again. It was easy to forget some of the first things you learned after you moved on to the more complicated concepts.

"These moves are deceptively simple. They're not hard to do, but they'll build your strength and flexibility. They'll also help focus your inner awareness. It's really worth taking the time to get them exactly right."

She stepped into a standing forward stretch. She kept her knees bent as she leaned forward, her chest a few inches above her thighs.

"Keep your elbows relaxed. Don't clamp them to your sides. This is a terrific stretch for releasing the back muscles. Keep your head relaxed. . . ."

A.J. slowly straightened her legs, letting her arms fall loose against her sides.

"Can you feel that? That release of stress and tension? We're going to hold the position for a count of ten. That's ten breaths. Slow and steady breaths—through your nose, if possible. Breathing is key. It may sound funny, but proper breathing requires thought, and if you concentrate properly on breathing while you're holding these positions, you'll receive greater benefits of relaxation."

She fell silent, demonstrating proper breathing.

After ten slow counts she drew back into a standing position. She stretched her arms over her head and pressed her palms together prayer style.

The students followed suit with a few staggers and gasped exhales.

"Very good! Now we're going to try a standing side stretch. Easy but so effective. Start in a standing position."

A.J. raised her arms overhead again, clasping her right wrist with her left hand.

"Inhale. Now exhale as you as you lean to the left, reaching your right arm past your ear, stretch—and hold for ten deep breaths. . . ."

After class ended, A.J. showered and changed quickly. Back in her office, she was dialing Andy to tentatively confirm Thanksgiving when Suze poked her head in. "Did you see that Oriel Goode signed up for the weekend retreat?"

"Seriously? Wouldn't her husband's funeral be this weekend?"

Suze lowered her voice. "The police haven't released his body yet."

A.J. shivered. "Oh."

Suze lifted her shoulders. "I guess you can't blame her for wanting to get away to the woods for a couple of days."

"I guess not. Although it just seems . . ."

"Weird? I thought so, too."

"When did she sign up?"

"She phoned this morning."

"Okay. Thanks for letting me know."

Suze departed, and instead of telephoning Andy, A.J. dialed the office number for the New Dawn Church. She had no idea if Oriel was taking over any of her husband's duties, but it seemed as good a starting point for tracking her down as any.

Lance Dally answered the phone in his pleasantly impersonal voice. A.J. asked for Oriel and Lance told her that Mrs. Goode was not there but he would take a message.

"I'd have tried her at home, but I don't have that number."

"No," he agreed. "Don't worry. I'll make sure she gets your message."

The problem with sleuthing was it required bad manners. A.J. forged on. After all, this was probably as good an opening as she'd get.

"I realize this is an awful time. You're probably swamped with calls from the media as well as everything else."

"Yes," Lance said coolly. "That's correct."

"I'm sorry to push, but a question has arisen over Oriel's membership."

"What membership?"

"I'd probably better discuss that with Oriel. At least . . . you're not her personal assistant, are you? I had the impression that you worked for the church itself."

"That's correct. Oriel doesn't have a PA, although I'm happy to do whatever I can to make things easy for her at this time."

"Will she be taking over her husband's ministry?" A.J. threw it out at random. She had no idea what questions to ask, but she felt instinctively that if she just lobbed enough balls, sooner or later Lance was bound to take a swing.

Lance gave a kind but dismissing laugh. "No. No way. Even if she wanted to, no one could take David's place. He was one of a kind."

"His death must have been a terrible shock to you, too."

"Yes." It was clipped in the extreme. "You've no idea."

"So no one is going to try and assume leadership of the church?" Now that she thought about it, usually a church had some kind of an executive board, didn't it? Church leaders? Very rarely was it a one-man operation. Even when

New Dawn Church had been under the leadership of Kirkland Bath, A.J. recalled seeing photographs of people listed as church elders in what appeared to be other positions of responsibility.

"I'm afraid I can't answer that at this time," Lance replied.

"This must be so difficult for you. What will you do now?"

There was a pause. "I'm sorry. I've got another call coming in. I'll make sure Oriel gets your message."

Lance hung up.

A.J. made a face at the dial tone. So much for that. Now what?

"Night, A.J.," Simon called, passing her office.

"Night, Simon," she called back absently.

For lack of any better ideas A.J. returned to reading what information she could find on Jill Smithy-Powell's murder.

The circumstances of the case were simple. Jill had returned from vacationing with girlfriends in Mexico on Sunday evening, January 20th. Much later that night neighbors had heard the sounds of two people arguing and then a woman screaming. The police had been summoned, and they'd found Jill dead in the bathtub. She'd been strangled with one of her own silk scarves. The door to the house was open. Jill's husband—and his car—was gone.

That was pretty much it. Most of what A.J. discovered was the same information recycled again and again. Jill had been successful, talented, and well liked. There seemed to be no apparent motive for her murder. She was an only child. Following her death, her parents bequeathed their considerable fortune to a number of charities for victims of violent crime.

"Are you still here?" Suze asked, looking in.

A.J. nodded. She glanced at the clock. It was later than she realized. "Is everyone gone?"

"Emma's still here and Jaci's upstairs, I think. Are you bringing Monster to Doga tonight?"

"I don't think so. It's been a long week. If we're going camping this weekend I need to get some things done."

"See you tomorrow then."

A.J. replied and returned to reading the laptop screen.

Jill's husband had naturally—as was typical with spouses in homicide cases—fallen immediately under suspicion. And the suspicion had mounted with his disappearance. But his disappearance was also the confusing element in the story. Max couldn't inherit if he wasn't present and accounted for. But then, he couldn't inherit *anyway* because the bulk of Jill's fortune was tied up in trusts. On top of that, she hadn't yet gotten around to changing her will, so even the money that wasn't tied up in trust wouldn't go to her husband.

The best guess of investigators was that Jill and Max had fought for reasons unknown, Max had killed his wife, and then fled. But according to everyone who knew them, Max and Jill never quarreled and loved each other dearly. The friends who had vacationed with Jill had all agreed that Jill was in love with her husband and appeared to be very happy.

Granted, friends and family had agreed that Jill was both a loyal and private person and might not have revealed problems with her marriage.

Reading between the lines of the various interviews and accounts of the murder, A.J. got the impression that Jill's father had not been overly impressed with Max and that a few of her friends had suspected him of fudging more than a few background details. But was that how people had initially felt or had those feelings been colored by Jill's murder? Difficult to say.

There was no proof that Jill had argued with Max or that he'd even been home at the time of the murder. According to neighbors, they hadn't seen him for two or more days. But there was no denying one thing—following Jill's death, Max was never seen or heard from again.

He seemed to simply drop off the face of the planet.

And that truly was weird. How, in this day and age, did someone disappear? Max's face had been plastered on television and in newspapers for weeks.

"Are you still here?"

A.J. jumped guiltily at the sound of Emma's voice. "No. No, this is my astral projection. I'm actually home doing laundry right this very minute."

Emma snorted. "That's good. You'll have something to wear when you have to hightail it back here three hours from now."

A.J. looked guiltily at the clock. Not quite as bad as Emma was hinting, but poor Monster probably thought he was going to have to make do with dry kibbles again. "I'll be out of here in just a few minutes."

"See you tomorrow."

"Night, Emma."

Of course A.J. could take her laptop home and do her research at Deer Hollow, but living alone in the middle of nowhere made her reluctant to bring murder and violence home with her.

A.J. Googled New Dawn Church again. She searched for the earliest photos of David Goode, squinting at the small and slightly fuzzy images. The earliest picture she could find was in 2003. She began scouring group pictures trying to find him in unlabeled earlier photos. Nothing.

But if Goode *was* Powell, perhaps he had still been wearing the beard when he joined up with the New Dawn Church?

She began studying the photos of young men with beards and decided that there were a few possibilities within the circle of devoted followers. Unfortunately, most of the pictures were thumbnail size, and the more A.J. tried to zoom in on them, the more blurry and distorted they became.

She decided to approach the problem from a different angle and began searching "David Goode," but that brought up a plethora of the wrong Davids. There was the British organist, the British sculptor, the Australian bank manager, and so on and so on. There were David Goodes on Myspace and Facebook and LinkedIn. There were David Goodes everywhere she looked, but there was no record of a Reverend David Goode before 2003. All references to the Reverend David Goode were in connection with New Dawn Church. In short, the existence of the Reverend David Goode began and ended with New Dawn Church.

Which meant what?

A.J. absently drummed her fingernails on the desk, thinking. If Oriel Goode had been murdered, everything would fit together. But David Goode was the victim. As suspicious as his past—or lack of past—was, it wasn't necessarily germane. Sure, it was possible that his death was the result of something in his mysterious background, but it was every bit as likely—probably more likely—that he had died because of the enemies he'd made since arriving in Stillbrook.

And he *had* made enemies. A lot of enemies for a supposed man of God.

Never mind Lily or any of the other irate yoga studio owners. There were other businesses that Goode had criticized and advised his flock to avoid. The owners of those businesses might also have taken a dim view of his continued existence.

And then there were all the women he'd had affairs with. Jake said that by most indications the women had ended the affairs—maybe they were merely flirtations?— but perhaps not in every case. Perhaps there were hurt and bitter feelings.

What about the husbands and boyfriends of these women? Not everyone was a good sport about infidelity. A.J. had not been a good sport. She hadn't been angry enough to want to kill Andy, but it wouldn't have broken her heart if something awful had happened to Nick. She was grateful that she had worked past that terrible period in her life. That much anger, that much bitterness, ate you up inside like a canker.

But she didn't want to dwell on that. What about this lunatic in the Jersey Devil costume? Anything other than the idea of a man in a costume was crazy, right? So was there some significance to the attempted break-in at the Goodes' home the night before the murder?

Maybe the aborted burglary had actually been a foiled attempt on Goode's life.

On impulse A.J. entered "Jersey Devil" in the search bar.

Yikes. She sat back in her chair as a variety of colorful and alarming images popped up. Nearly two million results in less than twenty seconds. And what kind of results. The different headlines read "See Videos for Jersey Devil," "The Mystery of the Jersey Devil," "Jersey Devil Hunt Club," "Timeline for the Jersey Devil" . . .

"You've got to be kidding me," she murmured. She began to scroll through the options. Clicking on one site, she read aloud, "The Jersey Devil was designated in 1938 as the country's only state demon." She snorted. Did that mean the thing collected Social Security?

The tall building creaked, settling as the night temperature dropped. A.J. glanced at the clock. Fascinating as this avenue of study would no doubt prove, it *was* getting late. In about half an hour the evening classes would begin and then she'd never get out of here.

She turned off the laptop and gathered up her things. The front lobby was deserted, the lights turned low.

She walked out to the parking lot. The night air was sweet with the scent of distant wood fires and damp earth. Jaci's Mini was still parked in its slot. Moonlight glistened on the dew-beaded hood. The lot was otherwise empty.

A.J. unlocked her car and started the engine. For a few seconds she sat letting the engine idle, gazing at the building surrounded by tall trees and open meadows. The bright lights in the many windows of Sacred Balance shone like a beacon in the cold November night.

It still surprised her sometimes that *this* was her life. That she had taken the opportunity Aunt Di had offered, that she had turned from the safe and familiar path and chosen something completely new.

How often did someone get that chance? How often did they take the chance if they did get it?

If David Goode was indeed Maxwell Powell, he, too, had received such a chance to reinvent himself. The question was . . . into what?

Eleven

A.J. was on her way upstairs to teach her Itsy Bitsy Yoga class the next morning when she was surprised to spot Oriel Goode.

Oriel, her hair pulled back in a ponytail, was dressed in nondescript yoga pants and a T-shirt. She walked among the other students, but she didn't seem to be part of the group. She was not laughing or talking with anyone as she made a beeline for the showers.

A.J. started to speak, then hesitated. She couldn't interrogate the woman in a public shower, and it would be better not to give her time to prepare for the chat that A.J. was determined they were going to have. She decided to wait and catch Oriel on her way out of the building.

Running downstairs, A.J. asked Suze to take her Itsy Bitsy class.

"Sure. What's up?"

"I want to talk to Oriel about her membership."

"Oh, right. Okay." Suze hesitated. "Denise said she talked to Lily last night and that Lily said you'd agreed to help her."

"I agreed to try. So far I haven't found anything that's going to be a lot of use."

"It's great you're doing it, though. It's what Di would have wanted."

A.J. nodded distractedly. She went out to the front desk and chatted with Emma, pretending to look through records while she waited for Oriel to come downstairs.

It took about fifteen minutes before Oriel appeared in a dark baggy sweater and pants, her hair piled in an unflattering bun on her head. Watching her coming down the stairs, A.J. thought that Oriel had just about perfected the art of invisibility.

Maybe Lily had had a point about how very mismatched the Goodes were. Whereas David Goode had sought the limelight at every turn, Oriel seemed to make every attempt to avoid attention.

A.J. moved to intercept her as the woman reached the ground floor and started for the main doors. "Oriel. May I have a word?"

Oriel jumped. She threw a startled look at A.J.

A.J. tried to look pleasant and nonthreatening, which shouldn't have been much of a stretch. Oriel glanced instinctively at the entrance, back at A.J., and then abruptly seemed to relax. Maybe *relax* wasn't the word. *Give up* was probably closer to the truth.

With a tight nod she preceded A.J. down the hall to her office. They went inside, and A.J. closed the door.

"Please, sit." She moved to the hot plate near the bookcase. "Would you like some tea?"

Oriel shook her head, although she took the seat A.J. indicated. "What is this about?" She spoke in a deep, musical contralto.

A.J. poured tea into her cup and took the chair across from Oriel. "I was so sorry to hear of your loss."

Oriel's eyes narrowed beneath the heavy brows. "Thank you."

"I only met your husband a couple of times. I'm afraid we disagreed pretty strongly on the subject of yoga—as I'm sure you're aware."

Oriel shifted minutely in her chair. "David had very strong views on most things."

"But you obviously didn't agree with those views."

"I agreed with most of his views."

A.J. smiled, persisting pleasantly, "But not his views on yoga, obviously."

Oriel's gaze veered to the jovial carved Buddha statue on the bookshelf. "No. I've been practicing yoga for five years now. I used to suffer from depression. Yoga was instrumental in my healing." She added quickly, "Not for any philosophical reasons. For me, yoga's benefits are strictly physical, but the mind and body are linked."

"Of course. Your husband didn't agree?"

Oriel chewed her bottom lip, clearly hesitating over her answer. She said at last, "David didn't know me when I was depressed. He only ever knew me happy and healthy, so he couldn't realize the role yoga played in my well-being."

"How long have you been married?"

"Three years."

"Oh?" A.J. tried to recall the timeline from the point Goode had appeared at New Dawn Church.

"*Oh* what?" Oriel asked with a hint of irritation.

"I just assumed you'd been married longer. I guess ministers always seem . . . married."

"Obviously you didn't know David." Oriel seemed to hear her own comment. Her expression was instantly blank once more.

"I've heard some of the rumors, of course." A.J. tried to say it sympathetically. "That's inevitable when someone dies so suddenly."

"Yes," Oriel said bitterly. "It is."

"This must be so hard for you. I mean, it would be hard under any circumstances, but having to deal with the police and reporters . . . I had something similar happen when my aunt died. It made what was already a terrible time even worse."

Unexpectedly A.J.'s sympathy seemed to hit a chord with Oriel. "I just want it to be over."

"Of course. First the investigation and then the trial. It must feel like it's never going to end."

"The investigation *is* over. The trial . . . Of course I want that over, but I meant . . . I want to stop *feeling*. I want it to be ten years from now when all of this is a memory and it doesn't hurt anymore." Oriel spoke with such intensity that A.J. was moved against her will.

"Is that possible?"

"Yes. I'm sure it is. Time heals everything."

"You have the comfort of your religion."

"Yes." Oriel's gaze held A.J.'s. It was almost difficult to look away.

A.J. spoke at random. "You said the investigation is over. Does that mean you believe that Lily Martin killed your husband?"

Oriel's dark brows arched. "That's a strange question. The police arrested her."

"I know, but no one who knows Lily believes she could have committed murder."

That was an exaggeration, but Oriel didn't challenge it. Instead, she seemed to think over A.J.'s words. "Frankly, I was surprised the police arrested her so quickly. I assume they had more to go on than the quarrel that you and I saw. Thank you, by the way, for keeping silent that day—and for the other day when my husband came here looking for me."

"Then he told you about that?"

Oriel's smile was sour. "Oh yes. David was very forthright when he was displeased."

"He didn't seem like someone who beat around the bush." The conversation was drifting from the expected channels, but the direction was interesting and might ultimately prove more revealing than A.J.'s original tack. "You said you were surprised that Lily was arrested. Does that mean you have your own suspicions about who killed your husband?"

"I did. I was obviously wrong."

"Who did you—?"

"My husband's assistant. Lance Dally."

That was a surprise. "Why?"

"Because David fired Lance that morning."

"You're kidding. Did you tell the police?"

Oriel's smile was pained. "Yes. Of course. They questioned Lance, but he was cleared." She winced at some memory. "Thank heavens he was gracious enough to overlook the fact that I accused him of murder."

"What made you so sure Lance had done it?"

"It wasn't . . . It was the first thing that popped into my mind when they told me David had been . . . David was dead. I thought that it couldn't be true because how would someone get past Lance without him seeing them? Then I remembered Lance was gone. And then I remembered why. You say things when you're in shock. . . ." Her voice faltered and died away. She said almost to herself, "It's so hard to believe."

"I can only imagine. I know what a shock it was when my aunt was murdered." A.J.'s gaze went automatically to the photo on her desk. "It's bad enough to lose someone, but to lose them to violence makes it that much worse."

Oriel nodded. "Anyway, once Lance understood that I didn't . . . that I wasn't . . . he agreed to return long enough to help me take care of all the arrangements."

"What will happen to the church now?"

"I don't know." Oriel's expression closed. "It's too soon to decide anything." She looked at the door. "Was there some reason in particular you wanted to speak to me privately?"

Realizing that her window of opportunity was closing, A.J. pretended to recollect herself. "Oh. Yes! I'm sorry. What I really wanted to know was whether you planned on continuing as a student at Sacred Balance?"

Oriel's smile held a hint of mockery. "You mean will I officially enroll and pay my fair dues instead of sneaking around on a guest pass?"

"I wouldn't put it quite that bluntly. I'm glad that you continued coming here however you had to do it. Yoga is obviously important to you. I know my aunt would have felt the same way."

"You're a kind person, A.J. Thank you. I do plan to continue attending classes while I live in Stillbrook."

"Are you planning on leaving?"

"I haven't made my mind up, but as you can imagine, my memories here aren't very happy."

"I'm sorry. I understand."

Oriel picked up her gym bag and rose. A.J. stood also. She reached for the office door, saying casually, "You also attend classes at Yoga Meridian, don't you?"

"Yes." Oriel made a face. "I attended a couple of local studios. I had to keep changing around in case David tracked me down. Yoga Meridian was my least favorite. A little too glitzy for me. The instructors all wear matching unitards and they call the place Yo M, which is just too . . ."

"Oh." A.J. and Oriel shared a wry smile before A.J. moved aside to let Oriel pass. "If I don't see you before, I guess we'll see you this weekend?"

"The retreat. Yes. I'm looking forward to it."

Oriel strode down the hall and out through the lobby. A.J. watched her go and then went back in her office and closed the door.

She phoned Jake and filled him in on her evening. "It was a better book than it was a movie. Also, you missed a really good margherita pizza from that new place in Blairstown," she informed him when he picked up.

"I'm sorry about the pizza. What are you doing for lunch?"

"Probably trying to avoid listening to my mother discuss wedding plans. What are you doing for dinner?"

"We're supposed to have a briefing on New Dawn Church's financial records."

"Speaking of New Dawn Church. How come Lance Dally isn't a suspect? I've just had a very interesting chat with Oriel Goode, and she said her husband fired Dally the day he died."

"He did. Dally came to us and volunteered the information. Along with the news that he's a reporter working
on an exposé of Goode and New Dawn Church."

A.J. nearly dropped the phone. "*What?* Seriously?"

"Yep."

"What was he exposing?"

"Yeah, well, we're having a difference of opinion on
that score. Dally's refusing to cooperate. He wants to keep
his story as exclusive as possible. He swears up and down
that nothing he discovered could be linked to Goode's
murder. Obviously we of the Stillbrook PD have a different take on the matter."

"But you've ruled him out as a suspect?"

"He doesn't appear to have a motive. He does appear
to have an alibi."

"What's his alibi?"

Jake sighed noisily down the line. "Why again am I
reporting to you?"

A.J. said in a sultry voice, "Because you grab every
chance you can to talk to me."

Jake laughed. "Right. That's gotta be it. Dally's alibi is
he was home packing. His neighbor verified seeing his car
parked out front all afternoon."

"That's not exactly watertight, is it?"

"You know, very often people don't have watertight
alibis for any given hour in a day. Dally doesn't seem to
have been angry about being fired. According to him he
was about ready to roll up shop anyway."

"Doesn't that seem a little strange to you? How did
Goode come to Dally's attention? As far as I can tell New
Dawn Church doesn't have a national presence."

Jake's voice was approving. "You're right. I asked Dally
that very thing. Apparently Goode was starting to build a

reputation for himself and the church in California. Dally saw him interviewed on a television special about the new breed of evangelists. Something about Goode aroused— Dally's words—his reporter's instinct. When he learned Goode was moving his operation east, he decided to go undercover in Goode's organization. And one of the first things he discovered was Goode didn't *have* much of an organization."

"I had that impression myself. So I was right!"

"According to Dally, Goode was a fanatical perfection-ist. He didn't trust anyone to do anything as well as he could do it himself. Dally said it took him weeks before Goode trusted him to so much as mail a letter without interrogating him. He said he'd never worked so hard at a job."

"Why was Dally fired?"

"Goode reportedly found out who Dally was really working for."

"Hmm. You're taking Dally's word for this?"

Jake said very patiently, "If you'll recall, we *have* our official suspect."

"So you're not looking any further than Lily at all?"

She could hear Jake's hesitation. "Look. Just between you and me, we're not completely ruling anyone out at this point. It turns out we hit pay dirt with your tip on the Jill Smithy-Powell homicide."

"Really?"

Jake's laugh was grim. "Don't sound so surprised."

"So Goode and Powell *were* the same man?"

"It looks like it. We sent Goode's fingerprints to LAPD and they came up a positive match for Maxwell Powell. Or at least for the prints they believe belonged to Maxwell Powell."

"That's incredible."

"What do you mean it's incredible? It was your theory."

"To be fair, it was Mother's theory. But I spent a couple of hours last night searching for David Goode, and as far as I could tell he doesn't exist before he showed up in the flock of New Dawn Church."

"Well, that makes it unanimous, because Max Powell doesn't exist either."

"Run that by me again."

"Maxwell Powell died in 2000 when he was eighteen months old."

A.J. had read about this kind of thing in credit card and identity scams. "You mean Goode stole someone else's Social Security number?"

"That's it in a nutshell."

"But how could he get away with it? It's one thing to try and fake an identity on paper. But in real life? Something should have flagged along the way, right?"

"That's one of the things we're waiting to hear. Hopefully by tonight's briefing we'll have some answers."

A.J. told Jake about her meeting with Oriel. He was unimpressed but sympathetic.

"What if Oriel Goode didn't know her husband's background? Or what if she *did*?"

"You mean you didn't ask her about her husband's uncanny resemblance to a missing California playboy?" Jake asked dryly.

"I couldn't think of a polite way to bring it up."

She heard his snort of amusement. "Whether Oriel knew or didn't know doesn't change the fact that *she* has an alibi."

"Until it's broken. It's not like we've never come across anyone who appeared to have an alibi before."

"Please don't say *we*. We're not partners in crime here. I wish you weren't getting involved again, but I know you well enough to know that you're going to poke around whether I like it or not. I'm hoping to share just enough information to keep you from getting into trouble."

"And I appreciate that. And I've been helpful so far, right?"

"You have." It was grudging, but honest. "And I'm not saying that it's not significant that Goode used to be somebody else, but it doesn't automatically mean his death is linked with his past. It's a tantalizing theory, but it's only one avenue of investigation. Our victim made plenty of enemies right here and right now as David Goode."

"But you have to admit that it's quite a coincidence. Most people are never involved in a single murder investigation, and Goode was involved in two. First he's the prime suspect and now *he's* been murdered."

"I agree it's one hell of a coincidence. But stranger things have happened. Somebody might even call that poetic justice."

"Exactly," A.J. said.

Twelve

"Isn't this lovely." Elysia smiled benignly as their waitress delivered a basket of fresh baked bread to their table at the Happy Cow restaurant.

A.J. met Dean's eyes and they both smiled automatically, politely.

Since this lunch had been A.J.'s first chance to see her mother without her, er, posse since her return to Stillbrook, she was a little disappointed to find Dean in attendance. Not that A.J. had anything against Dean. He seemed pleasant and intelligent if first impressions were anything to go by. He did have a tendency to watch his reflection in every remotely mirrorlike surface, but that was probably part of the job description.

"This place must make quite a change from Manhattan," Dean said when the waitress sashayed off with their drink orders. "Did you ever think about moving the whole yoga franchise to the big city?"

"No."

"Never?"

"Never."

"That's the first thing I'd have done. I'm a city boy through and through."

"Where are you from originally?"

"Bismarck, North Dakota, but my family moved to Los Angeles when I was sixteen. I've lived there ever since."

"You're the second person I've heard of from Bismarck this week."

"Who's the other?"

"Sarah Ray. You met her at dinner the other evening."

"Oh. Right. Yes." Dean wore an odd expression. "She mentioned something about that. So you grew up around here?"

Had Elysia not shared even this much information with him? A.J. said, "Oh no. I was a city girl. I don't know how to explain my conversion. I guess what it gets down to is I was ready for a change. I never thought I'd hear myself say this, but I like the slower pace."

"Now that she's used to it," Elysia put in, buttering a thick herb-crusted slice of bread.

"True. It did take some getting used to. Is LA really like it seems in the movies?"

"Pretty much." Dean launched into an entertaining account of his arrival in the big city and his first few acting jobs.

A.J. laughed along with Elysia. She began to see the appeal. Not only was Dean boyishly handsome, he was fun. And he was attentive. It was churlish to resent his presence today. There would be other lunches, other days spent with her mother. She wasn't losing a mother; she was gaining . . . a brother. A brother who would be sleeping with their mother.

Uh . . . probably better not to go there. Modern families, right? A least this newest boyfriend wasn't younger than A.J.

"So what about you?" A.J. tuned back in as Dean continued, "I understand this cop you're seeing is just about ready to pop the question."

"Huh?" A.J. said brilliantly. She turned to her mother. *"What?"*

Elysia's expression was bland, her pencil-thin brows arching in inquiry—although the look she threw Dean should have frozen him in his tracks. "Of course he is, poppet. A mother knows these things."

"Long distance? You haven't seen Jake in months."

"As the Bard says—"

"I wish the Bard would keep his nose out of my business."

Dean cleared his throat. Luckily the waitress arrived at that moment with their meals and drink refills. Glasses were handed round, plates distributed, and the ground pepper sprinkled liberally.

When they were on their own again, A.J. said, "Speaking of weddings, how are the plans for yours coming?"

Dean smiled tentatively at Elysia, who was neatly spearing olives from her salad plate. "It's up to the boss."

Elysia smiled noncommittally. "There's not a great deal to plan. We want something simple. Just our closest friends and family. We've both been through it before."

Dean said, "You can't really count my first time. I was only a kid."

"Me as well," Elysia said. "But mine lasted twenty years."

A.J. took pity on Dean. "Mr. Meagher certainly seems smitten with Sarah."

Elysia's smiled vanished. "Nonsense." She stabbed a final olive as though it had attempted to evade justice.

Dean said, "The old guy? I thought he was gay."

"No, he's not gay!" Elysia sounded quite indignant.

"*Old* guy?" A.J. inquired at the same time. Mr. Meagher was roughly the same age as her mother.

"Okay, okay." Dean smiled easily and turned his attention to his salad.

Whether through luck or design, after that the conversation gravitated to such neutral themes as the weather and property values and local theater, and they made it safely through their meal without anyone getting—in Elysia's vernacular—"up anyone else's nose."

The waitress brought the dessert menu. "I believe I'm in the mood for some of their delicious peach cobbler." Elysia looked around the table. "Shall we order something?"

"I have to get back." A.J. met her mother's eyes and sank back into the leather bench.

"Nothing for me." Dean slid out of the booth. "You ladies go ahead and order. I have to buy some razors and a couple of other things. I'll meet you back here."

Elysia smiled sweetly at him and accepted his kiss like the queen receiving the attention of courtiers. She ordered two peach cobblers and A.J. watched Dean stride through the crowded dining room, attracting glances and whispers as he went.

"He's very nice," A.J. said. "Can I go back to work now?"

"No. I didn't invite you to lunch to vet Dean. I wanted to find out how the case was progressing."

"And we couldn't discuss that in front of Dean?"

"No."

"Why not?"

Elysia made a little moue. "He doesn't approve."

A.J. laughed. "I think I'm getting to like him better every minute."

"Never mind that. Brief me."

A.J. rolled her eyes but related her meeting with Oriel Goode.

"Interesting." Elysia didn't sound particularly interested. "Did you pass the information we gave you to your Inspector Lestrade?"

"Yes."

"And?"

A.J. took Jake's request for discretion seriously, but it was hardly possible to conceal the information that David Goode and Maxwell Powell were one and the same from the person who had first brought it to her own attention. She comforted herself with the reflection that the Golden Gumshoes already knew the answer. They were simply waiting for corroboration.

"Marcie was right. Goode and Powell were the same man."

"Just as we thought. Cherchez la femme." Elysia dug triumphantly into her peach cobbler.

"Which femme? We've got a couple to choose from."

"This case is directly connected to Jill Smithy-Powell's murder. That's obvious."

"It's not quite that cut-and-dried. I agree that Goode's history makes his murder seem like an awfully big coincidence, but coincidences do happen."

"Oh bosh. It's perfectly obvious that someone from the past decided to even the score."

"There are a couple of problems with that theory. Jill Smithy-Powell was an only child. Her parents were elderly and in poor health at the time of her murder. Her father has since died and, according to the papers, her mother is bedridden. There don't seem to have been cousins or uncles and aunts to have gone seeking revenge—which, you have to admit, is pretty melodramatic anyway."

"Friends. An old boyfriend."

A.J. sampled her own peach cobbler thoughtfully. A bit of cinnamon, nutmeg, and a hint of lemon gave the sweetness a little bite. "There *is* one possibility. Goode fired his assistant, Lance Dally, the morning he was slain. Dally has an alibi, but it's shaky."

Elysia's eyes lit up. "Go on."

"Supposedly Dally is a reporter working on an exposé of New Dawn Church. What if he is—or once was—a reporter for the *Los Angeles Times*? What if he recognized Goode? What if he knew Jill Smithy-Powell and . . . I don't know. What if there's a connection there?"

"That's bloody brilliant, pumpkin!"

"It's complete conjecture. But . . ."

"Worth checking into."

A.J. nodded. "Maybe. It couldn't hurt."

"Right. The girls and I will take point on this angle."

"Oh God. Please, *please* be discreet, Mother."

Elysia's expression grew haughty. "I wrote the book on discretion."

"And it was a best seller. That's what I mean."

Elysia's hauteur gave way to a malicious grin. "Never you worry about me, pet." Her expression grew suspiciously innocent. A.J. didn't have to turn around to know that Dean was returning to their table.

"How long is the, er, team staying with you?"

"The girls are leaving on Tuesday."

"And is Dean going to be here all winter?"

Elysia said lightly, "Perhaps. As the Bard says, 'If winter comes, can spring be far behind?'"

A.J. muttered through her peach cobbler, "I don't know. I wouldn't hand my galoshes in quite yet."

Friday afternoon was not a particularly popular time for yoga and Sacred Balance always quieted down quickly after lunch.

"Here's the final head count for tomorrow." Suze offered the sheet to A.J. "Do you have a sleeping bag?"

"Jake is loaning me his." A.J. leaned back in her chair, examining the list. "What do you know about the Jersey Devil?"

Suze laughed. "Who on that list reminds you of the Jersey Devil?"

A.J. looked up with a smile. "No one. At least . . . I can't help wondering what Mrs. Goode was doing during the time that her husband was chasing off the Jersey Devil."

"What do you think she was doing?"

A.J. shook her head. "I have no idea, but it wouldn't be easy to sleep through someone kicking in your back door, right?"

"I guess. They have a pretty big house. Or maybe she takes sleeping tablets." Suze's gaze was curious. "So are we set for tomorrow morning?"

A.J. winced. "I guess."

"I think Denise is going to back out. She's been coughing and sniffling all day. I caught her popping DayQuil with her pumpkin spice latte."

"I know," A.J. said glumly. She handed the list back to Suze. "Oh well. It is what it is. We'll have fun."

"We will! Simon and Jaci have been great about communicating what clothes and equipment everyone needs to pack. They've really pretty much taken care of everything. All we need to do is show up."

A.J. nodded, though she doubted it would be that simple. Still, Simon and Jaci did seem pretty confident that everything was under control.

"See you at five a.m.!" Suze said on her way out.

A.J. groaned loudly, only partly kidding. She turned her attention to her laptop once more. She had been reading up on the Jersey Devil again—in particular the recent sightings.

The background on the Jersey Devil was, not unsurprisingly, sketchy.

According to legend, the creature was the thirteenth child of a local woman by the name of Leeds. Mother Leeds was reputed to have invoked the name of the Devil while giving birth. Never a good idea. The resulting offspring transformed into a devil and flew up the chimney and off into the surrounding woods where it spent the next couple of centuries spooking people by making weird noises at night, leaving strange tracks, and occasionally killing the odd cow or sheep. Just your average everyday supernatural juvenile delinquent.

A.J. had vague memories of watching an *X-Files* episode about the Jersey Devil with Andy, but in that version the "monster" turned out to be feral people living in the Pine Barrens.

As far as she could tell, the Jersey Devil was on a par with the Loch Ness Monster or the Abominable Snowman. Yes, there were those who would believe till their dying breath that such creatures existed—even that they had glimpsed them—but most people agreed they were either hoaxes or someone's imagination running away with them.

Except . . .

Except for those mutilated farm animals. A.J. clicked back to the online edition of the *Stillbrook Streamer*. She read again the account of John Baumann's slaughtered cattle.

It amounted to two dairy cows in a pasture. So . . . not wholesale slaughter and not exactly under the nose of the Baumanns. Still pretty horrifying. The cows were described as having their throats "ripped out." Was that an accurate description or was someone at the *Stillbrook Streamer* taking literacy license? Surely there would be a clear difference between someone using a butcher's knife and an animal using teeth and claws?

A.J. shivered and read on. Local police were described as "unwilling to comment" as to the nature of the attacks.

That stance had not changed, judging by the follow-up articles A.J. scrolled through. The only possibility officially ruled out by the police was that the Jersey Devil had perpetrated the crimes. Unfortunately, that was the only theory anyone wanted to hear about. Right beneath the article where the police chief categorically denied any culpability of—or belief in—the Jersey Devil, the *Streamer* ran an interview with a local Jersey Devil hunter who said just the opposite.

"These attacks bear all the earmarks of a classic Devil encounter."

A later edition ran a full history of the Jersey Devil, along with more interviews with local Devil hunters and a few anecdotal accounts from elderly local residents.

Obviously it was a lot more fun to think the Jersey Devil was hunting fresh meat than that local teenagers were running amuck again. A.J. could appreciate that.

The Reverend Goode's own encounter with the Devil had been lost in the bigger story of his murder. The only official account seemed to be the interview he had taped for Channel 3.

A.J. watched it again on the Internet, this time paying close attention to all the visual and verbal cues that were supposed to indicate someone was lying. These were things she had learned to observe back in the day when she was advising clients on how to best present themselves to a cynical public.

Goode's body language was relaxed and easy. He made eye contact with the interviewer. His smile was natural. He made simple, direct statements. He either believed what he was telling the at-home audience or he was a pathological liar.

A.J. suspected Goode was a pathological liar. What he hoped to gain by lying about seeing a monster, she couldn't imagine. Admittedly, she preferred to think he was lying rather than accept the possibility that the Jersey Devil existed when she was about to go camping in its backyard.

Thirteen

Something suspiciously like snow was falling from the lead-colored sky as the eleven members of the First Annual Sacred Balance Women's Retreat paused in a clearing of pines to catch their collective breath.

"It's just a little rain," Simon said, reading A.J.'s expression correctly.

A.J. gazed up worriedly at the heavy sky. Moisture kissed her face. "Are you sure? Because that looks pretty slushy to me." There were uneasy murmurs from some of the other women.

"It's not cold enough for snow," Jaci told her buoyantly. Jaci was obviously loving every moment of this expedition. She wore a knitted red ski cap with a snowflake emblem. Beneath it, her face was flushed, her eyes sparkling. In fact, as far as A.J. could tell, Jaci and Suze—who was wearing some kind of monkey sock puppet headgear—were having more fun than everyone else put together with the possible exception of Mocha. Suze and Jaci had taken the youngest member of the expedition under their wing and Mocha was clearly thriving with all the attention.

"It *smells* like snow," she said happily. She reached up, spreading her gloved fingers wide as though to capture the nonexistent snowflakes.

The three of them were certainly having more fun than A.J. Not that A.J. wasn't trying. There was no denying the beauty of the surrounding countryside. Beneath the dramatic skies, the fall foliage was vibrant with rich hues of gold and russet and red, in vivid contrast to the dark pines. The soft, sugary sand slipped beneath their boots as they walked along the narrow trail.

"See, now it's not even raining anymore," Suze said as the clouds parted and some fading rays of sunshine slipped through. Overhead the wind sang through the pines.

"Great."

Now and then something small skittered beneath the undergrowth or the occasional deer bounded out of a thicket.

Maybe it wasn't cold enough for snow, but it was more than cold enough for A.J. Her nose felt frozen. Her fingers and toes weren't far behind. On the bright side, she had walked on and off all day and was only bone weary and not ready to fall on her face like their seven students. Not so long ago A.J. would have been huffing and puffing like Oriel or Mocha or seventy-year-old Rose Ponte. Not that Rose wasn't doing wonderfully well for a seventy-year-old woman. But A.J. rejoiced in her own relatively newfound current state of fitness—and her lack of blisters.

Of the eight members in their party, four were Sacred Balance personnel, and three of those four were experienced campers. A.J. knew absolutely nothing about camping and would have been happy to keep it that way, but she had prepared for the trip with the same care she prepared for any business project. She'd done her homework, and she made sure to dress in layers and to wear soft, thick boot socks and sturdy footwear. In addition to a backpack and sleeping bag, Jake had loaned her a down-filled vest and his favorite green plaid flannel shirt. She wore her favorite New York Jets cap and a pair of Wayfarers to protect her eyes from the shifting sunlight.

"The break will do you good," Jake had assured her before kissing her good-bye that morning. "You might even have fun. You're only going overnight. What could happen?"

Ask a silly question. Never mind the potential for blisters and sunburn—not that sunburn looked to be an issue for the rest of the day—there was always poison ivy, snakes, spiders, swamps, cranberry bogs, falling trees, crumbling cliffs—okay, in fairness none of that had happened so far, but the day was still young.

Well, perhaps not that young, and, in fact, as they reached a ring of logs around a fire pit in a cleared meadow Simon suggested that this might be a good place to make camp for the night.

There were groans of relief from everyone. Packs were lowered to the ground—and bodies followed.

"Don't get too comfortable," Simon warned. "We want to get our camp set up now so we can relax and enjoy our evening." He threw an instinctive look at the darkening sky. Though his smile never wavered, it looked to A.J. like they were in for a rainy night.

"Mocha, come help me look for firewood," Suze called.

Mocha gamely, if wearily, pushed back to her feet. Jaci and Simon instructed everyone else in setting up the four small dome tents.

The tents were freestanding design and, to A.J.'s surprise, set up quite quickly and with minimal difficulty. Each tent provided snug—very snug—shelter for three adults.

Once the tents were ready, air mattresses inflated, and sleeping bags rolled out, Jaci, Simon, and A.J. started supper. Suze and Mocha returned with the firewood.

"You don't think there are bears out here, do you?" Mocha asked suddenly, staring at the dark, forbidding line of trees.

"No," said A.J., who had been wondering the same thing.

"It feels like we're a lot farther out than we are," Simon reassured. "Because we've been lugging our gear all day. Most bears aren't going to want to come this close to civilization."

"Civilization!" someone echoed doubtfully.

It did seem a very long way from civilization, A.J. had to admit. The closest thing they'd seen to another human was the ruins of a small abandoned town they'd passed through around lunchtime.

Suze laughed. "You'd have a better chance of seeing the Jersey Devil!"

There was an awkward silence while everyone tried not to look at Oriel Goode.

Oriel looked up from the veggie dogs she was piercing with dismantled wire hangers. She said nothing, only handed the wires over to Simon.

Someone tittered nervously. Mocha said, "Well, it was in the news, wasn't it?"

Simon replied, "Don't believe everything you read in the news."

"This was on TV."

That was almost touching.

"There's no such thing as monsters," Jaci said firmly.

"You're wrong there," Oriel said. "There are human monsters."

Not unreasonable that a woman whose husband had been murdered just a few days earlier might feel that way, but it did put a damper on the party. There was another of those abrupt silences.

A.J. rose. "Why don't we take a few moments to stretch and unwind from our hike with a few evening asanas?"

There was quick agreement, the students moving with alacrity to retrieve their mats. There was some discussion over whether boots or shoes should be removed, with the decision being footwear would stay on.

While the other instructors continued to prepare the meal, A.J. led the group through a series of warming, calming exercises.

She finished up, saying, "I nearly forgot. Here's a move that might have been created for our trip. I call it the Yogi Bear." She extended her arms, made wide circles, and thrust her hips out as though using a hula hoop.

Laughter and a few groans followed.

"Let me tell you, that move's a big hit with the Itsy Bitseys."

There was more laughter, especially from Mocha, and A.J.'s heart lifted. If nothing else came out of this trip, this fragile new connection with the girl made all the sore muscles worth it.

"Come and get it, ladies," Simon called.

The evening asanas finished, the group headed for the fire that was now blazing brightly in the ring of logs.

"Who's for veggie dogs and who's for turkey burgers?" Jaci asked as Suze dished out tomato soup spiced with garlic, celery, onion, and red pepper.

Maybe it was the fresh air or maybe it was all the exercise, but A.J. felt like she'd never had food as delicious as the soup and turkey burgers.

The others seemed to equally enjoy their dinners, although there were a few comments that a glass of wine would have made the meal perfect.

"Next time," A.J. promised, and as the words left her mouth, she realized that she didn't mind the thought of there being a next time.

She was enjoying herself. The stars had never seemed so huge, so brilliant in the sky—in between the looming rain clouds—and the dark silence beyond their campfire was . . .

Well, actually it was a little eerie. Depending on how you looked at it. Their cheerful voices seemed to bounce off the wall of trees lining the open field where they were camped. Beyond the trees was an impenetrable blackout of vegetation.

Beside A.J., Oriel said suddenly, "It's a relief to be away from everything. From reporters and policemen and . . . people staring."

A.J. had been hoping for some kind of opening where she could perhaps ask Oriel if she knew that her husband had once gone by another name—that he was suspected of killing his previous wife. But you couldn't ask someone something like that in public. It would be hard to ask at all.

Though Oriel had spoken quietly, her voice carried. There were some murmurs of commiseration. "Sorry for your loss," Simon said. Jaci and Suze spoke, too.

Oriel replied, "Thank you." She rubbed her face tiredly. "It still seems unreal."

Perhaps it was the intimacy created by the warmth and companionship of the campfire, perhaps it was simply that everyone was too tired and too relaxed to be on guard, but the other students began to express sympathy and ask Oriel what her plans were.

"I don't know. I don't see how I can stay now. Even if I wanted to. The memories would be unbearable."

"Don't you want to stay?" A.J. asked.

Oriel shook her head. "I grew up in the Pacific Northwest. New Jersey was David's idea. He said the Lord had summoned him here." Her mouth curled in the firelight. "I asked him why the Lord couldn't summon us to a metropolitan area for a change."

Rose chuckled and patted her knee. "That's a good question, if you ask me."

"If I had a choice, I'd live in Manhattan," Mocha said.

A.J. said, "I used to live in Manhattan."

"What was it like?" Mocha's eyes seemed to shine in the firelight.

"I loved a lot of things about it. The shopping, the nightlife, the wonderful restaurants, and museums and art galleries—and all accessible even without a car. But I like my life now, too."

"I hate my life."

Surprisingly, it turned out to be one of the best things Mocha could have said. Instead of shocking the other students, they began to talk about their own experiences as teenagers as well as their own children's insecurities and anxieties. As some of these kids were classmates of Mocha's, it was clearly an insider's look at her peers.

Only Oriel, sitting next to A.J., was silent.

It was a shame that the conversation had moved away from the Reverend Goode's puzzling insistence on sticking to backwaters for his proselytizing, but in the greater scheme of things, letting Mocha have this opportunity to vent and be heard by this many sympathetic ears was probably the greater good.

When Mocha had finally run down and the others had run out of advice, some useful and some merely well meant, Jaci asked who wanted s'mores. "We have vegetarian and nonvegetarian."

"Vegetarian s'mores?" Mocha asked.

A.J. said, "I know. That came as a surprise to me, too, but most marshmallows are made with gelatin which comes from boiled-down animal hooves and hides."

That had everyone opting for vegetarian s'mores. Jaci grinned at A.J. across the fire.

A.J. wasn't a big fan of s'mores. She contented herself with a hot mug of sugar-free cocoa and watched the others browning their Sweet & Sara marshmallows over the crackling flames.

"Who knows some good ghost stories?" Suze inquired. Her monkey cap had slipped sideways, and the button eyes glinted mischievously in the firelight.

Rose volunteered, "Has anyone ever been to the Colby Mansion in Byram Township?"

No one had.

"The story is that a wealthy railroad owner named Colby killed his wife—no one knows why exactly—and placed her head on his fireplace mantle."

Now there was an episode for *Divine Design*. A.J. wisely sipped her cocoa and kept her thoughts to herself. Her fellow campers looked, depending on temperament, either amused or spellbound.

"But the ghost of Mr. Colby's wife drove him to suicide."

"How did he do it?" Suze asked, wide-eyed.

"Er, I'm not sure," Rose admitted. "But I'm sure it was pretty gruesome. Now *both* their spirits roam the estate late at night." To Mocha, she said, "I had a cousin who lived in Byram. We went to the house with some friends when I was your age. It was all boarded up, but being kids, we broke in and had a look around."

"At night?"

"No. We weren't *that* brave."

Suze and Mocha asked at the same time, "What did you see?" Rose and the others laughed.

"The place was a wreck, but the big marble staircase was still intact. And there were three fireplaces."

"Did you see a ghost?" Suze asked.

"I saw something *much* worse. I saw Chester May trying to French-kiss my cousin C.J."

More laughter all around.

Someone else suggested, "How about the West Milford hellhound that will chase you through the woods and down Clinton Road."

"We've got plenty of hellhounds in Stillbrook," another student said, and there were chuckles. "One chases my car every morning when I leave for work."

"Well, there's always the Jersey Devil," Suze said cheerfully. She seemed unaware of the startled pause that followed her words. "That story used to scare the pants off me when I was a kid."

Jaci asked, "What *is* the story?"

Suze explained about Mother Leeds, who was some-times called Mother Shroud, and how her newborn devil child had eaten a couple of his twelve siblings before escaping out the window and into the woods.

"Yikes," A.J. said. "That's the first time I've heard *that* version."

"Oh, there are lots of stories," Rose said through a mouthful of s'mores. "Stories how the Devil came to be. Stories of it flying around the countryside."

"How could he fly with those little bat wings?"

"I don't know, but the legend is Commodore Stephen Decatur fired cannonballs directly at it, and the balls passed right through the creature and it flew safely away. Oh, and they say that Joseph Bonaparte, the brother to Napoleon himself, spotted it when he was out hunting one day."

"In France?" Mocha asked.

"Bordentown. I guess he lived in this country by then."

"Isn't the *Blair Witch Project* supposed to be about the Jersey Devil?" Jaci chimed in.

"I don't remember that," A.J. said. "I thought that was supposed to take place in Maryland."

"Yeah, that's right," Suze said. "There's *The Last Broadcast*. Except that's not *really* about the Jersey Devil."

"Did you get a look at it?" Rose asked Oriel.

"A look at what?"

"The Jersey Devil. Your husband said he saw it, isn't that so? He was on Channel 3."

A.J. could almost feel the struggle within Oriel. Oriel said, after a pause, "No. I didn't see anything. I go to bed early and I'm a heavy sleeper."

The campfire flared. No one spoke.

A.J. felt something wet against her face. She looked upward and another drop hit her brow bone. The fire sizzled as the rain began to fall faster.

"Uh-oh!" Suze exclaimed, getting to her feet.

Rose chanted, "It's raining, it's pouring, the old man is snoring."

The students began to retreat to their tents.

"Put your plates and cups out so the rain can wash them," Simon ordered.

There were a few sounds of dismay at this novel approach to washing up, but no one wanted to stay and argue. Plates and cups and silverware were spread out over the grass.

Inside the tent A.J. was sharing with Rose and Oriel it looked like one giant bed covered in a patchwork quilt of sleeping bags. A.J. held the flashlight as the other two crawled inside, sliding their shoes off and slipping inside their bags, giant shadows flashing against the plastic wall of the tent.

"What time is it?" Rose asked, smothering a yawn.

"Ten thirty," Oriel replied as A.J. took her turn pulling off her boots and wriggling into her bag. "It feels later."

"Hope I don't need to use the facilities."

A.J. and Oriel giggled as the rain began to patter harder against the roof of the tent.

"*I* hope this thing doesn't leak," A.J. said. "Does anyone want the light on?"

"Nope." Rose turned her back to them and snuggled down in her bag. "Good night, gals."

"I'm going to sleep. I was falling asleep out there anyway," Oriel said, following suit.

A.J. switched out the flashlight. The shadows of the tall pines brushed across the ceiling like dark wings. The silence was filled by the whisper of the rain on the plastic tent. The night smelled of cold, damp earth and cold, damp plastic and cold, damp flannel.

At least it was warm inside the tent. She closed her eyes.

The next time she opened them it was pitch-black and someone was screaming.

Fourteen

❧

There was a great upheaval of bedding around A.J. She sat up, groping for the flashlight. "What is it? What's wrong?"

"What in tarnation is going on?" Rose's gravelly voice drifted through the darkness.

A.J. switched on the flashlight. Rose was sitting upright, her gray hair standing in tufts. She swung the flashlight toward Oriel's sleeping bag. It was empty. "Where's Oriel? Where did she go?"

Rose shook her head.

The terrified screams were still echoing through the night, but now other voices had joined in.

"Here." A.J. thrust the flashlight at Rose and grabbed her boots, yanking them on over her thick socks. "Where's my coat?"

Rose lifted bedding with her free hand, searching. A.J. gave it up, crawling out of the tent.

The rain had stopped. The moon was as bright and perfect as a shiny new dime. It illuminated the rain puddles and shadowy clumps of grass. At the end of the row of tents more flashlight beams darted in a circle like fireflies.

A.J. ran, trying to avoid the puddles and scattered dishes, to the last tent. As she reached the little crowd around it, she could hear puzzled murmurs. From inside the tent came Suze's raised voice and Mocha's hysterical sobs. Simon knelt before the entrance, his deeper tones cutting through the shocked mutters of the other students.

"What happened?" A.J. gasped. She felt winded. Not from the short jog, but from waking up in a panic. Her heart was still thundering.

Mocha's gulped sobs drowned out Simon's response. Jaci seemed to take form in the pallid moonlight. "She says she saw the Jersey Devil."

"What?"

"I *did* see it!" Mocha cried. "I could see its silhouette through the tent and then it looked inside."

"No. No, Mocha," Simon said. "Too many s'mores before bed, that's all."

"It wasn't s'mores. It had horns and glowing red eyes. It looked right *at* me."

"I didn't see anything," Suze said, sounding bewildered. "You were sleeping. You were snoring."

"Why were you awake?"

"I don't know. I heard twigs breaking and then I heard something coming across the grass toward our tent. It sounded . . . weird. I heard it step on the dishes and silverware."

A.J. touched Jaci's arm, and beckoned for her to follow. "Shine your flashlight along here."

Jaci directed the beam along the side of the tent. The grass sparkled in the grainy glare of the beam.

"The *other* side!" Mocha cried from inside the tent.

Simon and Suze made shushing sounds.

A.J. led the way around the tent, Jaci shining the beam ahead of their steps.

"What's that?" A.J. halted, kneeling. Jaci squatted beside her. They exchanged looks. "What kind of print is that?"

"Hmm."

"Well?"

"It looks like a hoofprint to me. A deer print probably." Jaci frowned down. "There's only one indentation."

A.J. opened her mouth and then closed it. A one-legged Jersey Devil?

Reading her thoughts, Jaci said, "The other three hooves would have been in the grass so we can't see the prints."

"A deer, then?"

Jaci nodded. "Maybe even a small elk."

"It wasn't a deer," Mocha yelled. "It wasn't an elk. I know the difference between a deer and a devil. A deer didn't yank back the tent flap and look at me."

Simon and Suze made more soothing noises. A.J. said softly to Jaci, "I don't see Oriel anywhere. Do you?"

Jaci looked at the gathered group. The ghostly figures blinked back at them. "No."

"She wasn't in our tent when Mocha screamed."

"Maybe she needed some, um, private time."

"Maybe. But you'd think with all the screaming she'd have shown up by now. Is everyone else accounted for?" A.J. looked back at the students crowding around the tent Suze and Mocha were sharing.

With the exception of Rose and Oriel everyone seemed to be present.

Jaci said suddenly, "Aren't you freezing? Where's your jacket, A.J.?"

A.J. realized she *was* freezing. Her teeth were chattering. She hugged herself. "I didn't have time to grab my jacket."

Simon rose. "I think we're okay here now. I'm going to build a fire and sit up, so why don't the rest of you get some sleep?"

"You can't sit up all night, Simon," A.J. objected.

Simon laughed. "I hate to break it to you, but it's already four in the morning. It just feels like the middle of the night. You'll all need to be getting up for breakfast in another two hours yourselves."

A.J. went around the tent and peered into the opening. "Are you okay now, Mocha?"

Suze gave her the thumbs-up sign.

Mocha's dark head bobbed. "I'm okay. I know what I saw, though. It *wasn't* a deer or an elk or a moose or anything like that."

"Okay. Well, I don't think we're going to solve this mystery tonight. Shall we all grab whatever sleep we can?"

There seemed to be fervent agreement on that score. The other students began to slip away to their tents.

"Simon's going to sit up, so you're perfectly safe," A.J. told Mocha.

"Unless it gets him first!" Mocha flopped down on her back and closed her eyes.

"Don't worry, we're fine here," Suze said, which could have been directed to Mocha or to A.J.

"Sweet dreams." A.J. closed the flap and straightened.

"I'm going to get my jacket and look for Oriel. Will you come with me?" she asked Jaci in an undertone.

Jaci nodded. "Of course." As they headed for A.J.'s tent she said, "It had to be all those ghost stories and the talk about scary movies."

"And three s'mores."

Jaci huffed a little laugh.

When they reached A.J.'s tent they found that Oriel was back in her sleeping bag. She frowned into the flashlight beam directed her way.

"All present and accounted for," Rose said. "Can we get some sleep now?"

"Where were you?" A.J. demanded of Oriel.

Oriel looked mildly affronted. "I was using the ladies' room."

The idea of that dark untamed wilderness being referred to as a "ladies' room" was sort of funny, but A.J. didn't feel like laughing. "Didn't you hear all the commotion?"

"Of course."

"Didn't you think you should see what was going on?"

Oriel said coolly, "I could tell what was going on. I knew before we all turned in what would be going on. That child eats like a pig. And it seemed to me that there were more than enough people to deal with the crisis."

Certainly logical. A.J. couldn't fault her for that, but Oriel's reaction still seemed peculiar to her, not to mention a little harsh on Mocha. Then again, Rose hadn't felt the need to crawl out of the tent and see what was happening. Of course, Rose was seventy years old. Maybe she didn't feel up to staggering around in the middle of a wet, chilly November night. Even now she wasn't asking questions. Maybe theirs *was* a normal response.

"I guess we're okay here." A.J. turned back to Jaci.

Jaci swallowed a yawn. "Okay. See you all in the morning."

"Night."

A.J. crawled back into her tent and pulled off her boots. Her tent mates were already turned on their sides and hunkered down in their bedding, determined to make the most of what remained of the night.

A.J. slithered into her sleeping bag, which smelled ever so slightly and comfortingly of Jake. She turned out the flashlight.

Rose's muted snores drifted gently into the night.

Morning was wet and gray and came all too soon.

Simon's tending had produced a brightly blazing campfire to greet the washed-out dawn. A pot of coffee was boiling over the flames and a kettle of oatmeal with walnuts and apple pieces simmered away.

"This is wonderful. Thank you," A.J. told him. She hugged herself. "Is it colder this morning?"

"It is. Yep." Simon shrugged. "I forgot how much I like camping. This was an excellent idea."

"I hope everyone else still thinks so after last night." A.J. drew closer to the fire, holding her hands over the flames.

"You missed the deer," Simon said, perhaps by way of answer. "Two does and a fawn. They were halfway down the meadow before they noticed us."

"I wish I'd seen them. Did you happen to check the print marks next to Suze and Mocha's tent?"

Simon nodded. "I did, but it was too hard to tell in the dark and it rained again just before daylight, so whatever made those tracks, they're washed away now. From what I saw last night, it looked like deer hooves to me."

"I hope that kid's not psychologically scarred for life."

Simon made a derisive sound. "If she is, it's nothing that happened on this trip. Want some oatmeal?"

"Shouldn't we wait to eat until after the morning asanas?"

Jaci wandered up, warmly bundled. The tip of her nose was pink. "Coffee?"

Simon nodded to the pot and Jaci sighed in gratitude. To A.J., Simon said, "About the asanas." He pointed at a formidable wall of clouds moving in from the north. "We've had a change in weather conditions."

"What do you mean?"

"Snow," Jaci said succinctly.

A.J.'s mouth dropped. "You're kidding me."

Simon and Jaci both shook their heads.

"*Snow?* How soon? I thought this was the wrong time of year!"

"Weather malfunction," Jaci said. She sipped her coffee.

"We should have breakfast and get going," Simon said. "There's no cause for panic, but we don't want to mess around either. Most of us aren't dressed for snow."

A.J. nodded. "Okay. Let's eat and pack up."

By then the other students were making an appearance. A.J.'s news that they would be skipping the morning exercises was greeted with unseemly warmth.

"Hey, that *is* why we came, you know!"

The others laughed at her. "Nah, we came for the good company, for the fellowship," Rose said. There were assents from the group.

"And the veggie s'mores," Suze put in.

They made quick work of breakfast and quicker work of packing up, and were well down the trail when the skies opened up.

Rain, even slushy rain, was a lot better than snow, but it was still not optimum weather for mostly inexperienced hikers.

"There are some abandoned houses up ahead," Simon told A.J. "We can shelter there for a bit. Have our morning snack."

"Abandoned houses? That doesn't sound very safe."

The Pinelands were supposed to be the ideal hunting ground for those interested in ghost towns and ruins. In addition to graveyards and iron bogs and overgrown railroad tracks there were many crumbling foundations and tunnels of some of the industries that had once thrived there: lumber and paper mills, iron works, glass and munitions factories—more than forty-five industrial towns. And there were homes. Everything from farmhouses to stately mansions, all of them—with the exception of historically preserved and maintained Batsto Village—in various states of disrepair.

"I'm not suggesting we explore very far, but maybe we can wait out the worst of it."

"Unless the worst of it is still to come," Jaci said, joining them.

"True."

Suze joined them. "What's up?"

"How's Mocha holding up?" A.J. asked.

"She could use a rest. We could all use a rest."

A.J. nodded, combing the wet hair out of her eyes. "Okay. Let's find a place to hole up long enough to catch our breath."

They continued down the increasingly slick and muddy

road. Houses slowly materialized out of the rainy mist ahead of them, silvered by time and weather. The group strung out single file along a tumbled stone wall till they came to an opening that had once held a gate. They went up the path overgrown with weeds.

The roof was gone from the porch at the front of the house, but the steps and floorboards on the porch itself looked reasonably solid. Simon went first, shone his flashlight inside the building, and nodded approval. The rest of the group went cautiously up the stairs, following him into the black square mouth of the house.

The instant relief of being out of the pounding rain faded as flashlight beams played over peeling wallpaper, spiderwebs, and a pile of rubble. The windows were boarded up, but not very efficiently. Gray light filtered through the boards and pinpointed a broken rocker and another doorway leading deeper into the house.

The rain thundered down on the tin roof.

"Snack time," Jaci announced brightly, and there was nervous laughter.

It smelled weird and unwholesome, like freshly dug graves and rotting pantries and nesting animals.

"Well," A.J. said. "It could be worse."

"How so?" inquired Oriel.

"The building could be on fire."

"Not for long. Wow. Look at it coming down." Suze stood at the front door gazing out at the sheet of rain.

"How long is this going to go on?" someone asked.

Simon looked at A.J. and shook his head. "Hopefully this will only last a few minutes," A.J. said. "But we won't melt if we have to keep moving. It would be preferable if we didn't have to do it in a downpour, but I know we all want to get home before midnight."

Jaci unscrewed the cap of her canteen and took a swallow of water. The others began to follow suit.

Suze used her backpack as a makeshift seat. Jaci and Simon both had backpacks that converted to camp stools. The others dropped their packs and began hunting for water and snacks.

A.J. shined her flashlight through the interior door, checking out the next room. It turned out to be a short hallway. The hallway ended in a patch of watery daylight from one of the side rooms. She pulled her cell phone out and walked cautiously down the hall, sweeping her flashlight beam ahead of her. A fat spider disappeared into some dirty, faded fast-food containers.

The sight of trash, a reminder that they really weren't that far away from civilization, reassured her. They were only an hour or two away from the cars now, so assuming they didn't get lost in the rain, they'd be home and dry in time for supper.

She checked her phone and was surprised to see she had a signal. Not much of a signal, but she hadn't expected any. She speed-dialed Jake as she walked toward the light at the end of the hall.

Only she and Simon were carrying phones. The point of the retreat had been to get away from cell phones and pagers and laptops and all the other distractions of their normal, busy lives.

She put the phone to her ear, listening for a ring on the other end, but there was nothing. She looked at the screen but it was still showing signal bars. She dialed again, listening absently as she glanced inside the room at the end of the hall.

One of the rear windows stood wide-open, splintered boards scattered on the floor, so A.J. could see the ruins of a stone fireplace and what looked like an old framed picture hanging on the wall.

How had that picture not been grabbed or destroyed by vandals?

She crossed the floor. Checking her phone she saw that she was now getting the *No Service* message. Not exactly a surprise.

A rustling sound beneath her feet froze her in her tracks. A.J. stared down and realized that she was near the edge of a gaping hole in the floor. She had mistaken the dark patch for dirt. . . .

Staring down she could see there was some kind of cellar beneath the house and that it was filled with rubble and debris from the caved-in floor as well as a lot of broken furniture and wild vegetation.

She shined her flashlight into the pit and then did a double take as the beam was caught and reflected. A.J. bent closer and then gulped. A pair of eyes glittered back at her from a long, red face.

Fifteen

"A.J.?" Simon called from behind her.

A.J. started, turning from the gap in the floor. "Simon!"

"I didn't mean to startle you. The rain has stopped. I think we—"

She beckoned sharply, cutting him off. "Come and look at this." Simon crossed the floor in two steps. A.J. shined her flashlight into the dark. "There's something down there."

"What? What's down there?"

"I don't know, but its eyes were gleaming in my flashlight beam. Can you see it?" A.J. peered down. "I think it was right over there."

"It was probably a raccoon. They're all over the place. Or maybe a fox."

"No. The eyes were too big." A.J. swore under her breath and moved the flashlight slowly in the area where she had thought she'd seen something staring back at her.

"How big do you think it was?" Simon sounded more patient than interested.

"Big. I mean, maybe human-sized. Just for a second I thought I saw . . . features."

She could feel him staring at her in the gloom. "Human features?"

"Yes. Well, I can't say for sure. It was just a split second and then you called my name." She tried again to probe the darkness with her flashlight beam, but nothing reflected back. It probably *had* been a raccoon or a possum. The reflected light could have given an illusion of size.

"That's interesting," Simon said politely, "but I think we better seize this moment to get moving before the rain starts again. Besides, if what you saw was a wild dog or something on those lines, we don't want it following us down the trail."

"Right." A.J. stepped back. She clicked her phone off. "I was hoping we could call ahead and let someone know what's going on, but I can't get enough of a signal."

"No. Signal is hit-or-miss out here. When we get to the cars, we'll be able to phone. But we're not late yet. In fact, we're making pretty good time."

That was because no one wanted to spend a minute longer in the rain and mud than they had to.

A.J. agreed and with one final, reluctant look at the opening in the floor, she followed Simon back to the main room where everyone was donning their packs and hoods.

"I would kill for a hot pizza right about now," Rose announced and Mocha concurred in heartfelt tones.

"I'd kill for a hot bath," Oriel said as they shuffled onto the porch.

They went down the steps and picked their way through

weeds and broken walkway back to the opening in the wall and the trail beyond.

Though the rain had stopped at least for now, wet dripped from pine needles and beaded bare limbs. The *plops* sounded loud in the vast silence. Their footsteps made dull *thuds* on the soggy ground.

They walked in a straggling group, two and three abreast, and no one had much to say.

Something wet touched A.J.'s nose. She looked up as a soft feathery bit of white drifted down and evaporated against the ground.

It was snowing.

At the head of the group, Simon urged everyone to pick up the pace.

Groans and mutters followed this advice until someone pointed out the snow lazily floating down.

That was the incentive everyone needed. They sped up, pushing past their fatigue and sore muscles. There was little chatter now.

A bee buzzed past A.J.'s cheek and ploughed into the bark of a tree a few feet ahead and to the right of her. She thought vaguely that it was awfully cold weather for bees when the crack of a rifle split the rain-washed silence.

Pine branches bobbed, pine needles flew, and another rifle shot fractured the rainy afternoon.

Wait a minute, the rational, civilized portion of A.J.'s brain thought. *This can't be happening. This only happens in movies. . . .*

Startled faces were turning her way.

"Hey," Suze shouted. "There are people here!"

"*Holy shit*," Rose yelped. "Someone's *shooting* at us."

Yes. That was it. Someone was shooting at them. All around A.J., students were screaming, running. Of course.

That was the normal reaction to being shot at. No normal person was prepared for this, trained for this; A.J. certainly wasn't.

She joined the terrified flight down the trail. Ahead of her one of the gray sweatshirted figures lumbering beneath a backpack stumbled and clutched her arm, but kept running. There was another of those terrifying *bangs* that seemed to roll on and on forever echoing through the woods. The cries of the women sounded like frightened birds.

"Get into the trees," A.J. yelled breathlessly. "Go for the bushes."

Why hadn't they stuck close to home? The Skyland region had plenty of beautiful places to camp and commune with nature. *Why* had they decided to head for the Pine Barrens? Everyone knew the Pine Barrens were a weird and dangerous place.

They dived into the greenery lining the road and vanished—although the sounds of fear and alarm could still be heard as they thrashed around seeking hiding places.

A.J. found herself kneeling in a bed of pine needles behind a thick fallen tree trunk with Jaci and Suze. "Where's Simon?"

Jaci shook her head. Beneath the cheerful red cap her face was bone white.

A snowflake landed on the log—and stuck. Another drifted into place beside it.

Suze said through chattering teeth, "He grabbed Mocha. I think they're behind that big cement pillar."

"Could this be an accident? Is it hunting season?"

Jaci and Suze said at the same time, "Not for rifles!"

Not for rifles? What did that mean? Then what *was*

happening here? Why would someone fire at them? Were they inadvertently trespassing? It made no sense. No one could possibly think they could kill eleven people and get away with it—and certainly not this close to the outside world.

The rifle cracked twice more. This time its report was met with dead silence. The only stirring was the slow, steady drip of wet from the trees to the ground.

"What are we going to do?" Jaci whispered.

A.J. pulled her phone out and stared hard at the screen. There were a couple of bars of signal. *Work*, she willed it silently. She pressed speed dial for Jake.

No Service flashed up.

"Any luck?" Suze's blue eyes looked huge.

A.J. shook her head.

"We should arm ourselves." Jaci picked up a short stout branch.

Great. Sticks and stones against a rifle. That was going to go well.

A.J. listened tensely.

Plop.

Plop.

Plop.

Nothing but the rain splattering on fallen leaves. The snowflakes melted. That was good news. They had enough to deal with without heavy snowfall.

Something rustled in the bushes nearby and A.J., Suze, and Jaci jumped in accord. They relaxed as Simon joined them.

"He's moving away, back up the trail," Simon told them. "I spotted him through the trees."

A.J. asked, "Could you see who it was?"

"No."

"He must be crazy," Jaci whispered.

"Are you sure it was a he?" A.J. spoke.

"No." Simon stared at her. "Why?"

A.J. shook her head. "I don't know. I can't understand why anyone would fire on us. Even if the first shot was a mistake, the others couldn't have been."

"That wasn't a mistake," Suze said fiercely. "No one could have missed the fact that we were all screaming."

"She's right," Simon said.

"Is everyone safe?"

"A bullet grazed Oriel's arm."

"Oh my God." A.J. swallowed. "Is she badly hurt?"

Simon's head moved in negation. "It just nicked the fleshy part of her arm. She's scared and in shock. Like everybody else. We need to get down to the cars."

"Are you sure it's safe to move?"

"As far as I could tell there was only one shooter. Unless he's laying one hell of an elaborate trap—which seems unlikely—he's heading away from us now."

A.J. said, "Okay. Then let's move. But let's stay off the road and stick to cover as much as possible.'

"Good idea." Simon turned and they followed him, scuttling through leaves and undergrowth until they joined the huddle of students around Oriel.

Oriel had a white T-shirt wrapped around her upper right arm. The white cotton was spotted red. Not a lot of red, but even that spreading quarter-shape of scarlet made A.J. feel queasy. "How are you doing?"

"I'll live," Oriel said tersely. Her face was bloodless, her hair a rat's nest of leaves and twigs.

"Unless that maniac shoots us all," someone else muttered.

"We're going to go for the cars," A.J. told them. "But

we're going to stay off the road and stick to cover as much as possible. Simon thinks whoever shot at us is moving away, moving in the opposite direction, so I think this is the best choice."

"Maybe we should vote on it," Rose quavered. "What if he's circling round?"

"We're sitting ducks here," Suze said.

"Vote," A.J. said.

Hands went up. There were a few quick yeses. Rose bit her lip.

"You stick with me, Rose," Suze said.

Rose nodded.

"Let's move," Simon said, turning to lead the way.

Move they did. At first they stuck very close to the ground, but as they traveled farther and farther from the scene of the shooting, they began to risk standing upright as they darted from thicket to tree to bush to tree.

Snow began to fall again.

It seemed the longest journey of A.J.'s life. At last they spotted the main highway through the trees, saw the colored flash of passing cars, and knew the parking lot was just a few yards farther ahead. A.J. stopped behind a scrub pine and tried her phone again.

She could have cried her relief when Jake answered. "Hey, how's it going, Marco Polo?"

"Can you get us some help?" She steadied her voice with effort. "Someone shot at us. Oriel Goode has been wounded."

"Someone—?" Jake's voice changed. "Where are you now?"

A.J. told him. She did everything but give him longitude and latitude.

"Got it. Are you okay, honey?"

She had to fight the ridiculous urge to burst into tears at that "honey."

"I'm fine," she got out.

"Stay low. Help is on the way. So am I."

A few more words and he was gone. A.J. wished he could have stayed on the line with her, but of course that wasn't necessary. They weren't in any danger now, and if they had been, there was nothing Jake could achieve by staying on the phone. She was a big girl now. She could deal with whatever she needed to deal with until help arrived.

The students were running to their cars. A.J. sprinted after them. "Wait! You can't all just take off."

"A.J., I think I should take Mocha home." Jaci came back to meet her.

"I don't think any of us should leave yet. Everyone here is a witness. The police are going to want to take statements."

"Oriel needs medical help."

"Jake has an ambulance on the way. She seems to be okay for now."

Jaci bit her lip. "I still don't think this is any place for a kid."

"Okay." A.J. raked a hand through her damp hair. "Take her home. I'm sure she's still going to have to give a statement, but I guess it won't make much difference if she does it now or a few hours from now."

"Right. And don't worry. I'll be back, I promise." Jaci trotted to her car where Mocha waited inside. A few seconds later Jaci pulled out onto the main highway and disappeared down the road. A couple of the other women began to protest and insist they be allowed to leave.

A.J. tried to be sympathetic but firm. "Look, we're not

in danger now. The police are on the way. We need to wait."

"We don't know that we're not in danger," Oriel protested. "I've been *shot*."

"EMTs are on the way right now."

"Suppose that maniac is doubling back," Rose said. "I'm not going to stay here and risk getting shot."

"I can't force you to stay, but you're all going to have to give statements. Wouldn't you rather get it over with now?"

"I'm staying," Simon said, "so you're staying, too, Rose."

"I'm not going anywhere," Suze chimed in.

"Rose can drive my car." Oriel cradled her injured arm.

The wail of sirens floated in the distance.

Hearing that banshee lament, the other students fell silent, the incipient mutiny crushed. They waited, watching as the vehicles of State Park Police sped into view.

In a matter of seconds the cars of the Sacred Balance students were pinned in, whether by design or accident, by both State Park Police and the white sedans of State Police.

The troopers questioned everyone at length while Simon led the Park Police back up the trail to where the shooting had occurred.

The EMTs arrived and began treating everyone for shock and minor cuts and abrasions. Oriel had sustained the most serious injury.

"The wound itself is superficial," a rosy-cheeked young EMT informed A.J. when she walked up to see how Oriel was doing. "But her blood pressure is high and she's got a history of heart trouble."

"She *does*?" A.J.'s own heart skipped a beat. Well, that was fabulous. That was what happened when you didn't insist on a full medical history of guests and regular studio clients alike. What if Oriel had suffered a heart attack out there in the woods? What the heck would they have done then?

"We're going to go ahead and take her into Burlington."

"I'll follow behind, if that's okay?"

"It's not necessary," Oriel said. "I'm perfectly fine."

A.J. and the EMTs overrode her protests and the doors closed on Oriel's final exasperated objections.

By then the students had been questioned, the consensus being that no one had observed anything useful, and were being allowed to leave. A little caravan of cars edged past the official vehicles, departed the parking lot, and sped toward the main highway.

Suze trotted up to A.J. "Did you want me to follow you into Burlington?"

A.J. shook her head. "Jake's on his way. I'll call and tell him to meet me there. Can you call Jaci and tell her what's going on?"

"Sure. No problem. And don't worry about Rose. I'll take her home since there's no telling when Simon will be back."

"Thank you, Suze." A.J. hugged her.

Suze hugged her back. "You have to admit, it was definitely a bonding exercise."

A.J. gave an unwilling laugh. "Nothing like running for your lives to bring people together. I'm praying we don't get sued."

Suze shook her head. "Nah. Don't worry. It's not your fault some maniac happened to stumble over us."

"Or we stumbled over him." A.J. had nearly forgotten that weird glimpse of . . . something in the cellar of the abandoned house where they'd sheltered. Were the two things connected or was it just a coincidence?

"Right. Have a good night. I'll see you tomorrow." Suze loped back to her Beetle, waving to Rose.

A.J. climbed in her Volvo and let her head fall back against the seat for a few seconds. She didn't want to drive into Burlington. She didn't want to ever move a muscle again. She was beyond tired. She opened her eyes and looked at the crystal Mala beads hanging from the rear-view mirror. The smoky amber crystals sparkled with their own light on this gray, snowy day, like tiny suns.

It looked like everything had turned out all right, but the Sacred Balance retreat could have had such a very different ending. A tragic ending. It was just luck that they'd all made it safely.

Luck.

They were taking it for granted they'd had the bad luck to stumble on a lunatic—and the good luck to escape without serious injury.

But what if it wasn't luck at all? What if there had been some sinister design behind today's events?

A.J. sat up, reaching for her cell phone.

Sixteen

As wonderful sights went, Jake striding down a sterile hospital corridor had to be right up there with the Seven Wonders of the World.

In fact, the only thing better than the sight of Jake was the feel of Jake's arms around her. A.J. hugged him back with all her strength. Until this moment she hadn't really felt . . . safe.

"Sorry I couldn't get here any faster. How's Oriel?"

"She's fine. She's mostly suffering from shock. They're talking about releasing her if she wants to go home."

Jake frowned at that news. "For now she just might be better off where she is."

On the cell phone with him during her drive to Burlington, A.J. had shared her fears. The fact that Jake seemed to think her concerns held merit was not exactly reassuring. "I know. One thing's for sure: no hunter accidentally mistook our entire group for a herd of deer. But at the

same time, I don't see how anyone could have targeted
Oriel. We were all bundled up, wearing hoods and hats.
So unless someone followed us from our campsite—"

"Where was Oriel when she was hit?"

A.J. tried to remember. Her recollection of those hor-
rible moments when she'd heard the shots was blurred.
"She was a little ahead of me. I remember that. I'm trying
to picture everyone's position, but . . ." Her eyes met
Jake's. "The first shot nearly hit *me*."

Jake swore quietly.

A.J. put a hand to her cheek. "I felt the bullet go past.
I thought it was an insect."

If possible, Jake's face went grimmer. "Well. You do
have a habit of poking around in things that aren't your
business. It's possible you got on somebody's bad side.
Oriel getting hit might be a coincidence. How far was she
from you when she was hit?"

"It's really hard to judge. I know it's a cliché, but everything really *was* happening fast. She couldn't have
been more than a few feet ahead of me."

"Great."

"But we were all running in a pack. That's what I mean
about it being hard to target one person. We heard the
shots and we all took off. And we were all dressed very
much the same. A lot of us were wearing gray or navy
hoodies beneath our jackets. Oriel was."

Jake glanced at A.J.'s clothing. "You weren't."

"No."

He was silent, considering.

"I've been thinking. It's just as possible that some nut
was inspired by David Goode's preaching against yoga
and opened fire on all of us. *Or* maybe someone thinks that
because Lily was accused of his murder, yoga is somehow

responsible for Goode's death. We've been advertising this retreat all week. It wouldn't have been hard to track us down."

"Maybe." Jake sounded unconvinced.

"When I first moved here from Manhattan, not everyone greeted me with open arms. A lot of people thought Aunt Di was a kook and that yoga wasn't for 'regular folks.'"

"Assuming this wasn't a vendetta against yoga and women who wear leggings—"

"Funny."

"Did you notice anything else odd or out of the ordinary?"

"Beyond getting shot at?"

"Right."

"Does a sighting of the Jersey Devil count?"

Jake closed his eyes as though in pain. "Tell me you're kidding."

"No. Mocha Ritchie woke the whole camp up last night screaming that the Jersey Devil opened her tent flap and looked in at her. This was after three s'mores and an evening of telling ghost stories around the campfire, mind. She's fifteen."

"I think we can discount that sighting."

"Probably. The only thing is, during the commotion, Oriel was MIA."

"How's that?"

"Well, she wasn't in her tent when Mocha started screaming. I know because I was bunking with her. Her story is she was answering nature's call, which could certainly be true, but everyone else in camp came running to Mocha's tent. Oriel apparently finished up in the woods and went back to bed."

"I don't know that that proves anything. She was

probably freezing her tail off. It wouldn't be hard to figure out what was happening."

"That's what Oriel said."

Jake shrugged. "It makes sense to me."

"Maybe."

"You're not thinking that she scared the kid by peeking in at her?"

"No. That is, I can't imagine any reason for her to do such a thing. And Mocha was insistent that what she saw was neither human nor animal. She'd surely have recognized Oriel. That's on the assumption she saw anything at all."

"The whole thing sounds far-fetched."

"Believe me, I know exactly how it sounds. But then *I* saw something in the cellar of an abandoned house we took shelter in. And that wasn't very long before we were fired on."

"Whoa, whoa, whoa." Jake eyed her narrowly. "One thing at a time. Back to last night at the campsite. Did *you* see anything that looked like . . ." He apparently couldn't quite bring himself to say it.

"The Jersey Devil? No, Jaci and I found what looked like a hoof mark beside Mocha's tent, but Jaci thought it looked like a deer."

"Were there four prints or two?"

"One. That's the thing. The other prints, however many there were, were on the grass and we couldn't make them out."

They moved aside as an orderly wheeled an empty gurney down the hallway.

"Okay, so basically . . . weird sounds, bushes moving, dark shadows. Nothing that couldn't be explained away by the night and the wind—and nerves."

"Right. It was eerie out there, no question."

"In other words, no one really saw anything last night—
with the exception of one hysterical teenage girl?"

A.J. nodded.

"Okay. But today you think you saw . . . what in an
abandoned house?"

"I thought I saw glowing eyes in a long, red, horsey
face."

Jake's own face remained serious, but it was clearly a
battle.

Exasperated, A.J. said, "Assuming I saw anything at
all, I saw what could possibly have been someone in a
costume."

"A costume?" he repeated thoughtfully.

"I know it sounds ridiculous because no one could
know we would take shelter in that house, but I think
someone might have been masquerading as a monster for
their own purposes."

"What purpose would that be? You just said no one
could have known you'd take shelter in that building."

"There have been all these recent sightings of the
Jersey Devil, right? Maybe someone's doing it for promotional reasons—to bring tourists into the area. Everyone
keeps saying the economy is killing us and we need more
business."

"Visit the Pine Barrens and see the Jersey Devil?"

"Why not? People have come up with crazier marketing ideas than that. I ought to know. I used to be one of the
people coming up with them."

Jake laughed. "I won't ask what idea you came up with
that was as crazy as this one."

"The other possibility is someone is just getting a kick
out of scaring everyone."

"And slaughtering farm animals?"

A.J. swallowed. "I'd nearly forgotten that."

"Yeah. Well, forgetting the cruelty to the animals themselves, the Baumanns took a hit for several thousand dollars. That's no laughing matter."

"No, that's pretty horrifying."

"If not for those dead cows and the shooting today, I'd put these supposed Jersey Devil sightings down to teenage pranks. Do you think you could find the abandoned house where your group took shelter from the rain again?"

"I think so."

"You want to give it a shot?"

"Now?"

"The sooner the better. We've got local and state police combing the area, so there's no danger."

"But it's going to be dark before long. And it's snowing."

Jake glanced out the picture window that offered a view of the hospital complex and the wan sun making a halfhearted appearance through the trees lining the busy parking lot.

"It's not snowing anymore. And we've still got a good two to three hours of daylight."

A.J. groaned.

Jake's smile was grimly sympathetic. "I could go on my own but I might not be able to find the house. And if we wait till tomorrow reporters are going to be wandering over the park."

"And this isn't something we want advertised."

"Nope. For several excellent reasons."

A.J. sighed. "I can't believe I'm even considering this. If I agree to lead you back there, will you give me a foot massage tonight?"

"I'll be happy to massage anything you like."

A.J. expelled a long, weary breath. "I'm going to hold you to that." She reached for her jacket. "Okay. Let's get this over with."

Police vehicles still crowded the little makeshift parking lot when A.J. and Jake pulled up beneath the crooked pitch pines.

Being two counties away from home, they were far out of Jake's jurisdiction. He got out and went to have a word with the Burlington County Sheriff's Department officer in charge. In a couple of minutes he was back to the car where A.J. sat waiting.

"The State and Park Police are still combing the area, but we've got permission to hike in."

"Damn."

Jake laughed. "Come on. We'll be back before you know it."

And, in fact, they did make excellent time back up the soggy road, passing a number of troopers as they walked through the slushy drizzle.

"There it is." A.J. pointed to the last boarded-up structure in the straggling row that seemed to materialize out of the mist. "It's the one with the big yard behind the stone wall."

They went through the opening in the wall. This time A.J. spotted an iron gate lying rusting in the tall weeds.

"What made you pick this place?" Jake asked.

"It was the first one we saw in reasonably good condition. The skies just opened up and we went for the first shelter that looked like it wouldn't fall in on us."

"No one suggested this building specifically?"

"It was really Simon's call. But I don't think Simon is in the pay of the Jersey Devil."

Jake, having met Simon many times, snorted.

The porch boards squeaked noisily beneath his boots. A.J. followed more slowly. The hair on the back of her neck lifted at the memory of that creepy feeling of looking into darkness and seeing something looking back up at her.

"Which room?" Jake called.

"Down the hall and to the right. There's a big hole in the floor, so be careful."

Jake's mutter was lost as he moved down the hallway.

A.J.'s nostrils twitched at the scent of moldering decay. She stared around the room, remembering back to the morning, trying to think if there had been any warning of what was coming. She could think of nothing. Everyone had seemed perfectly normal.

Directing her flashlight through the black box of the doorway, she followed Jake down the hall. She found him kneeling beside the gaping hole in the floor, slowly sweeping his own flashlight from side to side.

A.J. joined him, adding her beam to the darkness. The light illuminated broken chunks of concrete, wooden crates, smashed furniture, and what looked like a small pine tree growing in the wet, black earth.

"See anything?" Jake asked.

"Happily, no."

"I mean, do you see anything you might have mistaken earlier for . . ."

He didn't complete the thought. A.J. pointed her flashlight beam to the right. "It was standing over there in the shadows. I mean, supposing I saw anything at all. Simon called to me, and I turned away. When I looked back, it was gone."

"Gone? Or maybe just the way you were holding the light had changed?"

"I honestly don't know. I don't believe the Jersey Devil was hiding under the house, so I'm perfectly okay with us agreeing that it was just the way the light fell."

Jake grunted and rose. "I might as well take a look."

"What?" Even A.J. winced at that note. She tried to moderate her alarm. "No. Way. No *way* are you going down there!"

"It's just a cellar. Hell, I could jump down."

"Have you missed the fact that half of this building fell in on that cellar?"

"Relax. If there's any danger I'll stop."

He was already walking back to the hallway. A.J. followed. "Why? Why do you have to go down there? There's nothing down there."

"Then there's nothing to worry about, right?"

"I mean nothing you need to check out. The roof could fall in on you. There could be snakes or black widow spiders or-or poison gas."

"Poison gas?" The grin Jake threw her was very white in her flashlight beam.

A.J. could only follow as he went outside and walked around the building to a pair of loosely hinged storm cellar doors.

"Not locked," Jake observed.

"Is that the good news or the bad news?"

Jake didn't answer. The doors opened with a hideous screech. The cellar seemed to exhale a gust of dank, musty air.

"What died in there?" A.J. looked at Jake. He shook his head.

They shone their flashlights into the gloom and spot-lighted a flight of rickety-looking wooden stairs.

Jake commented, "No dust."

"You're kidding, right? What do you call this stuff we're breathing? Besides *unhealthy*."

"On the steps."

A.J. followed Jake's indication and saw immediately what he meant. Though the steps were dirty, there was no untouched layer of dust. There was no real dust at all. The steps looked as though they were used on a fairly regular basis.

"Maybe the wind blowing through the cracks in the door keeps them clean?"

Jake made a spluttering sound. "You're not going to be winning the *Good Housekeeping* Seal of Approval this year, I can tell you that right now."

"You know what I—" A.J. broke off as Jake started cautiously down the steps. "Break a leg," she muttered. "You probably will if you insist on going down there."

Jake didn't reply.

In a few seconds he was at the bottom and then he moved from her view, though she could still hear him, hear the sounds of him shifting broken junk out of his path.

Then those sounds faded, too.

A.J. looked around uneasily. The woods were crawling with law enforcement, and yet it suddenly seemed very quiet and very isolated. The sky looked white and the trees stood out like ink silhouettes.

It began to rain again. The rain dripped from the eaves overhead and into the cellar.

"Unfortunately the ground is too uneven to make out

footprints or hoofprints or any prints." Jake reappeared. He
was holding something, a reddish scrap of material. Material or fur? The hair on the back of A.J.'s neck stood up.

"What did you find?" she asked as Jake reached the top
of the stairs.

He held the scrap out. It looked like a patch of hair on
very thin rubber.

A.J. wrinkled her nose. "What's *that*?"

"At a guess?" Jake's eyes were very green in the fading light. "I'd say it's a piece of someone's Jersey Devil
costume."

Seventeen

By the time A.J. and Jake got back to Burlington General Hospital they learned that Oriel had been released.

"How did she get home?" A.J. asked at the desk. "Her car is still at the park."

The nurse couldn't answer that question and was too busy with the usual weekend wounded to worry about it. She smiled apologetically and went to answer the summons of a harassed-looking doctor.

"She could have called a cab," Jake pointed out. "She could have called a friend."

"I guess that's true. I just feel responsible." A.J. smothered a yawn. She was so tired all she wanted to do was find someplace warm, curl up, and sleep for a thousand years.

"If you want to stop by and check on her, we can do that," Jake said as they walked back to the hospital parking lot.

A.J. stopped walking and eyed him suspiciously. "Oh really?"

He nodded.

"Since when?"

"Since when what?"

"Since when are you so agreeable to the idea of my sleuthing that you'll actually let me tag along?"

Jake shrugged.

"Ha! I know what you're up to. You want to question Oriel and you want to use me for camouflage."

"I wouldn't put it quite like that. Your presence might help put Oriel at ease. Plus, you're trying to help Lily, right? We might find out something we both want to know."

Lily. It seemed like a million years ago since she had agreed to help Lily. In fact, Friday seemed like a million years ago. This had been the longest weekend of her life—and apparently it wasn't over yet.

"I guess so," A.J. said. "I'll have to follow you in my car. It's easier than trying to figure out how to pick it up tomorrow."

"Sure. We can leave your car at Sacred Balance and I'll drop you off tomorrow on my way to work."

A.J. agreed and pulled her keys from her pocket.

The drive back to Stillbrook took a little more than an hour and a half, and by the time they pulled up in front of Oriel Goode's home, it was dark.

The Goodes had rented one of the oldest and loveliest historical homes on the outskirts of Stillbrook. It was a charming blue gray Victorian with a pink shingled mansard roof and gobs of gingerbread trim. Fake gaslight lamps dotted the pretty front garden.

Lights shone cheerily from behind draperies and wood

smoke flavored the damp night air as A.J. and Jake walked up the rose tree-lined walk.

A.J.'s phone chirped before they reached the front door. She checked the number.

"Oh my gosh. It's Andy. I never called him back about Thanksgiving." She accepted the call. "Hey!"

"I'm starting to take this personally," Andy replied.

"I know. And as much as I hate to say it, I can't talk right now either."

"You're going to have to do better than that. And why are you whispering? Are you in hiding?"

"If I was, asking me all these questions would not be helpful."

"True. One question only. *Are* you coming to Thanksgiving dinner?"

The front porch light went on, bathing Jake and herself in waxy light.

"Yes," A.J. answered, her eye on the door, which parted a cautious crack.

"Is Jake coming with you?"

"Yes. And that's two questions."

"Three o'clock on Thursday. Good-bye, A.J."

"Good-bye, Andy." A.J. pocketed her phone as Oriel opened the door the rest of the way.

She wore a pink dressing gown. One arm rested in a sling. She gazed at them doubtfully.

Jake glanced at A.J. Her cue, it seemed. She summoned a smile that she hoped conveyed the right mix of friendliness and concern. "Hi, Oriel. Are you all right? We were worried when we heard you'd left the hospital."

"I can't stand hospitals." Oriel looked sallow in the porch light. Her face was drawn, her eyes ringed in dark circles.

"I hope you don't mind our stopping by," A.J. said. "Do you have anyone staying with you?"

"No." Oriel hesitated, her gaze moving from A.J. to Jake.

"We'll only stay a moment," A.J. assured her.

Oriel stepped back, wordlessly, reluctantly inviting them in. "I'm all right on my own. I was lucky. A few inches farther in, and I could have lost my arm."

A.J. shuddered inwardly at the thought as they followed Oriel down an entry hall painted a sunny yellow. Framed prints of Van Gogh sunflowers lined the wall.

Oriel led them to an elegant room where a TV was turned to a reality show and a nest of blankets and pillows covered a long plaid sofa. There was a mostly untouched TV dinner on the coffee table.

Oriel lowered herself to the sofa and pulled the blankets over her lap. "Are you here to question me about the shooting? I didn't see anything."

"Wrong police force," Jake said. "I'm not here in an official capacity. A.J. thought we should stop by to make sure you were okay."

"Oh. I didn't realize you two were . . ."

A.J. sat in one of the chintz-covered chairs. Jake followed suit. "I guess I take it for granted everyone knows. But you're still relatively new to Stillbrook. Isn't there any kind of household staff or anyone here to look after you?"

She wasn't merely making conversation. Oriel did look haggard and wretched.

"I don't need anyone. To be honest, I prefer to be alone." She rubbed her forehead tiredly. "I don't know if this makes sense, but having people around me reminds me more that David is gone than being on my own."

"I'm sorry."

Oriel acknowledged A.J.'s words with a tight nod. "It wasn't a perfect marriage, but I don't suppose there is any such thing."

What was there to say to that? Some marriages were obviously worse than others, and in her opinion Oriel's had been in that category. A.J. knew what Jake *wanted* her to say, but as she had found on other occasions, sleuthing wasn't a particularly compassionate pastime.

It was left to Jake to speak up. "A.J. has been telling me about some of the more eventful moments of your retreat. Did you happen to see anything last night?"

"Last night feels like another lifetime." When neither Jake nor A.J. responded, Oriel sighed. "You mean that kid yelling about the Jersey Devil peeking into her tent?"

"Sure. That—or anything that struck you as suspicious."

"No. Of course not. There was nothing to see."

"You sound very sure of that. You must be aware of the report of an attempted break-in filed by your husband shortly before his death."

Oriel's expression gave nothing away. "I know what you're going to say. That it sounds too fantastic to be true. Isn't that right?"

Jake's tone was neutral. "I'm not challenging the fact that your husband saw *something*. I'm just wondering—naturally—whether he saw what he thought he saw."

"The Jersey Devil."

"Right."

"I understand why David's story seems strange to you, but if you believe in angels and miracles—and my husband did—then it makes sense to also believe in demons."

"Did you see this demon trying to get in through the side window?" Jake's expression gave nothing away. But then, neither did Oriel's.

"No."

"Did anyone in the house see it besides your husband?"

"No." Oriel's eyes narrowed. "There was no one else in the house. David wasn't a fanciful man. In fact, in many ways he was one of the most practical people I ever met. He was troubled by what he saw that night—and by the other reports of this devil or demon or whatever it was. He saw it as a sign, and he was trying to make people understand what it meant."

Jake nodded noncommittally. "Can you think of any reason someone might wish to harm you?"

"Me?" Oriel seemed genuinely taken aback. "No. What happened today couldn't have been directed at me personally."

"Why?"

"Why? Well, it just couldn't have been. There would be no reason for anyone to wish me harm."

"What about the person who killed your husband? Couldn't he or she wish you harm?"

Oriel stared as though she didn't understand the question. "Why should she?" she asked at last. "I'm not standing in her way. Whatever she misguidedly blamed David for would not apply to me."

"Did you know your husband had been married before?"

A.J. hadn't been expecting Jake to go for the jugular. Not while Oriel was still on the sick list. Oriel's eyelashes fluttered in confusion at the sudden change in tack. "Yes."

"Do you know what happened to his wife?"

"Yes. She died." Oriel's throat moved. "It was a terrible tragedy. David used to say she had been the love of his life."

A.J. couldn't help it. "He said *that* to you?" They could add tactlessness to all the rest of David Goode's sins.

Oriel nodded, her gaze pinned on Jake's face as though she knew the worst was yet to come.

"Do you know *how* your husband's first wife died? At least, we think she was his first wife. Maybe not," Jake persisted.

"W-what do you mean?"

"Do you know how Jill Smithy-Powell died?"

"Who?"

A.J. felt very sorry for Oriel. She understood that these were questions that needed to be asked, but she couldn't help feeling that Jake might have waited until Oriel was stronger—and that he could have broken the news more gently. She didn't like knowing that she was a party to this, although Jake hadn't had to twist her arm to get her to come along.

"Your husband's previous wife. The Los Angeles heiress Jill Smithy-Powell. Your husband was a suspect in her homicide."

Oriel went so white A.J. was afraid she was going to faint. Jake must have thought the same thing, because he started to rise. Oriel waved him off sharply. Her face twisted, but she got it under control.

"I don't know what you're talking about. My husband's first wife drowned. She died in a boating accident."

That hard smile on Jake's face reminded A.J. of when they'd first met, when she had been a suspect in his murder investigation. Being on the receiving end of that smile was not a pleasant thing. Oriel was still blinking and biting her lip, trying to make sense of what he was telling her, trying to avoid accepting the certainty in his face.

"Drowned, huh? Well, she was found in the bathtub. But she'd been strangled. Your husband's first wife was heiress to the Smithy Yacht fortune."

"That's . . . not . . . possible."

"I'm afraid it is. Your husband's fingerprints match those of Maxwell Powell, Jill's husband. Powell disappeared around the time of his wife's death."

"You're trying to make me believe that David and this Powell man are—were—the same man?"

"They were definitely the same man. The problem is we don't know who that man was. According to his Social Security number, the real Maxwell Powell died when he was a baby. And as far as anyone can make out, David Goode didn't have a Social Security number at all. The only Social Security numbers that show up in connection with New Dawn Church are yours and Kirkland Bath's."

Oriel said mechanically, "Kirkland Bath was my uncle."

A.J. rose and went to sit beside Oriel on the sofa. She didn't know what comfort she could offer, but it seemed apparent to her that whatever David Goode had been involved in, the news of it was coming as a shock to his wife.

"Right. Your uncle founded New Dawn Church, and David Goode came along and took over the leadership after your uncle died."

"David was my uncle's choice. He trusted David implicitly."

"A lot of people did. And a couple of them are dead now."

"How dare you?" Two spots of color appeared in Oriel's white face. "You have no right. David chose not to reveal his Social Security number because he believed the government would try to target the church through him. Government agencies track people like us."

"The government tracks everyone," Jake said. "That's part of its job. I only know of two ways you can legally change your Social Security number and that's if you're a survivor of domestic violence or if you've been the victim of identity theft. Far from being the victim of identity theft, your husband appears to have been a perpetrator of it."

Oriel pushed upright. Swaying slightly, she said, "I want you to leave. I want you to get out of my house *now*."

"Oriel." A.J. touched her arm.

Oriel shook her off. "No. I'm not going to listen to another word of this. It's ridiculous. It's *insane*. Now go."

Jake nodded. "Okay. Have it your way. I wish we could leave it there. I know you've been through a lot, and it looks to me like you're probably another of Goode's victims."

Oriel was shaking her head in steady denial.

Jake said, "We'll discuss it again when you're feeling better."

"Get out!" shouted Oriel.

They got.

"That was brutal," A.J. said as Jake started the engine of his sports car.

"Yeah. I know. Did you want to grab some takeout or did you have something else in mind for dinner?"

She stared at him in disbelief. His ruggedly handsome profile was limned by the lights of the dashboard. "I can't say I'm exactly starving after what we did to that poor

woman. Couldn't you have waited until she recovered
from the shock of being shot?"

Jake, who had been in the process of pulling away
from the side of the road, braked and turned to face her.

"I could have, yes. But the best chance of getting an
honest answer was to hit her when she was off guard and
vulnerable. I agree it wasn't kind, but it *was* a useful interview."

A.J. had to agree with that. "She didn't know about
Goode's other identity."

"Not unless she's one hell of an actress, and I don't
believe she is. I don't know many actresses who can actually turn white on cue."

"So Goode didn't have a Social Security number?"

"I'm sure he did, but not that we can find. Probably
because it's not under the name of David Goode. Who
knows how many times that guy reinvented himself over
the years. This could be the tip of the iceberg."

A.J. considered the implications. "You mean he could
have been a-a Blue Beard, marrying women, murdering
them, and moving on?"

"I don't know. It's possible," Jake admitted. "We haven't
been able to track him back past the point of Maxwell Pow-
ell. The only thing we know for sure is everything in his
Maxwell Powell biography was bogus. He never went to
USC, not under any name. He never served in the military.
Again, not under any name."

"Was that supposed to be part of his bio?"

"Didn't you read that far? Maxwell Powell had quite
the glamorous background. Graduate of USC, ex-Navy
SEAL, former architectural designer for Steven Holl
Architects."

"And none of it was true?"

"Not a damn word. His entire history was a fabrication of lies."

"So the question is, who was he before he was Maxwell Powell?"

"That's *one* of the questions," Jake said grimly, and put the car into gear.

Eighteen

It seemed to A.J. that she had been sleeping all of ten minutes when the alarm went off the next morning. She moaned and pulled the pillow over her head.

"Try this." Jake's muffled voice infiltrated the linen and down.

A.J. lifted the pillow away and gazed blearily up. The smell of coffee and aftershave reached her. Jake came into focus. He was holding out a mug. She sat up and took it, sipping gratefully.

"Are you sure it's morning? It looks awfully dark out." It had been so wonderful to be in a warm, comfortable bed again. Nothing like camping to make you appreciate civilization—even with all the pollution, overcrowding, and various death rays.

Jake grinned, sitting on the edge of the bed. He was already showered, shaved, and dressed. "I'm sure. It's raining again."

"I am *so* ready for spring."

"We haven't had winter yet."

"Still." She took another sip.

"You need a vacation." Jake's expression was serious.

"I know. It's hard to take time off."

"That's what Andy used to say, right? Before he got MS."

A.J. raised her head. "Wow. That's a little heavy for first thing in the morning."

Jake conceded her point with a lift of one broad shoulder. "I was just thinking it's funny how we don't make time for what actually matters the most until something happens. Something that forces us to make a priority of the things we should have made a priority all along."

It was a very long speech for Jake.

"You were just thinking that?"

Jake reddened, but said stubbornly, "Yeah. I was."

A.J. swallowed another mouthful of coffee. "Well . . . I agree with you. But it's still really hard for me to get away right now."

Jake nodded. After a second or two he rose and A.J. had the uncomfortable feeling that she'd missed a cue somewhere.

She put the coffee mug on the bedside table and threw aside the bedclothes. "Give me ten minutes and I'll be ready to go."

"Hey. Be wild. Take fifteen."

Again, A.J. had the impression that she was missing something.

A shower washed away most of the fuzzy-headedness. She lathered up with the Sacred Suds green tea and olive oil soap she pretended she'd bought for Jake, though he stuck to his Irish Spring with a devotion that would have warmed Mr. Meagher's heart. She rinsed in luke-warm water that was invigoratingly close to chilly without raising actual goose bumps, toweled off, and dressed in the jeans and raw silk sweater she left at Jake's for mornings like this.

He was on the phone as she gathered her freshly washed clothes from the weekend out of the dryer. She cleared away the take-out debris from the evening before and loaded the dishwasher.

She had just switched it on as Jake got off the phone. "We may have a possible lead on Goode aka Powell."

"What's the lead?" she asked over the rumble of the washer.

"According to a couple of people who knew him in Los Angeles, he had a way of pronouncing words that they thought might have been Canadian."

"*Canadian?* He didn't sound Canadian to me."

"Remember, this was over a decade ago, and they didn't say he had an accent, they said his inflection on a couple of words sounded like it could *possibly* be Canadian."

"Hmm. Well, it might partially explain the lack of a Social Security number."

"It's worth following up anyway."

"I'll say!"

He smiled faintly. "It's tempting to forget every other line of investigation, but the thing about murder is it's usually not like the clever, complicated stuff you see on TV. It's usually simple and stupid and obvious."

"Sure, but it's not like someone ran in off the street and clunked Goode over the head in order to steal his shoes."

"No." He looked at the paper bag with her freshly laundered clothes. "All ready?"

A.J. went to fetch her coat. "Will I see you tonight?"

Jake hesitated. "I'll give you a call?"

A.J. nodded.

Denise Farber was first in to Sacred Balance that morning. "I'm *so* sorry for flaking out on you this weekend. I swear I really was sick. I felt so terrible when I heard what happened on the news." Her still-pink eyes and raspy throat gave testament to her plea.

"It's okay," A.J. told her. "It's not like your being there would have changed the outcome. You'd simply have been miserable the whole time."

"No kidding. I was miserable at home the whole time. Have the police caught that maniac yet?"

"Not as far as I know."

"They will. Nowadays no one can hide for long."

"I guess that's true."

"Sure it is. Haven't you seen those programs where people call in and identify their neighbor as a former bank robber or their dishwasher repairman as an international hit man?"

"I need to watch more TV."

"That's all I've been doing for two days." Denise smothered a cough that would have alarmed Camille.

A.J. was still considering the truth of Denise's remarks after Denise went into her own office. The interconnectedness of all things seemed to boil down to technology. There weren't many places left to hide in the age of the information superhighway. Yet Maxwell Powell had managed it.

And, surprisingly, so had this woman Goode had been seeing before his death. Why couldn't the police locate her?

Did she even exist? Maybe there was no Madam X at all.

Or maybe there were too many Madam Xs to keep track of. Sarah Ray, for example. Where did she fit in? Her shocked reaction to Goode's death seemed too extreme to be merely that of a former member of his congregation.

But if the police hadn't yet connected her, maybe there was no connection to make. Maybe, despite Jake's words of caution, the only solution to Goode's murder lay in the distant past.

A.J. was still frowning over that possibility when Suze knocked on her door a little while later.

"Did Emma tell you Jaci's in Burlington this morning giving her statement to the police there? She took Mocha with her."

"She did. Yes. How are you recovering?"

Suze shrugged. "I feel fine. I admit I was kind of freaked last night. I still can't get over the idea that someone was deliberately shooting at us. How about you?"

"I need a weekend to recover from the weekend."

Suze giggled. "Too bad you're the boss. You could claim PTS. Not that you'd ever take any time off."

That gave A.J. pause. "I take time off. I take weekends."

"That's true," Suze agreed too easily.

A.J. frowned. "Do I really seem that driven to you?"

Suze laughed. "Seriously?"

"Yes. Seriously."

"You're a total workaholic. We're all taking bets on whether you'll take a honeymoon in the same year you get married."

"Honeymoon?" A.J. forgot the rest of it in the wake of that single, astonishing word.

Suze instantly went as red as though she was trying out

for a Christmas ornament. "Theoretically, I mean," she said hastily. "In case you and Jake ever do . . ."

Startled, A.J. considered the possibility that Jake might be getting ready to pop the question. First her mother and now her staff seemed convinced this was the case. Certainly it was the natural progression of their growing closeness.

It was sort of ironic, because when she'd first come to Stillbrook a few people had warned her not to get serious about Jake. That he wasn't the settling-down kind. But they spent most evenings and weekends together. She knew Jake cared about her and she cared for Jake. So what was the problem?

Was there a problem?

Not a problem, perhaps, but it didn't seem so very long since her first marriage had fallen apart. She certainly hadn't expected to be contemplating remarrying again so quickly.

Then again, she hadn't expected her marriage to fall apart or to leave her successful career in marketing to inherit a yoga empire.

Things changed.

It could happen. But did she want it to?

She changed the subject. "I wanted to ask you about Saturday night. The night Mocha thought someone opened your tent and looked inside."

Suze's expression was apologetic. "I sleep like a bear in hibernation. The Jersey Devil could have climbed inside that tent and played Twister over me and I wouldn't have noticed. The only thing I can say is I'm sure Mocha wasn't faking."

A.J. thought back. Suze was right. Mocha's terror had

been genuine. That didn't mean the cause of Mocha's fear had been genuine, only that Mocha's belief in it was.

"What about when that demented hunter or whatever he was opened fire on us? Did you get the impression that he was targeting any one person?"

"Are you kidding me? You think I stopped running long enough to take notes?"

"No. I just meant if you happened to notice . . . something."

Suze frowned. "Well, I think he was following us for a while. That's what I told the trooper who took my statement."

"Is that true? Why do you think he was following us?"

"Because someone was following us. At least . . . I don't know that he was *following* us, but there was someone way back behind us for a while before anything happened and then he didn't show up after the shooting, and he would have, right?"

"If it was some innocent hiker, you'd expect so. Or maybe he just took cover and hid till it was safe to come out? I don't know what I'd do in that situation. I think guns have to be one of the scariest things around. Were you able to get a good look at him?"

"No. Every so often I'd spot someone way back in the trees behind us. I even thought it might be a kid. He wasn't real big. Maybe my height, slender, and he had one of those olive hunting caps pulled over his face."

"Why didn't you say something?"

"What would I have said? *Oh look, another hiker?*" Suze's pale brows made one line. "We'd seen hikers on our way in and nobody thought anything about it. It isn't the kind of thing you think about except in hindsight.

Anyway, I think I did mention it to Jaci. It seemed odd that a hiker would be wearing camo."

"Was this guy carrying a rifle?"

"I don't know." Suze looked contrite again. "I wasn't watching him. I just noticed someone behind us. It wasn't until later that I realized he'd probably been following us the whole time."

It sure sounded that way, although it was possible this hiker or hunter or whatever he had been *had* simply been someone traveling behind their party.

"Oh well. I guess the State and Park Police will start looking for him, whoever he is."

"One good thing to come out of all this," Suze said cheerfully. "Mocha really seemed to blossom on our retreat, didn't you think?"

A.J. smiled faintly. "She did, yeah. Especially considering everything she went through."

"She's a kid. Once she gets over the drama, she's going to love having those stories to tell the other kids."

"I guess."

"Mark my words. She actually called first thing this morning to tell us that she's lost ten pounds since she started at Sacred Balance."

"Nine of them yesterday."

Suze laughed. A.J.'s cell phone rang and Suze excused herself.

A.J. fished around for her phone. Her mother's photo flashed up. She braced herself and clicked to accept the call.

"What on *earth* have you been doing?" Elysia greeted her. "You're all over the news this morning."

"*I'm* all over the news?"

"You and Sacred Balance studio. I *do* wish they'd use a more flattering photo of you, pumpkin. This one looks like a mug shot taken after a pub fight."

"Swell."

"They're saying some bloody madman opened fire on your students while you were on some kind of religious retreat."

"It wasn't a religious retreat. It was just a . . . retreat." Some parts more retreat than others. "Just a chance to get away for a couple of days and get in touch with—"

"The local crackpots?"

"You know, up until that lunatic opened fire on us it was a perfectly successful trip."

"You'll be lucky if someone doesn't sue you. According to that delicious young reporter, you had *children* with you." One would have thought they were an illegal substance from Elysia's tone.

"One child. A teenager."

"Was the child the one who was shot?"

"Oh God." A.J. closed her eyes. "Is that what they're saying? One student, Oriel Goode, was very slightly wounded. She's fine."

"Oriel Goode. *The* Oriel Goode? Now isn't *that* interesting?"

"I don't know if it's interesting or not, but Oriel was the one hit by gunfire."

"Speaking of interesting," Elysia said with one of those dizzying about-faces that always made A.J.'s head swim, "I thought you might be interested in what the girls and I discovered in our investigation this weekend."

"I'm almost afraid to ask. Who were you investigating again?"

"Lance Dally. Goode's right-hand man. Except since he was really an undercover reporter, I suppose that makes him Goode's right underhanded man."

A.J. snorted. "What did you find out?"

"Unfortunately our theories about Dally were all wrong. It's back to the drawing board."

After the weekend she'd had, A.J. could barely remember they'd had a theory regarding Dally, let alone what it was. She said as much.

"We thought he might have worked for a Los Angeles paper and known Jill Smithy-Powell."

"Right. I remember."

Elysia said patiently, "We thought he might wish revenge for her death."

"We did?" They must have had some reason, but it sounded a little convoluted now.

"However, as it turns out, Dally works for a paper in New York. The *New York Citizen*. He's worked there for seven years. He started straight out of college. Columbia University Graduate School of Journalism. He's held to be ambitious, relentless, hardworking, honest, la-di-dah and everyone on the paper loves him dearly, which is always suspicious, but as hard as we tried, we were unable to find any connection between him and Jill Smithy-Powell. Frankly, I don't think he's ever even been to California."

"Well, it was always kind of a stretch."

"I agree. I think it's far more likely that Goode was knocked off by one of his paramours. I think Sarah Ray looks good for it."

"Mother, I think you have it in for Sarah. You seem obsessed with her."

"*Obsessed?* Obsessed with *Sarah?*" Elysia's laugh of scorn would have given Lady Macbeth pause.

"It was very obvious the night she came to dinner that she had no idea Goode was dead."

"Nonsense. The girl is an actress. Of sorts. Any first year RADA student can spill a glass of wine and go wobbly chinned."

"I don't think she's—"

"Regardless, the reason I rang you up is we have tickets to her show this afternoon."

"Her . . . show?"

"Yes. That paltry made-for-cable thing where she gets up and smirks and preens her way through cooking a dish so elementary a five-year-old child could prepare it."

"Since you already know how to cook and I've given up on it, why are we going to watch your archenemy film her show?"

"That little miss is *hardly* my archenemy."

"That's right. I forgot how many people you actually hate."

Elysia's sniff bounced audibly from cell site to cell site. "We're going to observe Ms. Ray in her natural habitat."

"The scullery?"

Elysia laughed at that, but she said severely, "And then we're going to interview her."

"From the audience?"

A.J. would put very little past her mother once she was in full *221-B Baker Street* mode, so it was a relief to hear her make an exasperated noise. "Of course not from the audience. We'll speak to her after her show, when she's off guard."

A.J. sincerely doubted Sarah would ever be off guard with Elysia, but she kept the thought to herself. "What time does she tape her show?"

"One o'clock. We can have lunch and then dawdle over to the station."

"I can't do lunch. I've been gone all weekend. But I'll meet you outside the studio at a quarter to one."

"Roger. See you there, pumpkin." Elysia signed out.

A.J. rolled her eyes and got to work, but it seemed only a few minutes later that Emma buzzed her. "Lily Martin's here."

"Huh?"

"Lily Martin's here," Emma repeated without inflection.

"Okay. Send her back."

A few seconds later Lily rapped on the half-open door.

"Hi," A.J. greeted her. "This is a surprise. Have a seat."

"Hello. I thought I might as well stop by since I have nothing else to do." Lily gazed curiously around the office. "It hasn't changed at all."

"You've only been with Yoga Meridian a couple of months."

"True." Lily's mouth thinned. "If I *am* still with them."

"You haven't heard anything?"

"No one at Tussle and Rossiter will return my calls."

Waiting to see if Lily was exonerated, no doubt. But that was still better than firing her without even waiting for the outcome of a trial.

"I'm sure it'll work out." A.J. hoped that was true.

Lily stared at the fountain, the bookshelf, the desk with Diantha's photo. "It's so strange to be back here. You have no idea."

"No, but I can imagine."

"I never dreamed of, or wanted to, teach yoga anywhere but here at Sacred Balance." Lily seemed hypnotized by the fountain in the corner, the water murmuring gently over the bright, smooth stones. She made an effort to shake off her preoccupation, her black gaze turning to A.J. "Are you making any progress finding out who killed David Goode?"

"If you mean have I learned enough to clear all suspicion from you, no."

Lily's face tightened. "Have you discovered enough to create reasonable doubt?"

"*I* think I have, but I'm not the DA."

"What have you found out?"

Despite the fact that A.J. was only sleuthing in an effort to help Lily, she instinctively felt sharing everything she'd learned would be a mistake. Lily was too likely to fly off the handle, and leaking too much information might jeopardize Jake's investigation.

She said neutrally, "Well, for one thing, it sounds like Goode had a number of extramarital affairs."

Lily made a dismissive sound. "Is that supposed to be news?"

"The police seem to think it's significant. And it might have come as news to his wife."

"*Her.*" Lily's eyes kindled. "She's having an affair. Did you know that?"

"Says who?"

"Says the PI my defense attorney hired."

A.J. picked up a pen, ready to jot down notes. "Do you have any proof of that?"

"If you mean photos, no."

"What about phone records?"

"They don't prove anything."

"Why not? Who is she supposed to be having an affair with?"

"Goode's assistant. Lance Dally."

A.J. protested, "That can't be right. She initially accused him of murdering her husband."

"That just proves it."

A.J. resisted the temptation to rub her temples. "How does that prove anything of the kind? If they were having an affair, she'd hardly turn him in to the police."

Lily gave her a scornful look. "She would if she was just using him."

A.J. tried and failed to picture Oriel in the role of femme fatale. "I've seen and talked to her. I think she's genuinely grieving for her husband."

"Maybe she is. Maybe she regrets having him murdered. Maybe she did it in retaliation for all those affairs and after he was dead she realized how much she cared. Or maybe she's good at pretending to be what people want."

That sounded more like the late Reverend Goode, in A.J.'s opinion. "Why wouldn't she just leave her husband if she wasn't happy? And why would Lance Dally commit murder for her when they could just run away together?"

"Money." Lily's reply was succinct. "Do you know how much money that so-called New Dawn Church has collected in the months that they've been in Stillbrook? *Thousands and thousands* of dollars. All those fund-raisers for the big new church they were supposedly planning to build—you don't honestly think they were really going to build a cathedral, do you?"

A.J. was silent. This was an angle she hadn't had time to even consider yet. It didn't contradict the little they knew about David Goode. He had faked his identity to marry a yacht heiress. Then he had faked his identity to marry another kind of heiress. Kirkland Bath's niece was the key to the Reverend Goode's fame and fortune.

He had inherited New Dawn Church and its fund-raising potential, which sounded considerable.

And if Oriel had realized that she was being duped? Was it possible she might have reacted to betrayal by resorting to violence?

Even if Goode—or whatever his real name was—had experienced some kind of religious reformation after the death of his first wife, even if he was utterly sincere in his beliefs and his commitment to New Dawn Church, his penchant for romantic affairs might have been the one sin his wife couldn't forgive.

Except, according to Lily, Oriel was having her own affair.

A.J. said slowly, "Do you have any proof of this affair? E-mail records or security footage or good old-fashioned eyewitnesses?"

"No."

"Then how did this PI of yours come to the conclusion they were in a relationship?"

Lily said impatiently, "He's an experienced professional, A.J. He has an instinct for this kind of thing. He saw them together and put two and two together."

"You mean he guessed?"

"He has a hunch."

"A hunch?" A.J. sighed. "Does he have anything we could take to the police? I don't think they'll accept a hunch. Do you have *any* proof?"

"Of the fund-raising? Absolutely. It's not a secret. Goode was boasting about how much money they'd collected at the last service he conducted. Of Oriel's plan to get Lance Dally to kill her husband?" Lily shook her head. "No." She added, "Not yet. That's your job."

Nineteen

❧

Sarah Ray beamed into the cameras. "So as we've seen, there's just nothing quicker or easier for your summertime menu. Folks think of putting all kinds of meat on the grill, but not a whole chicken. And that's just crazy because roasted chicken . . . ? Mmm. Mmm. *Good!*"

Laughter, blinked the teleprompter overhead. *Laughter.*

The Channel 3 in-studio audience obediently laughed.

Elysia, sitting next to A.J. in the mostly empty tiered seating, gave a sniff like Mary Poppins confronting muddy galoshes. A.J. resisted the temptation to elbow her.

"See you next week, folks!" Sarah waved to the camera.

Applause, the teleprompter now urged. *Applause.*

The audience clapped enthusiastically.

The director cued the end credits. Sarah bustled around her TV kitchen, smiling happily as she transferred the roasted chicken to a carving board and checked on the pearl onions boiling in a saucepan. She hummed to herself.

"I believe that girl's simple," Elysia muttered as the applause died away and the overhead lights came on. "Why ever is she grinning like that? She looks like a fool." Elysia received a few curious looks as she rose.

A.J. stood, too. As Elysia opened her mouth again, A.J. said sweetly, "If you don't want me to push you down these steps, hush."

Elysia raised her eyebrows and did not deign to answer. They waited for the small audience to disperse. A few people maneuvered their way through the cameras to the stage, where Sarah greeted them warmly and offered thick chunks of warm herb bread.

"You have to admit, it smells wonderful in here," A.J. said.

"She didn't actually cook anything. The chicken was done before we arrived."

"I know, but it still smells wonderful. I think I'm going to try that recipe."

Elysia heaved a much-tried sigh.

They continued to wait until most of the audience had trickled away. Sarah and the director had a short private discussion and then the director left as well, the heavy soundproofed door swinging shut behind him.

Sarah went back to cleaning up her make-believe kitchen. She glanced up in surprise as A.J., followed by Elysia, edged her way around the lights and equipment.

"Why, hello! I didn't see you back there. Did you enjoy the show?"

"I did," A.J. said. "Very much. That chicken sounds delicious."

Elysia observed, "Pickled pearl onions are rather an unusual accompaniment to grilled chicken, don't you think?"

"They are, but they work great with the chicken. Just that added bit of tart sweetness." Sarah lifted the tea towel from the basket of bread. "Oops. Sorry. All out."

"We actually stopped by to see how you're feeling," A.J. said.

Sarah looked puzzled for an instant and then her smile faltered. "Oh. I guess I should apologize for breaking up your party the other night. I don't know what came over me. I guess I've been working pretty hard."

"Not a bit of it," Elysia said warmly. "Of course it was a terrible shock—given what you and David Goode were to each other."

"W-what?" Sarah looked startled and then her eyes narrowed. "I'm not sure what you're insinuating."

"We must brush up on our insinuation technique," Elysia remarked to A.J. "I thought our point was rather obvious. But then, I thought Sarah's feelings for the good reverend were rather obvious."

Sarah changed color. "I understand what you're saying, but it's not true."

It was such a patent lie that A.J. was moved to say, "Sarah—"

"Oh, I know!" Sarah interrupted. "You two are supposed to be some kind of idiot savants when it comes to solving crimes."

"Uh, I wouldn't put it like *that*."

"You know what? You know what you really are? You're just a pair of busybody bitches butting into other people's personal lives." Sarah picked up the empty bread basket and hurled it across the make-believe kitchen. It bounced off a stage prop cupboard and flew into the darkness beyond the stage lights.

A.J. and Elysia exchanged looks.

"Fine!" Sarah said. She put her hands on her narrow hips and faced them squarely in her flowered apron. "Ask away. What did you want to know? I'm sure you won't leave me alone till you find out whatever it is you think you have some right to know. Did I kill David? No. And, yes, I *do* have an alibi."

"We don't think you—"

"What is this supposed alibi?" Elysia interrupted.

Sarah bit out, "I. Was. Filming. My. Show."

"Your show doesn't begin filming till the afternoon. Goode was killed around nine in the morning." Elysia met A.J.'s gaze. "According to the papers."

"This was our special Thanksgiving show. It's a big production. Literally. We started filming at seven in the morning and we went all day. And I have a studio audience full of witnesses. I was never out of sight for more than five minutes at a time, and you can't even get out of this parking lot in five minutes."

Elysia continued to look skeptical. A.J. said, "Were you and David Goode still involved at the time of his death?"

"No. I told you that."

"You pretended you'd *never* been involved and we know that was a lie," Elysia said.

Sarah glared at her. "We did have an affair. It didn't last long. Most of David's affairs didn't last long."

"Who ended it?" Elysia asked.

"We came to a mutual agreement." Meeting their gazes, Sarah made a face. "Fine. David ended it."

A.J. got in before Elysia, "Do you know why?"

"Yes. He's easily bored. He likes the chase more than the conquest. He *did*, I mean."

"How long ago did your relationship end?"

"About a month ago."

"Do you know who Goode was seeing after you?"

Sarah shook her head.

A.J., knowing firsthand how it felt to be dumped by someone you loved, said, "You didn't try to find out? You weren't curious at all?"

"Of course I . . ." Sarah stopped. She sighed. "Yes. I was curious. I was curious and angry and hurt. We used to meet at the Hunter's Inn in Blairstown, so I went there a couple of times to try and spot him with her, whoever she was."

"Very enterprising," Elysia approved. "Did you succeed in finding them?"

Sarah nodded. "But don't ask me who she is because I don't know. I know her husband owns one of the big local construction companies, and that's all I know."

A light went off in A.J.'s brain. "Could you describe her?"

"She looked like she'd be right at home in thigh-high boots and a leather bustier."

"That could be *anyone*," Elysia said blandly, and A.J. breathed in the wrong way.

When she stopped coughing, Sarah was saying, "About forty, but takes care of herself. Not tall. Very trim. Sort of . . . military trim, if you know what I mean. Her hair was very short and silver, but it looked pretty good on her. I mean, *I* would color it, but I'm not into the whole Bad Nanny thing."

"Oh my God. I think I know who she is," A.J. said. "That sounds like Michaela Ritchie."

"Ritchie!" Sarah exclaimed. "That's it. Ritchie Construction. She's married to Leo Ritchie."

"I think we should go see Bradley as soon as possible," Elysia said once they were back in her Land Rover and pulling out of the Channel 3 parking lot.

A.J., in the process of calling Jake, paused. "Why would we need to see Mr. Meagher?"

"Why?" Elysia's profile was haughty. "For one thing, I need to make some changes to my will. Since Dean and I are going to be married."

"What's the emergency with changing your will?"

"No emergency. No reason to postpone either."

A.J. considered this doubtfully. "What am I missing? We just get a great lead and you want to go change your will? *Now?*"

"Your inspector won't let us talk to this Ritchie woman anyway."

A.J. clicked off her phone. "Okay. I'll wait to call Jake if that's what the problem is."

Elysia's mouth pursed but she said nothing.

"Wait a minute," A.J. said slowly. "You want to go *tell* on Sarah."

"Nonsense!" Elysia's ivory cheeks grew pink.

A.J. couldn't hide her consternation. "No, it's not. You can't wait to go break Mr. Meagher's heart."

"Now that *is* ridiculous," Elysia said sharply. "I merely want Bradley to understand what he's getting himself into with this . . . this . . . slag."

"*Slag?* You don't think that's a little harsh? Sarah was obviously in love with Goode. She wasn't just sleeping around with everything that moved."

"He was married."

"She wasn't. Okay. I'll give you that one. Sarah didn't show very good judgment. But . . ."

Elysia said tartly, "But what?"

A.J. bit her lip. "*Easy Mason?* It's not exactly like you built your career on living like a nun."

"Those silly tabloid stories." Elysia's foot slightly eased up on the gas. "Don't believe everything you read."

"I don't, but according to Mr. Meagher, you were a wee bit of lass in the old days." A.J. mimicked Mr. Meagher's Irish lilt.

Elysia's mouth struggled to maintain its severe line.

A.J. watched her, her own mouth curving. "Look, I know you're not asking for my advice, but don't do this. You know how much Mr. Meagher thinks of you. You're going to hurt him if you tell him that Sarah only got involved with him because she was on the rebound. It might not even be true anymore. Maybe she does care for him now."

"No, she doesn't," Elysia said darkly. "She's still rebounding."

"What's that mean?"

"Little   Cholesterol-Laden-Butter-Wouldn't-Melt-in-Her-Mouth-Sarah just *happened* to run into Dean last night when he went for a pint at Terry Mac's Pool Room. Does she look to you like a girl who plays pool?"

A.J. was wondering why Dean seemed to be making a habit of taking off for Terry Mac's. Was he uncomfortable drinking in front of Elysia? Once, A.J. had felt the same, unwilling to do anything that might tempt her mother. She had even agonized over whether to serve champagne at her wedding.

Or maybe there was another reason Dean was getting restless in the evenings.

"I don't know. Maybe. A lot of girls play pool."

"A lot of girls do not play pool at Terry Mac's. And no. She does not." Elysia answered her own question. "She's a sl—"

"Maybe she is, but it's for Mr. Meagher to figure that out on his own." Studying her mother's stubborn profile, A.J. said, "Why don't we go talk to Michaela Ritchie? We have this great lead. Don't you want to follow it up?"

Elysia said sulkily, "Shouldn't you call the inspector?"

"I'll call him afterward. Mocha, Michaela's stepdaughter, is a student of mine, so I have a legitimate reason for seeing her."

Elysia brightened. "Oh very well. We might as well interview her. The plod will only bungle it and put her on guard."

A.J. wisely let that ride.

"Lay on, Macduff, and damned be he who cries, 'Hold! Enough!'"

"Sir Francis Bacon?" A.J. pretended to guess.

Elysia smiled and patted her knee comfortingly.

As was only to be expected, the Ritchies lived in a newly constructed and ostentatiously oversized mansion built—according to the sign out front—by Leo Ritchie Construction.

Michaela was out in the leaf-strewn front yard when Elysia and A.J. pulled up in the driveway. She wore gray sweats and carried dangerous-looking loppers, which she was using to prune the long hedge of roses that lined the white picket fence facing the road.

She shaded her eyes from the shifting sunshine as she stared at the Land Rover in her driveway.

"She's not going to be easy to crack." A.J. lifted a hand in greeting. "Just so you know."

"We've faced tougher," Elysia said carelessly, reaching for the door handle.

They got out of the Land Rover and walked toward the side fence. Michaela strolled unhurriedly toward them.

"Ms. Alexander. Is there a problem?"

"Not at all," A.J. called back. "I was hoping you might be able to spare a few minutes to chat about Mocha."

Michaela's dark eyebrows rose. "Of course. You realize that she's with one of your instructors in Burlington today giving a statement to the police?"

"I do, yes. In fact, that's really why I wanted to speak to you."

Michaela opened the gate for them and A.J. and Elysia entered the yard.

"What lovely roses," Elysia remarked.

"Mrs. Ritchie, this is my mother, Elysia Alexander."

Michaela threw Elysia an indifferent look. But then astonishment came over her face. Her eyes widened. Her jaw dropped. "*Lucy Bannon*," she gasped. A nine-year-old in 1976 confronted by Farrah Fawcett, complete with red swimsuit, couldn't have looked more delightfully awed.

"Why, yes. Are you a fan of the show?" Elysia inquired graciously.

"Of course! I *love* the show. We TiVo it." Michaela led the way into the house, asking Elysia various questions about the other cast members and certain episodes.

Following a few steps behind, A.J. began to think Michaela was not nearly as tough a nut as she'd anticipated.

The house was immaculate and tastefully furnished. No dust bunnies lurked beneath Michaela Ritchie's seven-piece pedestal-style dining set, and even the thick pile of the chocolate brown carpet looked unsullied by mortal footsteps.

They settled in the spacious kitchen's breakfast nook. Michaela poured coffee and opened a bag of Pepperidge Farm Milano cookies. She might have gone on talking about *Golden Gumshoes* all afternoon—and Elysia might have let her—if A.J. hadn't finally broken in.

"How is Mocha dealing with what happened this weekend?"

"Mocha?" Michaela said vaguely. She contemplatively nibbled a cookie. "She views it as a way to skip a day of school, I imagine. That's usually her angle."

"She's not experiencing any symptoms of stress?"

"Hardly," Michaela said dryly. "Mocha doesn't experience stress. She's a carrier."

Lovely.

A.J. pressed onward. "Still. Most of us were shocked and scared being shot at. It's not a normal experience."

"No." Michaela shrugged. "No, it's not, but she's a kid. A weird kid at that. I think, if anything, she's enjoying a sense of celebrity." Her gaze went automatically back to Elysia, who was calmly consuming the last of the cookies.

"Did she tell you that she thought she saw the Jersey Devil?"

A.J. said it mostly to shake Michaela's self-satisfied poise. And she succeeded. Michaela's expression froze. Even Elysia did a double take.

"Yes. It's ridiculous." Michaela's voice was harsh.

"You know that and I know that, but Mocha was scared out of her wits."

"No, she wasn't. She said it for attention. That's why she does all the things she does."

"I was there."

Michaela said in that same harsh tone, "I know my stepdaughter."

"Well, after all," A.J. said mildly, "lots of people seem to think they've seen the Jersey Devil lately. You must have heard about the attack on the Baumann farm. And even your very dear friend the late David Goode claimed the monster tried to break into his home."

Elysia raised her coffee cup, hiding her expression.

Michaela stared at A.J. for long seconds. "What do you mean"—her voice steadied—"my 'very dear friend.'"

"You and David Goode were having a relationship, weren't you?"

In the sudden silence A.J. could hear the clock ticking over the refrigerator and, in the distance, the buzz of a power saw. Elysia's eyes met A.J.'s. She arched one eyebrow. A.J. looked back at Michaela, who was still wrestling with some kind of inner turmoil.

"Who told you that?" Michaela asked finally.

"Someone who used to see you together."

"It's not true. They're lying."

"You waited far too long to deny it, you know," Elysia told her cheerfully. "It obviously *is* true."

Michaela's lips parted. She licked them. "Why are you—this doesn't have anything to do with *anything*." Her eyes widened. "Are you telling me Mocha is the one who saw us?"

"No. Of course not." A.J. said it very firmly. Mocha and her stepmother had enough of a rocky relationship without adding that into the mix.

Michaela relaxed a fraction. "It doesn't matter. The affair was over before David died."

"Really?"

Michaela's brows drew together. "Why? What have you heard? What did this witness say?"

A.J. took a chance. "That you were still seeing each other. That it was still going strong on both sides."

"Then they don't know what they're talking about. I ended the relationship with David."

"Why?"

"Because I'm married!"

"You were married when you started the relationship."

Michaela licked her lips again. "I know, but that was different. You don't understand the . . . magnetism a man like David wields."

No, A.J. didn't understand it, but it was obvious from the little they knew of Goode's background that some women did find him all but irresistible.

"How did he take your breaking up with him?"

"He didn't believe it."

"When did you break the relationship off?"

"Two days before he died."

Remembering something Jake had said, A.J. asked, "How did you do it?"

"What do you mean?" Michaela looked aghast. "What are you implying? I didn't do anything!"

"I mean, did you break up with Goode in person?"

Michaela relaxed a fraction. She shook her head. "I did it by e-mail. I know that's not what Miss Manners recommends."

"I think she's down on the whole adultery thing," A.J. couldn't help observing.

Michaela didn't register it. "Frankly? I didn't trust myself to do it in person. David could be incredibly persuasive."

Not a bad thing in a missionary. Not so good in a philanderer.

"So someone else could have seen that e-mail?"

"We used a special Hotmail account."

No pun intended? A.J. kept the thought to herself. Just as she withheld the information that the police had already figured out Goode's Hotmail account and were checking into the alibis of his various lady friends.

"Did your husband know?" Elysia inquired.

Michaela started as though she'd forgotten Elysia was present.

"No."

"Are you sure?"

"Yes. For one thing Leo never stops working long enough to notice what anyone in this house is doing. And that includes his darling daughter. For another, if Leo *did* discover something like this, he'd never be able to keep his mouth shut. He's not what you would call *subtle*."

"Do you think, if he did discover the affair, your husband might have confronted Goode?" A.J. asked.

"No. I certainly don't. What are you suggesting? That *Leo* killed David? That's ridiculous. That yoga instructor killed him. It was all over the news."

"That doesn't make it true," A.J. said.

"It does in my book."

A.J. thought back to the beginning of the conversation. She remembered Michaela's odd expression when she'd heard about Mocha claiming to see the Jersey Devil.

"Why are you so sure that Mocha is lying about seeing something when we were camping? Goode claimed the same thing."

Michaela looked momentarily bewildered by the change of topic. "Because it's obviously not true."

"Goode thought it was. He went on TV claiming the Jersey Devil was a sign from above. Do you think he was saying it for attention?"

"Of course not. But . . . these sightings are pranks. Teenage pranks." Michaela lifted her chin. "And the reason that I think Mocha is lying is because I believe she's involved in these pranks."

Twenty

$\curlyvee$

"That was masterful, pumpkin!" Elysia threw the gears in reverse and backed out of the Ritchies' driveway with a fine disregard for the flow of traffic in the road behind them. "The way you segued from monsters to adultery was absolutely marvelous. I couldn't have done it better myself."

A.J. threw her mother an ironic look. "Thank you."

"Do you think it's true about your little protégée? That she's running about manufacturing these Jersey Devil sightings?"

"No. And she's not my protégée. She might be Jaci's protégée. And Suze's protégée. But that kid was definitely frightened out of her wits on Saturday night."

"Guilty conscience?"

"Maybe," A.J. said reluctantly. "But the thing I can't forget is that two of the Baumanns' cows were slaughtered. It's one thing to run around in a costume, pop out, and yell boo at people. It's another to kill animals. That's serial-killer-in-training-type stuff, from everything I've seen on TV, and I don't think Mocha fits that profile. She's a sweet kid underneath all the eye makeup and attitude. Not to mention the fact that she doesn't seem to have friends, so I don't see her being invited along on these juvenile delinquent outings that her stepmother suspects her of."

"*No* friends?"

"Not a one, that I can discover. She seems to be the classic case of the lonely fat kid. A lonely, rich, fat kid."

"That's a child who might be willing to do almost anything to fit in."

"Sure. Logically, what you're saying makes sense, but I was watching her, listening to her on the retreat. She might be willing to do anything to fit in, but part of her bitterness and anger at her peers is that no one is asking her to. She's being ostracized. And she reacts by making herself more unpleasant."

"It seems to me you're proving my argument."

"I know. I guess what it gets down to is I've been working with people, all kinds of people, for a long time. Both when I was freelancing and now that I'm teaching. Maybe it's naïve of me, but Mocha just doesn't strike me as malicious or mean-hearted. She was cooing over baby deer on the hike and pointing out every bird we came across. Kids like that are more likely to hurt other kids than an animal."

"That's a shrewd observation, pumpkin. Have it your way. Who *is* behind these sightings, then?"

A.J. sighed. "I'm not saying that it couldn't be local kids behind it. We've had problems with them before."

They were both silent for a moment.

A.J. said briskly, "But I don't think Mocha is involved. I think her stepmother has a warped view of her."

"I'm rather good with adolescents," Elysia said thought-fully, speeding around a slow-moving van. "Perhaps I should try to work with the girl."

A.J. squelched her instinctive alarm. As a matter of fact, Elysia *was* rather good with adolescents even if her approach was sort of unorthodox. "I'm not sure how we'd arrange that, but sure. She needs friends. People who care about her. Suze and Jaci have taken her under their wings, and I can see a change for the better already."

"We all need to be loved and appreciated," Elysia said. "Do you think there's a connection between Goode's mur-der and these Jersey Devil sightings?"

"I don't see how. And yet it seems too great a coinci-dence for them *not* to be connected."

"What could anyone hope to gain by running around the countryside impersonating a monster?"

A.J. shook her head. "The only thing that occurs to me is tourism. Obviously something like this gets attention." She felt around in her purse for her phone. "I guess I should call Jake and confess."

Elysia clicked her tongue dismissingly. "Are you com-ing by tonight?"

"The farm? Why?"

"The girls are leaving tomorrow."

"Is the slumber party over?"

Elysia seemed to consider this. She said at last, "It's been years since I've had close friends. It's rather nice."

"I know. I'm teasing you. I'm glad you're so happy. And, if you want the truth, I guess I'm a little jealous."

"Jealous?" Elysia threw a startled look A.J.'s way.

"Yes. Not of you being happy. I don't mean *that*. We've only in this last year really started getting to know each other again. Now you have a new career out in California.

You have a whole new social circle of friends there. And you're planning to remarry."

"Er, yes," Elysia said vaguely.

"So yes, I guess there's a tiny part of me that *is* jealous of all these other people and obligations claiming their share of you."

"You come first, pumpkin. You always will. That goes without saying. But you'll be getting remarried yourself before long."

"Why does everyone keep saying that?"

Elysia said dryly, "Maybe you should ask your inspector."

It turned out that A.J. couldn't ask her inspector anything because Jake didn't pick up his phone. Confessions were better made in person, so she hung up and reassured herself that discretion was the better part of valor.

Elysia urged her once more to come to dinner, but A.J. declined a final evening with the girls as she had to pick up Monster from Stella Borin, who had been watching him while she was away on the retreat.

"When is Dean leaving?" she asked very casually.

"You *do* keep asking that," Elysia said, equally casual. "Do you not care for him?"

"He seems perfectly nice. Not exactly what I was picturing when I imagined a future stepfather."

"Did you picture a future stepfather?"

"No. And I will say he's a big improvement over your last steady."

"Oh." Elysia's laugh was slightly self-conscious. "Poor Dicky."

"I don't even want to think about poor Dicky. Are you bringing Dean to Andy's on Thanksgiving?"

"I suppose so."

At the note of hesitation in Elysia's voice, A.J. said, "Or were you thinking you two needed some time alone? Andy will understand."

"No, no. Nothing like that," Elysia said briskly.

"What, then?"

Elysia made a small grimace. "Sometimes I wonder if I'm too old to remarry."

"Why would you say that?"

"You know, I've been on my own quite a while now. I rather like having things my own way."

A.J. chuckled. "Dean seems pretty easygoing."

"No man is *that* easygoing." Elysia added reflectively, "Dean was married before, you know."

"I gathered that from something he said at lunch the other day."

"I don't know how useful the experience was. He was quite young. Sixteen, as a matter of fact."

"Seriously? Sixteen. How does that even happen in this day and age?"

"In North Dakota it apparently happens with a notarized signature from your parents. Faked in Dean's case."

"Uh-oh. What happened? Well, there's a silly question. But what *did* happen?"

Instead of replying directly, Elysia said, "I think Sarah Ray might have been the girl."

"Sarah Ray? Our Sarah Ray? How did you deduce that?"

"It's obvious, to me at any rate, that they knew each other before."

"Did you ask Dean about Sarah?"

"Not directly. I keep hoping that he'll volunteer the information."

"Maybe there isn't anything to volunteer. Maybe he

just . . ." Liked Sarah? A lot? From the first there had been some kind of connection between Sarah and Dean.

A.J. blinked over the sudden, unbidden thought and decided it would be better to let it go. Elysia, too, seemed willing to drop the subject.

When they at last pulled into the Channel 3 parking lot so A.J. could retrieve her car, Elysia said, "Tomorrow we'll put our heads together and suss out how to get Mrs. Goode to confess."

A.J. dropped her keys. She found them on the floor of the Land Rover and sat up.

"When did you work out that Oriel Goode was the murderer?"

"As the Bard says, 'When you have eliminated the impossible, whatever remains, however improbable, must be the truth.'"

"I know for a fact it wasn't the Bard who said that. It was Sir Arthur Conan Doyle."

"Actually, it was Sherlock Holmes, pet, but that's beside the point. We've eliminated everyone else in the case. The only remaining possibility is Mrs. Goode. Our first and best suspect."

"You're going to have to show me your math on this one, because I don't get how you've decided we've eliminated all the other suspects."

"It's perfectly obvious. We have to rule Sarah out. Much as it grieves me. She has an alibi. Michaela Ritchie has no motive."

"According to her. And we don't know that her husband wasn't aware of the affair."

"A man would not use a pen as a murder weapon. Certainly not a man like Leo Ritchie."

"How do you figure that?"

"I've met Leo Ritchie. He built the add-on sunroom at Starlight Farm. He's a big macho bruiser. A bloke like that would punch Goode in the face or he'd use a real weapon. The pen was a weapon of impulse. Ritchie's impulse would be to smash Goode's face in."

"Interesting psychological profiling, but okay."

"It goes without saying you don't believe Mocha is involved, so that takes care of the Ritchies. I personally don't believe the Jersey Devil is a serious contender."

"I agree. There must be a connection there, but I don't know what it is."

"That leaves Mrs. Goode."

"Whoa. Goode had a number of affairs. All those women are possible suspects. Plus, aren't you forgetting your favorite theory? That the killer was someone out of Maxwell Powell's past?"

"There doesn't seem to be anyone. The only person who comes even close to knowing about Maxwell Powell was Oriel Goode. She knew him during what must have been his transition stage from Powell to Goode."

"Hmm." A.J. jingled her keys absently.

"Which leads us full circle. Who is the most likely suspect in any homicide? The significant other. In this case, the wife. Mrs. Goode had several motives that I can think of off the top of my head."

"Go on."

"Money. New Dawn Church has been fund-raising steadily since the day the Goodes arrived. Now all that money is Oriel's."

"True."

"Secondly, hell hath no fury like a woman scorned. Oriel was tired of the endless affairs."

"I would be, that's for sure."

"Any woman with a speck of pride would be. Which leads us to the final and most compelling reason to my thinking. Mrs. Goode knew her husband was eventually going to try and get rid of her—one way or the other—and she simply made a preemptive strike."

"The problem with that is, I don't think she did know about his past. And even if she lied about that, she has an alibi for the time of the murder. An unshakable alibi, by all accounts."

Elysia waved an indifferent hand. "Alibis were made to be broken. In any case, Lily's hired gun dug up the solution—and yet another motive. Oriel Goode had a lover. *He* killed her husband for her."

A.J. shook her head. "It makes sense up to a point, but I just don't buy the illicit lover angle. I think Oriel genuinely loved her husband. I think she did know about the affairs. You're right about that. She'd have to be oblivious not to know. But I *don't* think she was aware of Goode's past. You should have seen her when Jake gave her the news. She was stricken."

"Stricken that you'd discovered the truth."

"I don't think so."

Elysia made an exasperated sound. "Next you're going to tell me the woman couldn't have done it because she practices yoga."

"Weeelll . . . No. Of course not. But I can't see any justification for believing she was having an affair. Who would she have an affair *with*?"

"We've already been over this. With her husband's assistant."

"He also has an alibi."

"Alibi schmalibi."

"Huh?"

"That alibi is made of tissue paper."

"The police don't seem to think so. Dally's house isn't in walking distance of the center where Goode was killed—"

Elysia interrupted, "*And* as for Oriel being the only one who knew Goode's history, Dally is a journalist. It's possible he came across the truth while he was working for New Dawn Church."

"And killed Goode? What sense would that make? Why wouldn't he go to the police? It would be a huge scoop for him."

"Because he was having an affair with Oriel."

"So what? In fact, all the more reason for him to go to the police. Then he could have his scoop, have the woman he loved, and not take the risk of getting arrested for murder."

"The murder was obviously an impulse. No one sets out to commit murder using a ballpoint pen for a weapon."

"Unless he or she was deliberately trying to frame Lily."

"No. I don't think that's it."

A.J. laughed. "Well, *I* can't see any cause for believing Oriel was having a relationship with Dally other than Lily's defense team wants to believe she was having an affair with *someone*, and Dally seems like the only remotely possible candidate. Too remote, if you ask me. There's not a shred of proof against them. Lily admitted that. And given the fact that Dally is a respected journalist, it seems even more far-fetched."

"He was undercover."

"But there's a limit to things he could do undercover and not damage his own credibility."

"That's it. *That's* the motive."

"Plus, he could be married for all we know."

"So was she. Besides, he isn't. My team checked that. He's married to his work according to everyone who knows him. Well, there is a girlfriend, but I doubt if that means anything."

A.J. looked at her with disbelief. "That doesn't sound like someone about to engage in a career-damaging affair— let alone someone who's going to decide to commit murder for his lover. What would his motive be?"

"Le grand passion."

"Mother . . . have you seen Oriel Goode? She's not that type. She's a nice, ordinary, middle-aged woman. A little on the matronly side. She looks like she should be running the PTA or all those church committees that she does, in fact, run. She isn't the kind of woman who inspires *le grand passion*. Which, by the way, sounds like an oversized fruit smoothie."

"Now you're simply being obstructionist, Anna."

"But I'm not. I see that it would be beautifully convenient if Oriel and Lance had got together and knocked David Goode off, but going by my observations so far, I can't believe that they were having an affair. They aren't either of them the type."

"Then we must find proof of the affair."

A.J. groaned. "This is where my day began. Maybe Lily should hire *you*."

"I don't work for filthy lucre, pumpkin. I see a wrong and I strive to right it. Just as Lucy Bannon does on *Golden Gumshoes*."

A.J. rolled her eyes. "Don't worry, Lily doesn't actually pay. It's all pro bono."

Elysia said with unexpected and uncharacteristic sentimentality, "I don't need to tell you, Anna, that Di would be very proud of the way you've rushed to Lily's defense."

A.J. sighed. "I don't know about *rushed*. She had to call me. Anyway, Lily has her faults, but I don't believe she's capable of murder."

"Murder? No. I must agree."

A.J. glanced at the clock on the dashboard. "I've got to go. It's getting late."

Elysia protested, "We need to plan the next phase of our investigation. Somehow we must find the proof we need."

A.J. yawned so widely, her jaw cracked. "Not tonight, Mom. You've got guests leaving and I've got a dog that probably fears I've given him up for adoption. I haven't had more than four hours of sleep the last three nights. We're going to have to table this for now."

"'Delays have dangerous ends.'"

A.J. leaned over and gave her mother's cheek a peck. "So you and the Bard have said many a time. But tonight I'll take the risk."

Twenty-one

A.J. was curled up on the sofa in the front room drinking a cup of chamomile tea and reading Isherwood's *My Guru and His Disciple*, when she heard Jake's key in the lock.

She put the teacup and book aside, going to the front door to meet him, Monster padding at her heels.

"Hi! You didn't call."

"I know. I was on my way back from Blairstown. I figured I could be here in the time it would take to call." He hesitated. "I just assumed—"

A.J. said quickly, "Of course! You're just lucky I felt too lazy to slap a mudpack on my face."

"I can live with a little mud." Jake kissed her hello.

A.J. kissed Jake hello.

Jake kissed her hello again.

Monster grew bored with the proceedings and lay down on the floor with a groan.

Jake laughed against A.J.'s mouth and released her.

"Are you hungry?" A.J. asked. "I made a really tasty veggie manicotti for dinner, if I do say so myself."

"That sounds great. I didn't have time for lunch today."

Jake followed A.J. into the kitchen, leaning against the doorframe as she set about reheating the manicotti. "I heard you paid Michaela Ritchie a visit this afternoon."

A.J. threw him a guilty look. "I was just about to tell you about that."

"Mm-hm. You could have saved yourself some time and trouble." Jake bent to scratch Monster beneath his chin. Monster panted up at him. "We already knew about Michaela Ritchie, and she did break off the relationship with Goode before he was killed."

"It was worth a try. Does she have an alibi?"

"Everybody in this case, with the exception of Lily, has an alibi."

"Did you want a glass of wine with your dinner?"

"I'll get it." Jake retrieved the corkscrew from the drawer near the wine rack. "We got the information we were hoping for on Goode. Don't quote me, but whoever took that guy out may have done the world a favor."

A.J. automatically handed him two wineglasses from the cupboard. "Then you do think his death was the result of something in his history?"

"Not to get too philosophical, but everything that happens to us is the result of something in our history, wouldn't you say?"

"Yes. You know what I mean." A.J. swallowed hard. "Was he killed by someone out of his past?"

"I don't know. That was a guy with a lot of past."

"Tell me."

"David Goode started life as Raymond Grafton. He was a Canadian national, as we suspected."

"That explains the lack of a Social Security number."

Jake nodded. "He popped up on a FBI CJIS record request." He grimaced. "FFE. Foreign Fingerprint Exchange. When he was nineteen Grafton moved in with Marie Cloutier, a French Canadian woman fourteen years his senior. Cloutier and Grafton loved to go on long bike rides. One day she rode her bike right off a mountain and left Grafton an insurance policy in the neighborhood of half a million. Her family contested the will and it was eventually thrown out. Grafton disappeared."

The microwave *pinged*. A.J. opened it and removed the plate of manicotti. She grabbed silverware from the drawer and carried plate and flatware to the table. Jake washed his hands at the sink and pulled out a chair.

"The next time Grafton surfaced was in Washington. The state. He was teaching French at the School of Languages in Seattle. One of his students there was an older woman by the name of Terry Dan. Terry was a biophysicist whose husband had died in an industrial accident, leaving her the beneficiary of a life insurance policy worth a whopping three million dollars."

"What happened to him?"

"You don't want to know. And I don't want to think about it when I'm eating."

"Yikes."

"You're not kidding. Anyway Dan and Grafton move in together and all goes well for nearly eighteen months, and then Dan discovers, among other things, Grafton isn't a former instructor of the Lutece Langue in Paris. In fact, he's never been to France."

A.J.'s jaw dropped. "He was pretending to be *French*?"

Jake laughed. "Yeah. Can you believe it? And he got away with it for two years in Seattle, eighteen months of which he spent living with this poor woman."

"What happened when Dan found out he was lying?"

"She confronted him and he shoved her down a marble staircase. She was in a body brace for nearly a year. Grafton, meanwhile, disappeared again, taking all the cash he could liquidate from their joint accounts."

"But he didn't kill her. And the Cloutier woman's accident *could* have been just that. An accident." A.J. sipped her wine and lowered the glass.

"Correct."

"Didn't anybody check his references?"

"Sure they did. They checked all the forged documents he gave them. He looked great on paper. Nobody bothered to call the Lutece Langue."

"Oh no."

"Oh yes. After that Grafton drops out of sight. We don't know what he did during that period he's off the radar, but in 2001 his fingerprints pop up again, only now they belong to Maxwell Powell, the prime suspect in the murder of his wife of a few months."

"How did the LAPD not make the connection?"

"They checked school, military, and the California criminal records databases. He didn't come up clean—he didn't come up at all. Grafton didn't drive while he was living in Seattle and the language school was an adult school, so his fingerprints didn't pop up in the normal places you'd expect them to. The possibility that he might be Canadian apparently never entered anyone's minds until a few days ago."

"Jill Smithy-Powell must have discovered his glamorous background was faked."

"We're never going to know for sure what happened. I'm no psychiatrist—psychologist—whatever, but it seems pretty clear to me that Goode had problems anytime he was forced to confront his deception."

"As though he bought into his own cover story?"

"Right. And when he was confronted with the truth, unmasked, he snapped."

"Because he couldn't deal with the destruction of his fantasy persona?"

Jake shook his head. "It's possible. We could have fun playing guessing games all night, but the only person who knows for sure is dead."

"And that *can't* be a coincidence."

"Sure it could." Jake paused long enough to take another bite of his manicotti. "This is great, by the way."

"Thank you." A.J. rubbed her forehead. "Why didn't he just leave? Why did he have to kill her? Jill, I mean."

"I know you don't want to hear this, but Smithy-Powell's murder is still technically unsolved."

"Jake!"

Jake shook his head. "I know, but there's no proof that Powell killed her. We can draw some logical conclusions, but that's not proof. If Goode did kill Smithy-Powell, the answer to your question is pretty obvious. He's not—wasn't—right in the head. Why create these grandiose backgrounds for himself that almost guaranteed he'd be found out sooner or later? Think about how much he had to hide, and yet he courted the limelight as David Goode. Whatever was going on with him wasn't just about conning women out of their money. It went deeper than that."

"What if Oriel was lying? What if she did discover that Goode's background was a complete fabrication?"

"It's not Oriel's homicide we're investigating, it's Goode's."

A.J. finished her wine. "Right, but as terrible as this sounds, I can see why someone who discovered all these lies might want to kill him. Especially if she believed she was going to end up as one of his victims."

"But Oriel Goode didn't know. We interviewed her again today. In law enforcement we're trained to spot deception. Hell, we're trained to be deceptive ourselves when and where necessary in a criminal investigation. We had investigators in from Blairstown to observe, and we're all agreed, she had no idea who—or what—her husband really was."

"Apparently neither did he."

Jake gave a short laugh.

"Mother thinks Oriel was having an affair with Lance Dally."

Jake barely paused to swallow. "No way. I could more easily believe she knocked her husband off in rage over one of his affairs than that she and Dally were fooling around. Neither is the type."

"Is it possible Dally knew Goode's history? As a journalist he'd have done some background digging. Maybe he uncovered something."

"Not if his chagrin at hearing the truth today is anything to go by."

A.J. propped her chin on her fist and contemplated Jake's empty plate. "Then there must be someone else out there. Someone who recognized Goode and was so overcome with rage they walked in and stabbed him with the first available weapon."

Jake nodded. "It's a tempting theory, I agree. But who? Who is this mysterious person from Goode's past? You're the last person to move here from out of state."

"It might be a . . ." A light went on in the back of A.J.'s brain. She closed her mouth so hard her teeth clicked.

"It might be a what?"

"Visitor."

"That's possible. In a perfect world, someone just passing through." Jake drained his wineglass. He smiled at A.J.

She smiled feebly back. She was mentally flipping calendar pages. When had Elysia and her posse arrived? The day before Goode's murder. No. The *night* before Goode's murder. So there really hadn't been opportunity for any of them to go into town. Right? She tried to remember if anyone had mentioned a trip to Stillbrook.

"Something wrong?" Jake asked.

"No! Nope. Nothing. Not a thing."

His smile was faintly questioning. "Are you sure? You have a funny expression on your face."

"I just remembered there's something I need to ask Mother."

"Now?" Jake glanced at the clock, which indicated it was well past midnight.

"Er . . . no. It can wait till morning, I guess." She rose, picking up their glasses and Jake's plate, carrying them to the sink and running water over them.

Jake came up behind her, wrapping his arms around her and nuzzling her neck. A.J. closed her eyes and leaned back against him for a moment.

"Bed?" he murmured.

She nodded. She opened her eyes, turned the water off, and moved away from the sink.

Jake followed her, turning off the lights after them. As

the last light went, leaving the hall in darkness, he said suddenly, "Damn."

"What's the matter?"

"I forgot. I've got court tomorrow and I don't have a tie here."

"Oh."

A.J. nearly tripped over Monster as Jake added off-handedly, "It would sure simplify things if we lived to-gether."

Elysia cleared her throat and said in a voice like spilled gravel, "'Lo."

"It's me. I have to ask you something. Are you alone?"

Against a background of mattress springs and tossed bedclothes, Elysia said indignantly, "Anna, do you realize what time it is?"

"It's just about six o'clock. Are you alone?"

Elysia expelled an exasperated breath. "No, I'm not alone. Hang about."

A.J. waited, foot tapping nervously, as she was placed on hold. A few seconds later Elysia came back on the line sounding more alert but still exasperated. "All right. I'm alone now. It's just me and a goldfinch with insomnia. What's this all about, Anna?"

"The day after you arrived back from LA, did you all drive into Stillbrook for any reason?"

"You expect me to remember . . ." Elysia's voice trailed to a stop. She asked in a very different tone, "Why?"

"Just answer me. And please tell me the truth. Did Marcie or Petra or . . . Dean come into Stillbrook for any reason?"

"No." The word came too quickly and too forcefully after the shocked pause.

"Mother. Please."

"No," Elysia repeated. "I drove in to pick up groceries."

"No one went with you?"

"No."

"It's going to be easy enough to verify one way or the other."

Frost chilled Elysia's next words. "Are you suggesting I'm lying?"

"I'm suggesting that you would do whatever you thought you had to in order to protect people you love."

Silence.

Elysia said stonily, "I drove into Stillbrook on my own."

"How did you find out about Goode's murder? Marcie recognized him . . . when?"

"When she bloody stabbed him with her pen, of course! This is utterly ridiculous. Marcie recognized him when we turned the telly on. We already know who killed David Goode. His unfortunate wife and that journalist."

"Did anyone else recognize Goode? Was Marcie the only one who knew him from before?"

Elysia said wearily, "No one recognized him. No one left the house. Now may I return to bed and get some sleep before I have to drive my friends to the airport?"

"Yes. But . . . Mother?"

"Anna?" The word was clipped.

"Jake hasn't thought of this yet, but when he does . . ."

"He'll be his usual charming self. Yes. I realize that. He seems to be rubbing off on you."

The phone was replaced with a soft but very final click.

A.J. chewed her lip, gazing at the framed photo of

Diantha. "She's lying. I know she is. That's why she's so angry."

Diantha smiled back with enigmatic serenity.

The building creaked as the front door opened. A.J. heard the sounds of someone moving around the lobby, heard the front desk computer turning on, heard the slide of drawers opening and closing. She glanced toward the window. The rising sun bathed the morning meadow in amber light.

Staff and students were arriving. It was time to greet and embrace another day. Time for Sunrise Yoga. All else would have to wait at least until class was over, and the realization was a relief. Very soon she was going to have to deal with this, but not now. The moment of reckoning was postponed.

For now.

Twenty-two

A.J.'s phone was ringing when she returned to her office. She eyed it uneasily and then reached for the handset.

"A.J. Alexander."

"A.J." The voice was male and vaguely familiar. "This is Dean Sullivan. Is your mother there?"

"Here?" A.J. instinctively glanced around her office. "No. Is she supposed to be?"

"No. That is, I don't know. What did you say to her earlier?"

"I . . ." A.J. tried and failed to think of a way to put the gist of her phone call with Elysia diplomatically. "It was a personal matter."

Dean didn't respond for a moment. Birds seemed to be squawking in the background of the wind tunnel he was traveling through. He came back on the line. "Look, was it something to do with this murder investigation you're all messing around in?"

As A.J. tried to think of a way to answer without compromising her mother's possible safety, Dean said, "I don't know what's going on here, but I'm starting to get worried. Lucy—Elysia, I mean—was supposed to come with us to the airport, but she changed her mind at the last minute. Now the girls are telling me she said something about going to get proof of my innocence. What in the name of the Almighty is going on? Why would Elysia think she needed to prove my innocence? What am I supposed to be guilty of?"

Surely if Dean was guilty he wouldn't need this spelled out? Wasn't the fact that he had to ask a good sign? "Did you go into Stillbrook the day after you arrived from LA?"

"Sure. Lucy and I drove in and had lunch and picked up groceries."

"Did anyone else go with you?"

"No."

"Did you go by the shopping center where the New Dawn Church is located?"

"How would I know?" Dean made an obvious grab for his patience and clarified, "Not that I know."

"Did you see the Reverend Goode and recognize him?"

"Recognize him from what? What is this? An interrogation?"

"Had you ever seen him before?"

"No. Is that what this is about?" In the silence that followed, A.J. could hear the birds shrieking again. She deduced Dean was on his way to the airport with Petra and Marcie. Dean's voice came back on the line. "Are you telling me she thinks I'm a *murderer*?"

He sounded furious. A.J. said, "Obviously she *doesn't* or she wouldn't be trying to find proof of your innocence."

Dean began to swear. There was more gabbling from Petra and Marcie.

A.J. said quickly, "Don't worry. I think I know what her next move will be."

"Of course you do," Dean said. "You're the one who dragged her into this mess."

Dean probably had a right to be irked even if he was unfairly putting all the blame on her shoulders. But if he really thought Elysia was the victim of A.J.'s machinations he was in for one or two unpleasant shocks once they married. That reminded A.J. of something else.

"What's going on between you and Sarah Ray?"

"Sarah? Nothing."

"Dean, there isn't time for this!"

"How the hell is anything to do with me and Sarah your business?"

"Where do you know Sarah from?"

"We grew up together."

"Where? Los Angeles or North Dakota?"

"North Dakota. Look, I don't know what this is about, but I hadn't seen Sarah since I was sixteen. She's not involved in this, whatever you imagine this is."

"Are you sure about that? You moved to Los Angeles. Couldn't Sarah have moved to Los Angeles, too?"

"She didn't. Her family moved east. Mine moved west."

"Why? To keep you apart?"

A stunned silence followed. "How did you know that?" Dean demanded.

"I didn't. Mother guessed."

"Elysia knows?" Dean sounded horrified.

"She figured it out when you kept running into Sarah every time you went into town."

"That wasn't anything—there's nothing going on. Sarah and I are just . . ." He couldn't seem to find the words to explain exactly what they were.

"Save it for Mother. I'll find her and call you back as soon as I know something."

A.J. didn't wait for Dean's answer. Even before the handset hit the cradle, she was clicking on her laptop to find the phone number for New Dawn Church.

The church site came up. A.J. scanned for the number and began to dial.

"New Dawn Church," Lance Dally's pleasant voice stated.

Why was he still working there? How much tying up of loose ends was there to do? Surely Oriel could have hired someone to replace him by now? Really, why would he *want* to continue working there with all that had happened? Especially given his real day job?

"Oriel Goode?" she inquired briskly.

"I'm sorry she's not in today. Is there something I can help you with?"

Still gazing at the New Dawn Church website, A.J.'s eyes suddenly focused on a sidebar link. *Tour de Christ led by Lance Dally.*

"No, thank you," she said mechanically and hung up. She clicked on the link.

Photos of helmeted bikers sweating cheerfully in their formfitting Lycra outfits appeared before her along with the information on when and where the New Dawn Church cycling club met and rode.

It seemed to A.J. she sat blinking at the screen for a very long time, running through all the possibilities, but in fact it was only one minute before her screen saver came on with its calming pictures of the meadows and trees at Deer Hollow. She blinked.

Lance Dally was a cyclist. He owned a bike and he rode well enough to lead the New Dawn Church Tour de Christ club.

And *that* was how he'd managed to get over to New Dawn Church and kill David Goode while his car remained parked out front of his house, providing him with an alibi.

"Where are you going?" Emma cried behind her as A.J. shoved through the glass doors and ran to the parking lot.

As she turned the key in the ignition, A.J. reminded herself that there was no danger. Dally was safely across town manning the phones at New Dawn Church. Elysia was in danger from no more than arrest for breaking and entering—even assuming she'd correctly figured out Dally's involvement. Hopefully she was staking out Oriel's house. That would be safest of all because she was hardly foolhardy enough to break into the house with Oriel there.

A.J. found her phone and speed-dialed Elysia. The phone rang and rang and went to voice mail. "It's me," she said. "I'm sorry. I was wrong about Dean. Jake and I were speculating that Goode's killer was someone just passing through, and of course I remembered the *Golden Gumshoes* cast was visiting from Los Angeles, and Dean was always disappearing to go into town. It was just . . . circumstantial. But I'm almost positive now that Lance Dally killed Goode. I know how we can crack his alibi. Call me as soon as you get this."

She disconnected. Then she hit redial. "Please don't do anything foolish! Call me."

Disconnecting that time, she dialed Jake and got his voice mail as well. "Lance Dally owns a bike. That's how he managed to get across town and back without his car. I'm on my way to his house right now because I'm afraid Mother might do something . . . might try to find proof. I don't know. She might be staking out Oriel Goode's. Anyway, call me!"

She tossed her phone to the passenger seat and pressed harder on the gas.

Early in her fact-finding efforts A.J. had tried Google Mapping Dally's house and calculating the distance to the shopping center where New Dawn Church had set up their base of operations. She remembered the address and was able to find the street without too much trouble, although it felt like an eternity before she was turning onto the right block.

Maybe her mother was right. Maybe it was time to buy a new car with an up-to the-minute GPS system.

She drove slowly past the house Dally was renting. It was a small, ordinary two-bedroom one-bath recently renovated Colonial surrounded by tall bushes and bare trees. Elysia's Land Rover was parked four houses down, but there was no sign of Elysia.

A.J. parked even farther down the block, having to wedge in behind a pickup truck on wooden blocks and a battered black Toyota.

She got out, looking up and down the street. A yellow school bus trundled past her, and a man with a briefcase left his yard and climbed into his red MG.

A.J. checked her phone, but no one had left her a message.

She locked her car and walked briskly up the leaf-strewn sidewalk, eyes peeled for her mother. She paused by the Land Rover and glanced inside, but there was no sign of Elysia. A.J. continued toward Lance Dally's house.

In the house next door to his, a woman stood at the sink doing dishes. She stared at A.J. and A.J. smiled and raised a polite hand. The woman nodded, unsmiling.

Dally's yard was not fenced. A.J. walked up the straight cement path, still keeping an eye out for her mother, although it was hard to picture Elysia lurking in the bushes and not speaking up.

A.J. climbed the steps to the porch and knocked. No one came to the door—she'd have been startled out of her wits if they had. She rang the doorbell.

Same response.

That was, of course, the good news.

She went back down the porch steps and walked around the side of the house. A tall wooden fence and fruit trees provided concealment from the neighbors on both sides.

"Mother?" she called softly, stepping over a garden hose.

There was no answer. In fact, there was no hint that Elysia had ever been on these premises, let alone that she still was.

Behind the house was a long, cracked cement driveway with a detached garage at the end of it. A.J. considered it, then turned back to the house. A narrow flight of stairs led up to what must be a mud porch. The basement was a full walkout. Its narrow windows peeked up over the patchy lawn and driveway.

A small dog began to bark from behind the tall fence on the other side of the driveway.

A.J. ignored it and tried the basement door. It was locked.

Okay. Not a surprise. Now what?

She stepped back from the house, and as she did her gaze fell on one of the basement windows. She looked closer. The window was slightly open. So slightly that she'd missed it the first time.

Next door a man called to the dog, and A.J. heard the jingle of its tags as it trotted away still growling disapproval.

She squatted down and pushed the glass. The window panel opened with a jarring squeak. A.J. looked nervously around but there was no sign that anyone—including the neighbor's dog—had heard it.

"Mother?" she whispered.

Nothing.

Great. What now? If she went inside and was caught trespassing, she could get arrested. Jake would not be happy, to say the least. But if Elysia was here—and where else could she be with her car a few yards down the street?— she was inside this building.

A.J. made a couple of uncomplimentary observations on her esteemed parent as she thrust her legs through the opening and wriggled through. It was a tight fit, but not impossible.

Dropping down a couple of feet to the basement floor, she brushed her hands off and stood, looking around. There was a dusty AG oil tank in one corner and a new hot water tank in another. There was a barbecue pushed to the side, a couple of Styrofoam coolers, and patio furniture stacked on top of itself. A couple of wooden tennis rackets hung from the wall along with a couple of empty picture frames.

Nothing remotely sinister.

"Mother, are you here?" A.J. called, more because she wanted Elysia to be there than because she actually thought she was.

She went to the door leading out to the back patio and unlocked it, poking her head out and listening.

There was no sound to indicate anyone was aware of her trespass. The wind sent a few dead leaves scraping across the cement drive. The dry tree branches rattled.

A.J. closed the door but left it unlocked in case she had to leave quickly. She didn't plan on climbing through those windows again if she could possibly help it.

Turning, she spotted the stairs leading to the upstairs. She started toward them when something red caught her eye. She stopped and stared, then stepped forward to get a closer look.

Her first thought was that she was looking at a Halloween costume, but as she took in the crimson, misshapen head, the limp and drooping wire and rubber wings, she realized it was more sinister than that. She was staring at the latest incarnation of the Jersey Devil.

The sudden unmistakable squeak of a floorboard sent A.J.'s heart rocketing into her mouth. She ducked down and waited, still trying to make sense of the costume hanging a few inches above her head.

Had this been what she'd seen in the abandoned house in the woods? Was Lance Dally the Jersey Devil? Who was walking around upstairs? Had Dally shot at the Sacred Balance students? Her thoughts tumbled over and over one another, and all the while she listened to that soft, steady approach of footsteps.

The door at the head of the basement steps swung open, hinges creaking spookily.

"Anna? Are you down there?"

She'd recognize that hiss anywhere. A.J. rose. She could just make out the slight figure in black at the top of the stairs. Elysia blended in nicely with the shadows. Nothing went with a life of crime like basic black.

"Mother, what on earth are you doing here?"

Elysia jumped, but instantly regained her poise. "I might ask you the same question."

"I'm here looking for you."

"I'm collecting the evidence I need to prove Dean's innocence."

A.J. quickly climbed the stairs. "Didn't you get my phone message? You don't need to prove his innocence. I already know Dean isn't involved."

"Very heartwarming, I'm sure. But what about the rest of the world?"

"I already told you. Did you not pick up your messages?"

"I put the ruddy thing on vibrate. Didn't want to take a chance of getting nicked when it went off at the wrong moment."

"Well, if you'd bothered to check your messages, you'd have heard me telling you that this stunt was totally unnecessary. I know how to crack Lance's alibi."

But Elysia was staring past her. "What on earth . . ." She moved past A.J. and went down the stairs to the red costume.

"Bloody hell," she breathed. Wide-eyed, she met A.J.'s gaze. "Is this what I think it is?"

A.J. nodded.

"Of course," Elysia said to herself. "Makes perfect sense, I suppose. The reverend found out what Dally was up to and threatened to expose him. Dally had to kill him."

"It *doesn't* make perfect sense. To start with, why would Dally be impersonating the Jersey Devil?"

"Because it makes a fabulous story, and he's in the fabulous story business."

"But his newspaper isn't that kind of paper. Anyway, he was already doing an exposé on Goode. That seems like all the fabulous story anyone would need."

Elysia shrugged. "Who can know the workings of the criminal mind? The main thing is, we have the proof right here."

A.J. studied the misshapen horse head. Yes, they did have proof of . . . something. What?

Elysia said with satisfaction, "Now all we have to do is set a trap for Dally."

A.J.'s head snapped up. "No, we don't. We don't need to set any trap. The fact that Dally rides a bike is enough for the police to take another, closer look at him. That, and the fact that he has this thing hanging here—although I suppose he could always claim someone planted it. But if he's ever worn it, there will be DNA."

Elysia was following her own train of thought. "Rides a bike . . ." Her frown faded and her eyes lit. "Yes. I see. That's how you plan to break his alibi. Oh very good, Anna!"

"I'm glad you're pleased. Now let's get out of here."

"Get out of here?" Elysia looked taken aback. "We still have to find evidence that Dally and Oriel Goode were having an affair."

"For the last time, they *weren't* having an affair."

"You what? But of course they were having an affair. What else would his motive be? You've just said he didn't kill Goode over Goode's discovery that Dally was impersonating this devil creature. Right. But he had to have *some* reason for sticking that pen into the good reverend."

"I don't know what the motive was. It doesn't matter, though. We've got enough here to prove Lily wasn't involved. That's the only thing I care about. The rest of it is for the police to deal with."

Elysia tilted her head, studying A.J. "What is it you're not telling me?"

"I'll tell you when we're safely out of here." A.J. had hold of her mother's arm and was trying to usher her to the exterior basement door.

Elysia freed herself. "D'you mind, darling? You've a grip like a stevedore. I never realized yoga was a contact sport."

"Mother, we need to get out of here before someone calls the police. Before *we* can call the police, I mean."

"I can't leave without my jacket."

A.J. looked at her with disbelief. "What jacket?"

"My Tommy Hilfiger leather jacket. Never mind the fact it cost me three hundred quid, it's got *my* DNA all over it."

"Mother."

"Besides," Elysia said with aggravating calm, "if Dally finds that jacket—and he can't miss it—he'll know that someone has been snooping around and he'll get rid of every bit of evidence before your precious inspector can get his search warrant together."

"Where did you leave this jacket?"

"In the bedroom. I was searching for love letters."

"I'll get it. You get in your car."

"It'll be faster if I get it."

A.J. looked heavenward for guidance, gave up arguing,

and sprinted up the staircase. She could hear her mother following leisurely in her kitten heels. Yes. B&E in heels, black leather jeans, and a cashmere turtleneck. Elysia must be channeling Honey West this week.

The basement opened onto a kitchen. A.J. had a brief impression of old-fashioned appliances and gingham curtains and then she was in the hall, looking for the bedroom.

The hall ended in a long living room with hardwood floors, built-in cabinets, and walk-in bay windows. A.J. did an about-face and started back the other way, past a bathroom with a marble-topped cherry vanity, and a large dining room with no furniture.

Her cell phone vibrated and she nearly jumped out of her skin. She snatched it up without looking to see the number.

"Jake?"

"It's me," Suze replied buoyantly. "A.J., I had to tell you. Mocha sent a Thanksgiving basket to the studio. It's full of fruit and flowers and it's got this great big felt turkey with the funniest face. And there's the sweetest thank-you card. It's addressed to all of us. She says—"

"Suze, that's *great*. It's totally a credit to you and Jaci. Can you call Jake?"

"Can I . . . huh?"

"Can you call the police department and try to get hold of Jake? I called earlier but he hasn't called me back. I really need to talk to him. I'm over at Lance Dally's house."

"Why?"

"Long story." There were two staircases, one front, one back, leading to the second floor. A.J. started up the front staircase. "Can you tell Jake to get over here?"

"To get over to Lance Dally's house?"

"Right." A.J. reached the second floor. Another staircase led up to the attic. She eyed it uneasily. God only knew what Dally might have hidden in there.

"Sure," Suze said doubtfully. "I'll tell Jake. What time are you coming back to the studio?"

"Er, soon. I hope." A.J. hurried down the narrow hall past a family room, a bedroom that had been turned into an office, and came at last to a large master bedroom. Elysia's black leather jacket was lying on the blue chenille bedspread.

"Okay. See you then."

"See you." A.J. dropped her phone in her coat pocket, snatched up Elysia's jacket, and ran down the hallway. She was starting downstairs when she heard the front door open.

A.J. froze. She looked across and saw Elysia on the back staircase also motionless and listening.

For an instant the rushing of blood to her head kept her from hearing where the intruder was. She heard a cabinet open. She looked at Elysia. Elysia sat down on the steps, making herself as small as possible in the shadows. There was just a chance she might get away with it. Anyone coming in would go automatically to the front staircase in order to go upstairs.

The front staircase where A.J. currently stood frozen in place like a misplaced lawn ornament.

A.J. heard a drawer slide open and a rattling sound. What was the intruder searching for?

Oh wait. *She* was the intruder.

A.J. took a cautious, careful step backward. If she could get back upstairs and down the hall, she might be able to get to the back staircase, too, and then they could make a try for the mud porch entrance. Or perhaps she could hide in one of the rooms until Jake or the police showed up.

She inched back and up another step.

A floorboard squeaked. A.J. looked down. A shadow fell across the wooden planks in the hall below. Lance Dally stepped into view. He gazed up at her for a long moment.

A.J. gazed back though her attention was focused not so much on Lance as the rifle he held. It was pointed straight at her.

Twenty-three

"**Come** down." Lance's voice was flat.

A.J. found her voice. She tried to say with confidence, "I've already called the police."

"Really? Did they get caught in traffic?" Lance called to Elysia, "You, too. I see you crouched down over there. Get down here."

Elysia rose and, with surprising dignity for a woman who had just been discovered cowering behind the banisters, started slowly down the stairs. A.J. said, "Lance, shooting us would be incredibly stupid. There's no way you could explain it."

"It would be," Lance agreed. "And you wouldn't enjoy it much either. I suggest you don't force me to pull the trigger." As Elysia reached the bottom, he glanced at her. His brows rose. "Who are you supposed to be? Diana Rigg?"

Elysia made a very British and very rude gesture.

Lance looked briefly taken aback. His eyes narrowed. "Yeah, I know you."

Was it the vulgar gesture that gave her away? A nervous laugh nearly escaped A.J. She swallowed it and said with a semblance of calm she didn't feel, "How did you know we were here?"

"My neighbor called to tell me the star of *Golden Gumshoes* was running around my yard, peeking in my windows and trying my doors. It wasn't hard to put it together with the two phone calls this morning asking for Oriel. Obviously someone was hoping I wouldn't be home today." He gestured with the rifle. "Get down here. I won't ask nicely again."

Elysia said briskly, "Since you're obviously going to kill us, you might as well tell us everything."

Lance laughed. "Really?"

"Yes," Elysia stated as though it had been a genuine question. "Granted, we've already figured most of it out ourselves. We know you cycled across town to kill the Reverend Goode and then cycled back here."

"Big deal. I don't know how that escaped anyone's attention as long as it did. It doesn't prove anything. The fact that I *could* have biked across town doesn't mean I did. No one saw me."

"So you think."

"I don't think. I know. Where are the witnesses? There aren't any. No one pays attention to cyclists—except as a traffic nuisance."

"We know you were the one who shot at my group in the woods," A.J. interjected.

"How do you figure that?" Lance asked.

"Well, first clue is you're pointing a rifle at us."

He snorted. "You're kidding, right? Every other person in this hick town owns a gun of some kind."

"But I bet every other person in town doesn't have a gun with ballistics that match yours."

He shrugged.

"The only thing we don't know," Elysia said, with a glance at A.J., "is why you did it. Was it because of your affair with Oriel? Or because you wanted to avenge Jill?"

"Jill? What are you talking about? Who's Jill?"

"Jill Smithy-Powell," A.J. said.

"Oh. No." Lance blew out a long, unsteady breath. "Can you believe that? All those months I was working for that ass, building my story, and he turns out to be on the FBI's wish list."

"So then it *was* the affair with Oriel," Elysia said. She couldn't help a triumphant look in A.J.'s direction.

"Lady, what are you smoking? No, it wasn't an affair with Oriel. She's practically old enough to be my mother."

That annoyed Elysia no end. "Then why *did* you kill Goode?" she demanded. "*What* was the motive?"

Lance's face tightened to bones and hollows. "I didn't have a motive. It wasn't planned. It was . . . mostly an accident."

A.J.'s cell phone, tucked in her pocket, vibrated again. She surreptitiously reached her hand in as Elysia said with hauteur, "Like this, I suppose?"

Lance's face darkened. "No. Not like this. This isn't what I wanted, but . . . it's out of my control now."

A.J. felt the face of her phone and pressed what she hoped was the flat incoming call button. "That's not true," she told Lance. "There's a big difference between killing someone in the heat of a fight and cold-bloodedly, deliberately murdering two people to conceal the first crime. You know that."

"What I know is, I've told you to get down here three times. If you don't come down now, I'm going to hit Her Majesty in the head with my rifle butt."

A.J. didn't fail to note that Lance did not say *shoot*. She began to suspect that one reason he hadn't hit anyone when he fired on their group in the woods was because his heart wasn't completely committed to murder.

A.J. slowly walked down two more steps. "What did you and Goode fight about if it wasn't anything to do with his past? Why did he fire you?"

"He fired me because he found out I was a reporter and I was gathering enough information on him to put him out of business permanently."

"Why would that matter to you?"

"It didn't. Except . . ."

"Except what?"

"In order to get the goods on him, I had to go along with a couple of things that I probably shouldn't have gone along with."

"I knew it!" Elysia exclaimed. "Didn't I say this from the beginning?" She looked from Lance to A.J.

Neither Lance nor A.J. responded. A.J. was thinking of the costume in Lance's cellar. "You mean you went along with things like impersonating the Jersey Devil?"

"No. That is . . ."

"Yes," Elysia said uncompromisingly.

Lance's face twisted. "Yes, have it your way. That and other things. It's a fine line between covering the news and becoming part of it."

Let alone fabricating it. But A.J. knew enough to keep

her mouth shut. "So Goode threatened to reveal your part in the Jersey Devil hoax?"

"My *part*?" Lance grew indignant. "He was going to claim that the whole idea was mine. That I'd come up with it to discredit him, that he knew nothing about it. That when I couldn't come up with a legitimate story, I resorted to smear tactics and fabricating my facts. It was crazy, but I'd seen him in action. I knew how persuasive he was. And I had let myself get in too deep." He stopped.

A.J. said, "John Baumann's cows."

"I didn't touch those cows, but . . . I was there. I saw Goode slaughter them. It was the most sickening thing I ever saw. But afterward I helped him rig that scene to look like a wild animal attacked them. I had to do it to preserve my cover. I didn't have a choice, but it made me an accessory."

"You were an accessory to killing a cow. That was certainly preferable to being guilty of murder," Elysia said.

"I know! I didn't mean to kill him. I didn't even intend to talk to him that morning. I was out riding, clearing my head, and I decided to stop by the church and talk to him. See if I could . . . I don't know. Defuse the situation. I didn't want to be involved in a huge lawsuit and I knew what my editor would think of some of the things I'd done in pursuit of my story. So I thought I'd try to talk to him, reason with him. Maybe strike a compromise."

Movement outside the bay windows caught A.J.'s attention. Her heart leapt in relief. The police. It had to be the police. The cavalry had arrived.

Lance was saying, "But Goode was worse than he'd been the day before. His ego couldn't take the idea that he was going to be exposed as a fraud. He was ranting and raving about my betrayal. He called me a Judas. *He* attacked me. Physically, I mean. He grabbed me and, I'm telling you, there was murder in his face. It was there. I've never seen any human want to kill anyone as much as he wanted to kill me. And he would have. But I grabbed the pen off his desk and I jammed it as hard as I could in his throat."

"Then it was self-defense," A.J. said. "Why didn't you call the police?"

"Because I'm a reporter! I know how it works. I'd have been ruined. Everything would have had to come out. Everything I worked for would be lost."

"As opposed to now?" Elysia inquired.

At the same time, A.J. said, "Is your career really worth committing murder? Why did you try to kill Oriel?"

The rifle wavered for an instant. "I didn't know how much she knew, how much Goode had told her. At first I thought I was safe. She apologized for suspecting me of murder and asked me to stay on for a while at the church office. I thought it would be smart to hang around long enough to make sure I'd covered my tracks with the police. Then she started acting funny. I think she'd begun to suspect me. But I couldn't be sure. I decided the only thing to do was make it look like it was some antireligious nut out to destroy the church."

"Completely the wrong approach!" Elysia objected. "What you should have done wa—"

But Lance would never know how a criminal mastermind would have handled his situation because the front door crashed open, hinges shrieking, doorframe splintering. The whole house seemed to shake as uniformed officers burst into the living room.

Lance turned, bringing his rifle up, but he was knocked to the floor before he could fire. He went down under a pile of uniformed law enforcement. His muffled curses could be heard beneath the shouted warnings to not move a muscle.

Elysia sagged back against the wall. "It's about bloody time!" Her irritation faded in the wake of the attentive young officers rushing to her side.

"A.J." Jake pounded the staircase. A.J. met him halfway, flying into his arms.

"I was praying you'd get my message!"

Jake hugged her tightly. "What did you think you were doing? Don't *ever* take that kind of chance again. We could have gotten a search warrant—we *did* get a search warrant!"

A.J. shook her head. "I know. I know." She gave a shaky laugh. "But as the Bard says—"

Jake's mouth covered hers.

"**Wait**, wait, wait," Andy interrupted. "So Goode's murder had absolutely *nothing* to do with his previous life?"

A.J. shook her head. "Not a thing. It was a—"

"Red herring," Elysia supplied.

"No. It was a—"

"MacGuffin."

A.J. threw her mother an exasperated look. "I was going to say it was a dead end."

Jake supplied, "False lead."

"I was going to say it was ironic," Nick put in.

"Poetic justice, in fact," Elysia said, reaching for the dish of olives Jake passed her way. She popped an olive in her mouth. "Mmm. Lovely."

It was Thanksgiving Day and A.J., Jake, and Elysia were gathered around the sumptuously laden table in Andy and Nick's elegant Manhattan brownstone. Barber played softly in the background, and the Wedgwood china and silver gleamed in the warm candlelight.

A.J. was glad to see Elysia seemed much her usual self. She had turned up at Deer Hollow that morning without Dean. When asked, Elysia had said that she and Dean had decided to call it quits. Later on the drive she had volunteered the information that Dean and Sarah were going to give their long-lost relationship another try.

She seemed philosophical about it. A.J. couldn't help wondering how Mr. Meagher was taking that news, and she resolved to call him soon.

"So Goode was behind the Jersey Devil sightings?" Andy sounded so disappointed, everyone laughed.

Nick grinned. "Scratch a cynic, find a kid who still believes in monsters."

Andy's mouth quirked, but he shook his head, denying this. Glancing down the table, he said, "Ellie, your glass is empty. More mineral water?"

He started to rise. Nick was already on his feet, a friendly hand clamped on his shoulder, keeping him seated. "Relax. I live here, too. I know where we keep the mineral water."

Andy rolled his eyes and met A.J.'s gaze. He winked. Then he glanced at Jake and wiggled his eyebrows in inquiry.

A.J. shook her head.

Andy's expression managed to capture astonishment and aggravation. A.J. hoped that hers communicated something sufficiently dampening, but there was no repressing

Andy. He was a born tease, and apparently he was yet another person convinced that Jake was about to pop The Question any moment.

Jake was saying, "Yep, it's not clear whether Goode was manufacturing demon sightings to give his own church publicity for fund-raising or simply because he had a taste for the limelight. He enlisted Lance to help, and in an effort to get his story and probably to preserve his undercover role of devoted assistant, Lance went along taking notes and not interfering with anything Goode did. Including slaughtering the Baumann cattle."

"Did he think there was a Pulitzer in his future?"

"Something like that." A.J. picked up the story. "When Goode discovered Lance's real agenda he fired him. When Lance tried to talk him down, Goode threatened to discredit him by blaming Lance for killing livestock and perpetuating the rest of the Jersey Devil myth."

"You know who had a narrow escape." Elysia took the glass of mineral water Nick handed her. "Oriel Goode. And I don't mean Lance's attempt to shoot her."

Nick agreed. "Leopards don't change their spots."

"I'm not so sure," A.J. said. "I think no one bought into the Reverend Goode's con like the Reverend Goode. I think he believed completely in the persona he'd taken on—and I think Oriel believed in it, too. And I think in a funny way that was part of what kept her safe. She did last longer than his other relationships."

"Intriguing," Elysia mused. "Perhaps there's some truth in that."

Jake smiled at her across the table. A.J. smiled back. For a moment it was as though they were the only two people at the table.

"Was Lily properly grateful for everything you went through on her behalf?" Andy asked.

Jake laughed and reached for his glass.

A.J. made a face. "In her own way, I think she was. You know Lily. I think she feels she really solved the whole thing herself by putting me on the trail of Oriel Goode's affairs."

"But Oriel Good didn't have any affairs."

"I know. Anyway, the good news—and Lily and I are in total agreement on this—is that she's got her job back at Yoga Meridian. She couldn't be happier. And I couldn't be happier for her."

"A toast to Lily," Nick said. "Before the food gets any colder."

They touched glasses in a succession of musical clinks.

"Wait a minute," Andy protested suddenly, setting his glass down. "What *did* A.J. see in the abandoned house? Was that Dally or not?"

"No," Jake said. "He swears up and down he wore camos and fatigues when he tracked the Sacred Balance group through the woods, and I can't see why he'd lie about that when he admits to shooting at Oriel Goode."

"His story confirms what Suze reported about seeing him following us," A.J. said.

"Okay. So it wasn't Dally at the campsite and it wasn't Dally in the abandoned house. Who was it?" Andy looked from A.J. to Jake.

A.J. also looked at Jake. "Come to think of it, what did you do with that scrap of hide or fur or whatever it was you found under the house that afternoon we hiked back?"

Jake cleared his throat. "I had it analyzed."

"And?"

"The closest the lab could get to identifying it was . . . equine."

"There was a horse in the cellar?" Andy looked at Nick. Nick raised his brows.

Jake said, "Not exactly. The sample had equine characteristics. It also had, er, characteristics of *Canis lupus.*"

"*Wolf?*" Nick said disbelievingly.

Elysia began to laugh. "You mean the lab couldn't identify it?"

Jake was laughing, too, albeit reluctantly. "Not so far."

"Good God. Well, as the Bard says, 'There are more things in heaven and earth than are dreamt of in your philosophy.'"

"Speaking of heaven and earth," Andy said, reaching out his hands to Nick on one side and A.J. on the other. "How about a prayer before the meal?"

They all clasped hands and bent their heads.

Andy said quietly, "Lord, thank you today for this feast. Thank you for the food for our bodies, and thank you for the food for our souls: a chance to spend time with those we love, friends and family."

A.J. raised her lashes. Jake gazed at her across the table.

"Amen," she said.

Exercises

❧

I realize that not everyone who reads the Mantra for Murder series plans to enroll in the nearest yoga class. I also realize that yoga can seem intimidating from the outside looking in. But as we age (and so far I haven't discovered how to avoid that) our bodies grow tighter, stiffer, and yes, heavier.

The three exercises that follow are basic yoga moves, but more important, these are basic exercises that just about anyone can do, and they'll help you preserve your flexibility and limberness while also helping to trim your waistline. Do these every morning and every evening, and you'll be pleasantly surprised at the results.

Sideways Bend

If you ever took a gym class, I know you know this one. You didn't realize you were doing yoga, did you?

Step One: Stand with feet about two feet apart. Balance weight equally, lightly on feet.

Step Two: Inhale as you raise your arms over your head and clasp hands in prayer position (you can interlace your fingers if that feels more comfortable).

Step Three: Exhale as you bend to the right. Focus on the pressure of your feet touching the earth, concentrate on your breathing—slow, deep breaths—and think about how good it feels to lengthen your spine as you stretch.

Step Four: Hold the position for eight deep and even breaths—relax into it if possible.

Step Five: Inhale and return to standing position, lower arms to your sides.

Step Six: Breathing in, return to standing position.

Now repeat bending to the left.

Forward Bend

The key to this one is to really focus on your hips and back.

Step One: Stand with hands on hips. I find this move easier to do with feet apart. Exhale and bend forward—you should be focusing on using your hips, not your waist, for this move. As you lower, all your focus should be on lifting and lengthening your spine.

Step Two: Keep your knees straight. Touch your palms or fingertips to the floor, positioned slightly in front of or beside your feet. Try to press your palms to the floor. Or, if you're feeling flexible, clasp your ankles. Press your heels firmly to the floor—really concentrate on feeling grounded, centered.

Step Three: Inhale slowly and evenly. With each in-drawn breath, lift and lengthen the front torso if you can. With each exhale, relax a little more deeply into the bend. Let your head hang down. Relax.

Step Four: Breathe softly, deeply, evenly, eight times.

Step Five: Lift yourself from your hips as you rise back into standing position.

Do this three or four times.

Cobra Pose

I have to say that I used to think this pose was useless—until I stopped doing it for a time and then tried to pick up where I'd left off. I was shocked at how my spine had tightened up! It really is a good move for keeping your back supple.

Step One: Lie prone (facedown) on the floor, legs stretched back, arms stretched in front, elbows to your side, and torso braced as though you were about to read your favorite yoga mystery.

Step Two: As you inhale, straighten your arms and push your chest off the floor, not rising up so far that your hips leave the ground.

Step Three: Tilt face ceilingward. Relax your shoulders. Breathe slowly, deeply, for a count of eight. Lower yourself to the floor.

Step Four: Inhale and rise up again, this time looking over your right shoulder. That's not so easy! But hold the pose and breathe slowly, evenly, deeply.

Step Five: Lower yourself to the floor.

Step Six: Inhale and rise up again, this time looking over your left shoulder. Hold the pose and concentrate on keeping your shoulders down and expanding your chest cavity as you breathe slowly, deeply, evenly.

Step Seven: Lower yourself to the floor. Don't just flop down. Keep the movements controlled.

Do this three or four times on each side.

Recipes

❧

Baked Manicotti

(Serves 6ish)

Ingredients for crepes

5 eggs
1¼ cups all-purpose flour, sifted
¼ teaspoon salt
1¼ cups water

Ingredients for filling

2 pounds ricotta cheese (whole milk is best,
    but may be sacrificed for health/artistic
    license :-p)
1 pound mozzarella cheese, shredded
2 eggs

2 tablespoons Parmesan cheese
1 teaspoon salt
¼ teaspoon pepper

Directions for crepes

Combine all ingredients in medium bowl with electric mixer. Lightly grease a 7-inch skillet and place over low heat. Pour in 2 tablespoons of batter, rotating pan to evenly coat bottom. Cook until top is dry, but bottom is not brown. Using a spatula, turn crepe over and allow reverse side to cook, approximately a few seconds. Turn onto wire rack to cool. Repeat with remainder of batter, stacking crepes on wire rack to cool.

Directions for filling

Preheat oven to 350°.

Combine all ingredients in medium bowl with a wooden spoon. Once crepes have cooled, spread 1 to 2 tablespoons of filling in each crepe and roll up. Place rolled-up crepes in shallow baking dish (either a broiler pan or jelly roll pan works well). Cover with foil, and bake until steaming, approximately 30 minutes. Serve with favorite marinara sauce and grated Parmesan cheese.

Thanks to my old friend Gillian Houde for supplying this yummy recipe!

Chocolate Clementine Cake

(Serves 12–16)

I can't pretend that this cake doesn't take a bit of preparation, but it can be made a day or two in advance. Being culinarily challenged like A.J., I buy a nice brand of chocolate sauce, heat it up, and pour it over, but some of you will choose to make your own). I personally think if you use the best ingredients, you get the best results—especially when it comes to chocolate.

By the way, a clementine is a type of mandarin orange!

Ingredients

12 ounces bittersweet chocolate

1 cup butter

7 large eggs (separated)

1 cup sugar

¾ cup all-purpose flour

2 teaspoons grated clementine zest (about 2
   clementines)

2 medium clementines, peeled and coarsely
   chopped

3 tablespoons orange liqueur (orange juice may
   be subbed)

¼ teaspoon salt
warmed chocolate sauce
sweetened whipped cream for garnish

Directions

1. Preheat oven to 350°. Grease a 9-inch springform pan (or line bottom with parchment paper and grease that). Flour. Tap out excess flour and set aside.

2. Melt chocolate and butter in a heavy saucepan over low heat until smooth. Remove from heat.

3. Beat egg yolks and ¾ cup sugar in a large bowl at medium speed with an electric mixer until pale and thick. Add melted chocolate mixture, beating until blended. Add flour, beating until blended, stopping to scrape down sides. Stir in zest, chopped clementines, and orange liqueur.

4. Beat egg whites in a separate bowl at medium-high speed with an electric mixer until foamy. Slowly add salt and remaining ¼ cup sugar. Beat until stiff peaks form. Fold one-third egg white mixture into chocolate mixture. Pour mixture into prepared pan.

5. Bake for 50 to 55 minutes or until slightly firm to touch. Remove from oven and set aside to cool in pan for five minutes.

6. Remove from pan by running a sharp knife around edge and tapping bottom of pan gently. Remove sides of springform pan. Tip cake onto serving plate, and remove springform bottom and parchment paper. Serve while still warm with hot chocolate sauce and whipped cream garnish.